I0692654

IN

LOVE
AND WAR

TARA MILLS

Copyright

Sherman Hills Press

Stories with a heartbeat.

Dedication

*For those who report the truth
despite the risks.*

Chapter One

Summer—2006

Daylight was fading fast when Dylan Bond sat down at his computer and shot the smuggled USB driver home. As he slowly peeled back layer upon layer of evidence, the room fell dark around him. The only illumination left came from the computer screen. The unnatural glow sharpened and defined his features, the planes of his face, the clean line of his nose. Dylan's eyes, lost in shadow, flashed black, all pupil, the lapis blue of his irises obscured by the lack of light.

Glancing at the sleeping golden retriever sprawled next to him Dylan reached out with his stocking-covered foot and gave the animal's belly an affectionate rub. "You wouldn't believe what I'm reading. This scumbag started setting things up over three years ago."

The dog's eyes flickered and closed. His tail flopped on the floor a couple of times while his satisfied groan rose and fell with the tummy rub.

Smiling, Dylan turned back to the screen and opened the next document. He leaned in and continued to read, though he quickly sobered, his outrage growing with every new paragraph.

———

Ariela Perrine's face fell when she saw the dark blue, checked necktie hanging from the doorknob. Pressing her ear to the wood, she could hear the unmistakable sounds of an action flick on the television inside. What was she supposed to do now? Were they actually watching the movie or was it just playing in the background? Her gaze dropped to the necktie once more and she bit her lip, undecided.

Screw it. She was home now. If those two wanted privacy, they could move things into Jean's bedroom.

She knocked three times—hard, so they'd hear her over the movie and announced, "I'm home. Zip up."

"Hang on!" Jean shot back.

Time seemed to drag while Ariela waited, though it was probably no more than two minutes. Feeling impatient to get inside and leave the memory of her latest failed date on this side of the door, she gave another hopeful rap. "Are you decent?"

"All clear."

Ariela dropped the looped necktie over her head, accessorizing her smirk, and went in. Jean and Ron were still making wardrobe adjustments when she hung her purse on a hook behind the door and flopped into the easy chair with a dejected sigh.

Jean tucked her legs beneath her on the sofa and sank against Ron. He snuggled her even closer and she sighed even though she was frowning pointedly at Ariela.

"You're back early. What happened? I thought you were going dancing tonight. Didn't you like Randy either?"

Ariela sent her roommate a long look. "Where would I even start?" Withdrawing into the cushions, she turned to the television. "What are you watching?"

Ron glanced over. "Split Infinity."

"Never heard of it." She struggled to figure out what was going on for ten minutes, but having missed the beginning, she couldn't catch up. What was the point? "I'm starving. I'm going to find something to eat."

Jean stared at her. "You just *came* from dinner."

"I couldn't eat. The guy ruined my appetite. He never stopped talking, not even when his mouth was full. I swear, it was like watching a front-load washing machine, except with a washer you're not in danger of getting hit by something flying out of it."

Jean looked revolted. "Tell me you're joking."

"I wish. He was disgusting."

"So, how much did you drink?" Jean knew her so well.

"Two glasses of wine. When Randy asked why I wasn't eating, I told him I was coming down with something. Thank god I thought of it. It saved me from having to kiss him later. There was no way he was getting anywhere near me with that tongue of his." Just the idea was enough to make her shudder.

Ron chuckled and broke in. "There's pizza on the counter—help yourself."

"Thanks." Ariela popped up to go investigate. "Anything I have to pull off of it?"

"'Shrooms," said Jean.

Damn. "Mushrooms?" She hated the ungrateful whine in her voice.

Jean arched an eyebrow at her. "Hey, we didn't order pineapple because you bitched so much last time."

"I did? Oh…I did. Sorry." Ariela gave her friends a fake perky smile. "Mushroom pizza? Fantastic."

Sputtering on another chuckle, Ron stood and stretched, letting out a deep groan with his full extension. "Well, I suppose I should clear out. I have an early morning."

Ariela flipped up the top of the cardboard pizza box, though it didn't block her view of Jean's theatrical pout through the kitchen doorway. Amused by it, she reached in and tore a slice of pizza free and peeled back the cheese so she could pick off the mushrooms. She flicked every single one she found back into the box.

"See you later, Ron," Ariela called as the couple kissed goodnight.

There was a pause before he answered. "Be good, Ariela."

"I'm always good," Ariela muttered under her breath. She was tired of being good. She wanted to be bad, to be a rabble rouser, to get into a little trouble for once in her life. Too bad it didn't come naturally. She needed someone to corrupt her. Yes, a bad influence to shake up her boring routine would be great.

Jean wandered into the kitchen and took a glass down from the cabinet. Going into the fridge, she held up the carton. "Milk?"

"I'd rather have juice."

Jean looked over the shelves. "Don't see any."

"Figures. Guess I'll have milk too."

She was off to a good, rebellious start. Well, at least she was getting her calcium. Tomorrow, she'd better get to the store to pick up more of her favorite cranberry blends.

Jean set Ariela's glass down in front of her and took her usual chair at the table. Reaching into the pizza box she helped herself, playfully wiggling her eyebrows as she bit the mushroom at the very tip clean off.

Ariela quivered in distaste. "Do you mind? I'm eating here."

"So am I." Jean laughed and dabbed her mouth with a napkin. "You know…I think I like cold pizza best."

"I get into moods." Using her freshly polished fingernails, she picked off a tiny chunk of black olive and wiped it on the inside of the box.

"It's not a booger, Ariela." Jean kicked back in her chair and contemplated her roommate.

Wary, Ariela lowered her second slice of pizza. "What?"

"Nothing."

Ariela slowly shook her head. "Oh no, no, no, no. Tell me."

Jean breathed in and out first. "Fine. It's just, well, I figured Randy was going to be a bust. And he was—just another dud in a pattern of duds for you."

"What's that supposed to mean?"

"Face it. You go out with losers, knowing they're losers and they're going to disappoint. It's like you set yourself up on purpose."

Ariela gave a dismissive snort. "Don't be ridiculous."

"I'm just saying. You know what you want, and you refuse to go there." Jean took another bite of her pizza.

"I go out with the guys who ask me."

"You turn down any guy who might be interesting."

"I haven't met any of those."

"You don't want to." Jean tossed her crust back into the empty box and wiped her hands on her napkin. "I think you're afraid to fall in love."

Ariela scoffed at the idea, unconvinced. "Is that right?"

"We've been friends a long time. I know you better than you think. You're afraid you'll end up like your mom."

Sitting up, her eyebrows raised, Ariela deflected the charge. "I don't think this is how a psych session is supposed to work. I believe *I'm* supposed to be the one talking and you're supposed to take notes and nod occasionally and say things like 'hmm,' and 'I see. Very interesting.'"

"I've just made some observations over the years, that's all. Maybe it's time to admit you don't go deep with men. You keep them shallow, where they can't hurt you."

Ariela laughed. "Okay then, point me in the right direction, because I'm obviously mucking things up on my own."

"Be serious." There was an understanding look in Jean's eyes. "You can't run away forever."

———

It was well over six hours since Dylan gave any thought to his aching back. All sense of time and discomfort were lost in a flurry of mental activity. Armed with damning evidence, he was in his zone, a master of political commentary as his words flowed across the screen.

> *'—and unfortunately for the American people, Senator Norton has never acted on any legislation before his financial terms have been worked out first. The Carpenter Bill is a prime example. It makes this jaded journalist pine for the days when money was passed discreetly under the table, instead of brazenly and unapologetically in the open.'*

With a dramatic flourish, Dylan lifted his hands off the keyboard and kicked back in his chair with an exhilarated smile. "Take that you bastard. Hope it stings like a bitch."

He dated his column and sent it in.

"Oh yeah." Reaching for his long-neglected beer, he took a swig and his face contorted with a wicked grimace. "Warm and flat." He shuddered and rolled back his chair, grunting stiffly to his feet. Only now did he notice the daylight streaming in the windows.

"Jesus. What time is it?" He scrubbed his tired eyes with the heels of his hands.

Max sat up and scratched himself, his attention centered on his human. When Dylan swept up the open bag of cheese puffs on the desk and shook the last two into his hand, the dog's tail beat the floor in double-time. Chuckling at the animal, he popped one into his own mouth and tossed the second to him. Max snatched it out of the air and swallowed it whole.

"You could at least *pretend* to taste it for my sake," he said dryly.

The dog followed him into the kitchen and parked himself directly behind Dylan when he threw open the refrigerator door.

The pickings were slim. Dylan pulled out a container of forgotten lunch meat and opened the lid. He took a cautious sniff, jerked his head back, and sent the bologna sailing across the room. It landed in the trash with a satisfying *whump*. Max stretched up and gave the garbage an interested look.

"Don't even think about it," he warned.

Shit, there was nothing to eat. He slammed the refrigerator door and stretched through his spine, finally attuned to the stiffness he'd managed to ignore while working. Rubbing his lower back in a distracted fashion, he looked at the dog.

"I've gotta get something in my stomach. How does a breakfast sandwich sound?" Max wriggled with excitement and pounded his tail on the floor. Laughing, Dylan patted his leg and invited the dog over. "Yeah, like you know what I said." Max leaned his weight against his thigh while he rubbed his ears. "Come on boy." He grabbed the leash off the counter and snapped off the kitchen light.

——

Two blocks away, Jean shuffled into the kitchen and found

Ariela curled over a mug of coffee, a magazine open on the table in front of her. When Jean saw the headline, *Are you getting enough Niacin?* she gasped in alarm. "Oh my god. Put that away!"

Ariela glanced up with a frown. "Why? It's just a health article." She returned to her reading.

Jean snorted. "I know. That's what worries me." She got a bowl down and reached for the cereal.

"Ha-ha. Very funny."

But as Jean silently predicted, it wasn't long before Ariela made another of her ridiculous suggestions.

"We should have green tea on hand. It's supposed to be good for you."

"You don't like tea."

Without looking up from the page, Ariela shrugged. "I could learn. I *should*."

Jean groaned. "Not this again. Do me a favor, stick to the makeover tips. Stop reading those health updates. I don't need you imagining you've got a wheat allergy next. And I'm through, I mean it, I'm through with all those stupid fad diets."

"You make it sound like I'm a hypochondriac or something."

Jean slowly turned and gave her roommate a significant look.

Ariela rolled her eyes. "I'm not that bad."

"Debatable. So, what time is Mrs. Corley coming in?" Jean pulled out a chair and sat at the table.

"Nine."

Ariela's listless reply made Jean smile. Sprinkling sugar on her flakes, she asked, "Are you going straight down after breakfast?"

"Actually, I'm going to run to the market first and pick up something for later."

Jean's spoon hovered in front of her, milk dripping back into the bowl. "But I have to bring some sample books over to Banks Brothers at eight."

"I'll be right back. Just go do what you have to do. I've got it covered."

"Good."

———

As Ariela dressed for work, she thought about her appointment that morning. Though it was their policy to fawn over their clients, Mrs. Corley was a woman who appreciated a bit more fuss than normal. Unfortunately, that didn't mean she made it any easier on them. Her habitual indecision was maddening, but the money on the line made it worth the trouble.

Their last appointment was particularly frustrating. The knotty-pine cabinets Mrs. Corley had chosen were suddenly out. Now she wanted a radical new look for her kitchen, something sleek and modern. Maybe in oak? Ariela had crossed off the tile countertops without blinking and listened patiently while the client asked about granite, but not necessarily granite, instead. Could she do that?

"That's no problem," Ariela assured her with a tight smile, then brought out examples for Mrs. Corley to look over.

Then they moved on to wallpaper samples. That alone took well over an hour, even with Ariela steering the woman in the right direction again and again.

If Mrs. Corley didn't commit to this kitchen plan today, there was no telling what Ariela would do. She could almost picture herself escorting the impossible woman out and giving her a boot in the ass as she waved her off. Ariela sighed. No way could she ever do anything of the sort. Still, it was an enjoyable fantasy—hours of pleasure without the blowback and guilt.

Being Friday, Ariela would be on her own for lunch. Jean had a standing date with Ron.

Her roommate and business partner was already gone when Ariela slipped out the front door, locking it behind her. Heading down the front steps, she turned left at the sidewalk.

Gorgeous, the day was simply gorgeous—warm sunshine, clear, deep blue sky, and the lazy hum of bumblebees on the old-fashioned roses growing along the neighbor's fence. Ariela drew the fragrance deep and sighed at the unexpected subtle finish of freshly mown grass that followed. It was a perfect day to play hooky, or maybe enjoy a picnic.

Truth be told, she didn't mind the Friday routine. She had an hour, one whole hour, all to herself and she liked to stroll over to the little market at the end of the block. They usually had something good in their deli case, and a nice selection of sparkling juices and waters to go with it.

———

Pushing his way out the doors of the Spiffy Mart, Dylan wolfed down the last bite of his breakfast sandwich. There were two newspapers caught tight under his left arm and a second unwrapped sandwich in his right hand. He felt a wave of relief to see Max still waiting exactly where he'd left him, tied to the bike rack.

"Good boy."

Dylan tore the sandwich into thirds and fed it to the dog. He had to shove the excited animal back in order to untie the knot and free him. The instant Max felt slack in the leash he took off, nearly jerking Dylan's arm out of its socket. He struggled frantically to keep his newspapers from raining down on the sidewalk one section at a time.

"Max, wait! I said, *wait*, damn it."

If he lost anything, Max was going to pay. A newspaper was a treasure. Even though he could get all the information he needed off the internet, there was something deeply satisfying about holding a paper. The pleasure of having to wash the inky residue off his fingers after he finished reading could never be replaced by a screen. Another drawback to reading online was his habit of making notes in the margins would naturally end. Harsh. Then there was the daily crossword, of course. He'd missed those the most while he was overseas.

Dylan hauled the dog back at the corner to keep him from darting into traffic. Giving up the fight for the moment, Max waited, happily fanning the air with his tail. When the light changed, Dylan eased up on the leash and the golden retriever took the lead, this time striding as regally as a show dog. Anyone who saw them might be fooled into thinking Max was domesticated, but Dylan knew better. His dog was a disaster waiting to happen.

Crossing the intersection, Dylan looked up from his dog and his smile evaporated when he saw a bike messenger shoot out of a dental-office parking lot and barrel into a woman on the sidewalk. The large hedge growing next to the lot must have blocked her from view. The impact threw her backwards and Dylan winced when he heard her head strike the concrete.

He broke into a run and reached the accident scene as the stunned bicyclist fought his way back to his feet. Still straddling his bike, the man stared bug-eyed at the woman lying in front of his tire.

Max, always the friendliest of dogs, chose that inopportune moment to leap on the guy and nearly knocked him over again. Aghast, Dylan dragged Max back by his collar.

The stunned messenger clutched his helmet. "I didn't see her. I swear. She was just there." They both turned to look at her. "Is she okay? Please tell me she's okay."

The woman lifted her head, her confusion palpable, and mumbled something.

Dylan went to one knee next to her. "Hey there. Are you all right?"

Her hand went to her forehead. "I think so." The sun caught her directly in the eyes when she squinted to look up at him. She grimaced and closed them again, turning her face away.

Despite his concern, Dylan couldn't help but notice how pretty she was, how nice she smelled. Her delicate perfume invaded his head with his next breath. A little shaken by it, he rose and gave the bicyclist an uncertain shrug.

"She seems okay, but I'm not a doctor."

One thing was certain—she was going to have one whopper of a goose egg on the back of her head.

The courier checked his wristwatch. "I'm so sorry, but I really have to fly. I'm on the clock here."

Since the woman wasn't asking for herself, Dylan spoke up. "Do you have a business card, just in case?"

"Yes." Reaching down, he pulled one out of a ridiculously tight pocket and handed it to Dylan. He started to go into another apology.

Dylan raised his hand, stopping him. "It's cool. I'll stick around."

"Thank you. Thanks a lot. I really appreciate it." The messenger took off and rejoined the early traffic.

"Okay." Dylan turned back to the woman and a sudden chill sliced through him. She was too quiet, too still. Why wasn't she sitting up? He dropped to his knee to take a closer look. "Hey. Still with me?"

Nope. Or she was doing one hell of a Sleeping Beauty impersonation. The stray thought left him wondering if a kiss would actually wake her.

"Better not try it," he said to Max. Dylan patted her soft cheek instead. "Miss, miss? Can you hear me?"

Max nudged his way in and licked the young woman from chin to hairline in long slobbery strokes.

"What the hell?" Dylan wrestled him back, banishing the dog to the nearby grass. If an animal could sulk, Max was certainly doing it now. "You stay there. I mean it." Dylan pointed sternly at the dog.

The woman jerked awake with a gasp. "I'm bleeding!"

Dylan whipped around and saw her feeling her damp face, a look of outright panic in her eyes.

"You're not bleeding," he assured her. "That was just my dog. He licked you. Sorry about that."

Who could blame the animal? Dylan was having similar thoughts himself.

"I feel wet," she said weakly.

"I know, that's because my dog—"

"What?" Then she began to fade.

"Hey! Can you focus on me?" Dylan took her head in his hands and stroked her cheeks with his thumbs.

Her lashes fluttered open and she locked onto his eyes.

"Wow," she whispered before going limp.

Tara Mills

Two

Dylan cradled the woman's head in one hand while he fumbled in his pocket for his phone. As he placed the emergency call, he gently lowered her onto his left hand, cushioning her skull from the concrete. Within minutes, an ambulance and a squad car stopped along the curb. Apart from a soft moan, the woman had been eerily silent while he waited for help.

The EMTs moved in and took over, shunting Dylan aside. Suddenly cast adrift, he turned to find the police officer next to him. They walked over to the squad car and Dylan gave his statement. He was distracted while answering questions and kept watch over the woman from a distance.

They had her on a stretcher now, though that was as far as they'd made it. Obviously conscious, she fought to sit up, against the advice of the paramedics. Dylan grinned when she impatiently brushed the flashlight away from her face and demanded to know what happened. Finished with his statement, Dylan wandered over.

She spotted him. Ignoring the others, she asked him directly, "What happened?"

Before he could explain her lashes fluttered and she seemed to stare at him, though he couldn't say if it was a vacant stare or not. He thought so at first until one of the EMTs shined his flashlight in her face again she swatted it away with an annoyed, "Do you mind?" She turned back to him.

Intrigued, Dylan took another step forward. "You were in a battle with a bike messenger. You lost. Do you remember? I got his business card for you."

She squeezed her eyes shut for a moment. "Hmm, vaguely."

When she tried to sit up, the EMT stopped her. "Please—we think you have a concussion. You should come in for observation."

"I can't. I have to work. I'm sure I'm fine." She shook her head and let out a groan. "Whoa, woozy."

"We can make a call for you," the EMT offered, giving her the hard sell.

"I don't know." She sought Dylan again.

He slowly nodded. "Do it."

To his surprise, she agreed, finally resigned to the idea. "Okay."

The medics moved fast, strapping her down, not allowing her a single second to change her mind. As they rolled her to the back of the waiting ambulance, she turned her head, fighting to find...*him*?

She gave a weak smile. "Thanks for staying with me."

He closed the distance. "Wait—what's your name?"

"Please," she pleaded with the medic pushing her stretcher. She stopped rolling, leaving her hanging halfway out of the vehicle. Her hand reached for Dylan's.

"Ariela Perrine." Then she laughed and blushed. "And who's my champion?"

He grinned and squeezed her hand. "Dylan Bond."

"Thank you, Dylan Bond."

"My pleasure."

"This is so embarrassing," she muttered as the stretcher rolled all the way inside, pulling their fingers apart. One of the medics climbed up with her. The other closed them in.

Dylan returned to the sidewalk as the ambulance drove away without fanfare. Feeling oddly and abruptly excused he looked around and finally noticed the small crowd dispersing. His talent for observation had failed him for the first time.

Suddenly remembering Max, he spun and saw the dog lying in the shade, patiently waiting with the remains of the newspapers torn and creased beneath him.

———

"A concussion?" Jean asked as she drove Ariela home.

The call from her roommate an hour ago had shocked her almost as much as hearing she needed a ride home from the hospital. It explained why she wasn't running their office when Jean got back.

"A *mild* concussion." Ariela touched her scalp with care. "It's like a bruise on the brain. I just have to take it easy—no sudden movements, no field hockey or soccer."

"I know what a concussion is."

Ariela groaned. "Oh god, how much is this going to cost me?"

Her question made no sense. Frowning, Jean's eyes cut to her friend then back to the road again. "Why would it cost *you* anything? The messenger service is responsible. Their insurance should cover it."

Ariela ran her hands up and down her thighs, squeezing them. This did not bode well. "Um, I didn't actually get his business card from the guy."

"What guy?"

"There was this other guy there too. With his dog. They stayed with me. He's the one who called the ambulance."

"Did you get *his* name?"

Ariela bit her lip. "Yes…*sort of.*"

It was Jean's turn to groan. "You forgot his name, didn't

you?"

"Hey, I have a concussion, remember? I have an excuse."

"What's your excuse every other time?" Jean muttered under her breath.

Ariela scowled at her and crossed her arms.

She was apparently still miffed when they pulled into the driveway. Ariela jumped out of the car and made a beeline for their back door.

Jean sighed, regretting the timing of her dig. Scooping up the sample books from the backseat, she hurried after Ariela. Her roommate was already heading up the flight of stairs to their apartment.

"I'm sorry," Jean called after her.

Ariela stopped, still facing forward. "Forget it. You had a point."

"But ragging on you doesn't exactly accomplish anything."

"Right again."

Jean threw out her hand, rattling her keys at the same time. "I guess it's not the end of the world. All we have to do is call the dental office and find out which messenger service they use. Piece of cake."

"Yeah, that'll work." Ariela turned slowly, looking relieved. "I'll call them when I come down."

"About that—I was thinking maybe you should take the rest of the day off. I'll make the call for you and handle the office myself. Take it easy, okay?" If she'd blinked she might have missed Ariela's quick forgiving smile.

"You twisted my arm."

Jean watched as she let herself into their apartment. "I'm right downstairs if you need anything. Don't be afraid to call me."

"I won't. Thanks." Ariela quietly closed the door.

Hitching up the sample books in her arm, Jean went straight through to their business. The light on the answering machine was blinking. She let the message play while she unlocked the front door and switched on the open sign for their design studio. Hearing the carpet they'd ordered for an important job had been discontinued sent her mind scrambling for options. Damn. She dropped heavily into her desk chair and reached for the phone. Fortunately, Jean was able to head off a full-blown panic attack when the third warehouse on her list told her they had one roll left. She claimed it on the spot.

Crisis averted, she hung up the phone and glanced out the front window. There was a strange man loitering on the sidewalk, clearly confused about something. He looked at a slip of paper in his hand then back at the house. What was that all about? Curious herself now, Jean went to investigate.

She opened the front door and peeked out. "Can I help you?"

"Maybe, I'm looking for someone. The address I have led me here, but I think there's been a mistake. This is supposed to be a residence."

"Actually, it's both. Who are you looking for?"

"Ariela Perrine."

Ah ha. Now she understood. "Were you the one who helped her today?"

He gave her a modest smile and nodded. "The same."

"Come in. Ariela's my business partner and roommate."

Jean stood back so he could pass and closed the door after him. She examined him with interest; nice height, good build, great face, filled out a pair of jeans like a god, and his aftershave was doing its job. Noting the damp hair, she suspected he'd showered just before coming here. Ooh, this was getting even more interesting. Delightfully amused now, she offered her hand. "I'm Jean Myers."

"Dylan Bond," he said, shaking it. "I brought the messenger's card for her."

"Ariela's upstairs taking it easy for the rest of the day. Why don't I show you the way and you can give it to her yourself?"

She led him through the back and showed him the staircase leading to their apartment. Standing at the bottom of the stairs, she watched him climb, thoroughly appreciating how his worn and faded jeans moved with him. Only when she heard Ariela's surprised, "Hi," did Jean turn and go back to work with a happy little spring in her step.

———

"Please, come in." Ariela grabbed her sweater off the hook on the wall and slipped it on, feeling a little underdressed in her pajamas.

What on earth was *he* doing here, and how had he found her? Not that she was complaining. Oh no, far from it. He'd made a startling impression on her earlier today. When he'd smiled at her, she could have sworn his brilliant blue eyes were dancing like fairies at a midsummer frolic. Odder still, when he spoke she'd imagined butterflies circling her head. She'd heard tinkling bells. At the time, she hoped it was because of the knock on her head. Now she wasn't so sure. Just looking at him again was doing crazy things to her mental and physical circuitry.

The guy entered the apartment and gaped at the furniture right out of the sixties. Very familiar with this reaction, Ariela laughed.

"Yeah, I get it. The Jetsons meet Beetlejuice, right?

Probably not the décor you'd expect two interior designers to have."

He shook his head, still blinking as he took it all in.

Overlapping the edges of her unbuttoned sweater, she hugged herself, painfully aware she wasn't wearing a bra. "Well, there's a simple explanation. When you're cash poor and starting a business with next to nothing, you can't exactly go wild in your own apartment right off the bat. We're still living with the furniture we had during college, courtesy of Uncle Henry and Aunt Rose—with a few freebies thrown in to make it really eclectic."

She gestured to their space-age teal sofa. "Please, have a seat. Appearances aside, it's actually quite comfortable. Can I get you something to drink—juice, tea, coffee maybe?"

Anything, anything at all?

Turning, he flashed a little dimple. "No thanks. I'm fine."

He'd get no argument from her.

They sat down and he looked pained when she settled into the bright tangerine-colored armchair. Understandable. It did clash jarringly with her pajamas—pastel balloons floating across a soft pink background. The poor guy blinked several times, seemingly trying to handle the color overload. Biting her lip so she didn't break out laughing, Ariela tucked her feet up and gave him a slow, curious smile.

He sat up straight, recognizing his cue. "Right. Sorry. I suppose you're wondering why I'm here."

"It crossed my mind," she admitted.

"I didn't get a chance to give you that business card before they carted you away."

"Oh, and you brought it to me? That's so nice. Thanks."

He peered at her intently, more serious now. "How are

you?"

Even though she didn't know him, there was something in his expression that made her believe he could be trusted, and more importantly, he wouldn't have asked about her if he didn't honestly want to know. The naked concern radiating out of his deep blue eyes transformed his handsome face into something miles beyond devastating.

"I have a mild concussion." Why was she blushing?

The corner of his mouth curled up a smidgen. "Headache?"

She felt her warm cheeks flare hotter. What was wrong with her? "Not anymore."

"Good." He broke into a full-blown smile and settled back on the sofa, apparently satisfied.

Still reeling from the power of his smile, Ariela shifted uneasily in her chair. "I have a confession— I can't remember your name. It's really bugging me."

His head dropped back and he laughed. "Dylan Bond."

She brightened. "Like in Bond, Dylan Bond?" She'd remember it now.

His eyebrows flicked up in amusement. "Something like that."

"Dabbles in international intrigue?" She was toying with him, but it was fun.

He flashed a sexy-assed smile. How many kinds did the guy have? "I'm comfortable being in the middle of the action, but I'm back to working domestically again."

Say what? Ariela's eyebrows rose so high she felt her hairline shift. "I think I need a translation. What is it you do?"

He had a great laugh. "I'm a journalist. I just finished a stint in Iraq, but I'm back now. It's nice not having to deal with body armor and helmets."

Looking skeptically back at him, she assumed he was putting her on. "Is that right?"

"Actually, yes." He shifted onto one butt cheek and pulled out his wallet. A second later, he handed her a press pass from a recent event. "I'm working out of my house now—mostly covering the political side of the war."

She read the pass, her doubts dissolving. "You actually live around here?" She handed the card back and he put it away.

"Sure, why not?"

Shrugging, she said, "Well, Lewiston isn't exactly Washington DC."

"With the internet and a telephone, you can stay connected from pretty much anywhere. Still, I do plenty of traveling and Washington is only a two-hour drive. I can be there and back before Max even notices I'm gone."

"Max?"

His blue eyes were dancing again. Hello tinkling bells. "My retriever."

"Ah yes, I remember him now."

Dylan grinned. "He's probably the reason you woke up wanting a wet wipe."

She laughed and his smile deepened. That dimple of his was growing on her.

"Listen," he said, leaning forward, elbows on his knees. "How about going out with me sometime? We can do something gentle—bumper cars maybe?"

She waited for her retreat mechanism to kick in. It was strangely silent. "Here I was, hoping you'd suggest hang gliding or bungee jumping."

"Anything you want. I'm flexible."

Another perfect smile flashed at her and Ariela's heartbeat

spiked. "Sure, why not?"

"Good." He stood and pulled the business card out of his front pocket. "Here, before I forget."

Ariela unfolded her legs and reached for the floor with her bare feet. When she rose he was right there with the card. Taking it, she noticed he was taller than she'd initially thought. She supposed that made sense. How well can you judge anyone's height when you're on your back?

She walked him to the door. Opening it before she could, he turned and asked, "When?"

"When what?" She watched his eyes move as he took an unabashed tour of her face.

"When can I take you out?"

The birds in her stomach were back, fluttering away. Good thing they were keeping the noise down. "Whenever?"

Dylan gave her a meaningful look, full of promise. "Expect a call."

Ariela closed the door behind him and fell against it. If she hadn't locked her knees, she would have been a puddle of melting woman on the floor. As Dylan's footfalls faded out and the back door shut, she pressed a hand to her excited heart. Something told Ariela that she was in for a wild ride with this one. Hell, just sitting in a quiet room with Dylan was exhilarating. Now she knew it wasn't just the concussion. There was far more at play here. Scary.

She was about to find out whether Dylan's hands were capable and steady on the wheel, because he was already in her driver's seat. She knew it, and judging by the look he gave her on the way out, he knew it too. Suddenly the Beatles were singing *Drive My Car* in her head.

Ariela pulled herself up and wobbled on shaky legs into the kitchen for a cold drink of water with loads of ice.

Tara Mills

Three

Ariela was startled awake by the ringing telephone at her bedside. She peered blearily out from behind heavy lashes and read the clock. Six-thirty? The phone had beaten her alarm by thirty minutes.

Her hand landed heavily on the receiver, and she yawned through a deep, "Hello?"

"Did I wake you?"

A man's voice?

Confused, Ariela gave a cautious, "Yes. Who is this?"

She heard soft chuckling on the other end. "It's Dylan. Dylan Bond."

"Dylan? Is there something wrong with you? Why would you call anyone this early? What were you thinking? And FYI, I *never* get up before seven." He might be hot, but she needed to establish some ground rules with the guy.

"*What?* I called to see if you'd like to have dinner with me tonight."

Now she was completely lost. Tonight? "What time is it?"

"It's six-thirty—p.m.—Friday night. Are you hungry?"

She pulled herself up and smoothed back her messy hair. "Six-thirty in the evening? Really? Wow." She tried to get her head around that information.

"Maybe I should just let you sleep."

His suggestion zapped a hit of adrenaline into her sluggish bloodstream. "No!" Calming herself, she went on. "I mean, I've been sleeping for hours, but I haven't eaten since breakfast, so yes, I'd love dinner."

"How much time do you need?"

Her shrug was automatic. "Thirty minutes?"

"Done. I'll be waiting outside."

She stifled another yawn. "Use the alley. I'll be coming out the back."

"Got it. See you soon, Ariela."

She hung up and swung her legs out from under the covers. Walking like a stiff zombie over to the window, she raised the blinds.

"Oh my god," she gasped as brilliant light pierced the room, making her squint in pain. She let go of the cord as if it had stung her, and the blinds dropped back into place, shutting out the searing sunshine. It was too soon for that.

There was a note from Jean stuck to the television. She didn't expect to be home until late, which meant she probably wouldn't be home at all. Jean's notes usually implied a sleepover at Ron's. Better his place than theirs.

Ariela walked out of the bathroom dressed and primped with four minutes to spare. Standing at her dresser, she picked up her favorite scent and gave her wrists a dab. At the sound of a car pulling up outside, she turned and set the bottle down. She pulled back the edge of the blinds and saw a strange Saab in Jean's parking space.

"Here we go," she said, none too confidently, and grabbed her purse.

The sunshine blinded her when she went outside. She had to shade her eyes to safely navigate the short flight of steps. Once she touched down on the path of pavers she chanced another look at the cars and was startled to see Dylan staring at her as he climbed out of his car. Looking down at her creamy linen pantsuit and butterscotch camisole, she understood why. She was bright enough to burn his retinas.

They met up at his front bumper and he escorted her to the passenger side, opening the door for her. Before she could duck into the car, he held up his hand, stopping her for a moment while he looked her up and down more personally. His bold approval made her quiver.

"You're breathtaking, luminous," he told her.

Stunned and speechless, she sank onto the passenger seat, and with a smile, he closed her in.

Joining her in the car, Dylan caught Ariela eyeing him with equally frank interest.

He swiveled his body in his seat, giving her a better view. "Do I meet with your approval?"

Laughing, Ariela took him in, from his dark blue, button-down shirt and plain, black jeans to his simple, dark Nike's. "You'll do." She imagined it was probably her warm tone, more than her words that pleased him.

"Good." Dylan fired up the engine and winked as he threw his arm behind her seat to back out. "I cleaned my car for you too," he added, looking over his shoulder.

Flattered and amused, Ariela laughed again. "Be still, my heart."

"I thought you were worth it."

"And you're admitting this to me?"

He shifted into drive and snickered. "I wanted to make a good impression."

She was on to him. "How's your house?"

"You won't be seeing that tonight."

Laughing, Ariela ignored the passing scenery. Her date's handsome profile was far more appealing. "I didn't expect to hear from you so soon."

"Ah." Dylan nodded as he signaled his turn. "I meant to give you more time to recuperate, but then I got a call and found out I'm heading out of town early Monday. I didn't want to put off seeing you again since I'm not sure when I'll get back."

"Where are you going this time?"

"Back to Iraq."

Ariela's blood cooled. "I thought you were doing domestic stories now."

"Primarily, but this is intertwined. There's a small group of senators going over next week and I need to be on the ground before they arrive."

"Does that make you nervous—going back?" She was nervous for the guy and she didn't even know him!

In her mind she saw her parents again, as clear now as that day sixteen years ago. Her mom had been wearing her ruffled, pink robe. Right behind her stood Ariela's dad, looking so handsome in his uniform. He'd been pressed against her, nose buried in her hair as she rinsed out a coffee cup in the sink, while Ariela ate her breakfast at the table behind them. Her father's arms had wound around her mother's waist, and they'd swayed side to side to a silent tune. Ariela remembered how she'd smiled when he nuzzled her mother's neck and started her laughing. Her parents had been playful and completely in love. Like an otter, Ariela had swum in the overflow of that love, amazingly content.

"Gotta go," was the last thing her father said as he bent to kiss her on the top of the head.

Dylan's voice pulled Ariela back to the present.

"Not really. Besides, nearly everything we do involves some risk—even driving to the restaurant tonight."

"I suppose, but you're going back to a war zone. Doesn't that make you a bit anxious?"

He smiled. "No. It's not something you want to get overly confident about, but if you use your head, you'll be ahead of the game. Experience minimizes the risks. There's less chance you'll blunder into something if you know what you're doing."

"Well, I wouldn't want to go."

"Good thing you don't have to." He glanced over and flashed a smile. "If it makes you feel any better, this should be my last assignment over there. I'm not sorry about it…though probably not for the reasons you might expect."

Ariela frowned. "What do you mean?"

"Basically, I was in lockdown for the last year because of how dangerous it got to venture out. We had to rely on trusted Iraqi stringers to do all our important legwork. It felt like I was under house arrest. When you can't do your own investigating, it's frustrating and the job isn't as satisfying—pretty tough to feel like a journalist under restricted conditions."

Oddly enough, Ariela *was* glad he wasn't going to cover the war anymore, whatever the reason. Still, she didn't understand why his personal safety concerned her. He was a virtual stranger, yet it really bothered her to think of him in such an unstable and dangerous place.

Dylan seemed to pick up on it. "Listen, I'll be fine. I won't even be outside the green zone this time around, so the risks are minimal."

She gave him a weak smile. "You're going to think this sounds weird, but I don't think I could handle being involved with someone who's always heading into danger. The stress would be too much for me."

He grinned and his gorgeous baby blues were dancing when he asked, "Are you suggesting that if I can keep from getting my ass shot off you might consider falling for me?"

Ariela laughed. "I've already fallen for you," she said, making light of how they'd met.

"Good, because I'd like to see more of you."

"I'd like that too, but you know my terms."

"Get my ass out of danger, and we'll talk," he said with a nod, then flipped on his turn signal and cut across the intersection.

"That about covers it."

They pulled into a crammed parking lot and drove around and around, looking for an open space.

"Let me drop you at the door, and I'll find something," Dylan said on the next pass.

"I'd rather walk in with you."

He smiled at that. "Your call."

The space they eventually found should have come with shuttle service, but any further complaints were forgotten when Dylan's hand settled comfortably on the small of Ariela's back as she walked up the steps to the restaurant. That touch made her float the rest of the way.

Ariela waited by a large palm while Dylan spoke with a host. He returned with a suggestion.

"Since we hit it on the wrong night and the wrong time, this could take a while. How about waiting in the bar?"

"Sounds good."

They cut through the crowd and lucked out when they passed another couple leaving. Ariela and Dylan claimed the vacant stools.

A bartender stopped over and set out fresh coasters. "What can I get you?"

Dylan looked at Ariela with raised eyebrows.

"I'll take a Seven-Up or Sprite—whichever you have."

"And I'd like a glass of your house pinot noir."

The bartender moved off to fill their order.

Dylan snapped his fingers. "I forgot. You probably can't have alcohol tonight, right?"

"The doctor discouraged it."

"Are you still fuzzy on the details or can you remember things now?"

"As far as I can tell, I'm fine." When the guy looked at you, he *really* looked at you, but without being creepy about it. Interesting. It probably helped in his line of work.

"You're lucky it wasn't more serious," he said, bringing her out of her thoughts.

She scoffed at the idea. "I don't know. Athletes go right back into the game all the time after getting hit harder than I did."

"Most wear helmets and still have to be medically cleared first."

Good point. "I *was* checked out." Closing the subject, she smiled sweetly at the bartender when he set her fizzing glass down in front of her.

Dylan drew his wine toward him, not finished studying her. There was something in his expression she couldn't quite read.

Finally, he moved his glass aside and asked, "Can I touch you? Would you mind? I've wanted to check something out since I picked you up."

Touch her? What did he expect her to say, *"Grope away?"* Considering where they were, she felt relatively safe. *Still.*

After a lengthy delay, she asked carefully, "Touch me where?"

It was tough to say which was sexier, his chuckle or his grin. "Indulge me." With that, his fingers slid under her hair and brushed her scalp. Their gazes locked. Her heartbeat accelerated as he located her bump and gently traced it. "That's not as bad as I thought it would be." He gave her a reassuring smile and withdrew his hand.

Okay, that was strangely arousing.

"You're a little peculiar," she told him, refreshingly pleased with *this* date.

Clearly amused, he raised his glass. "Judging by your smile, I'd say that's a good thing. Here's to being in the right place at the right time this morning."

Those astonishing lapis blue eyes shimmered over the rim of his glass, beckoning her into dangerous depths as they tapped their stemware together.

———

The surprises continued during dinner. At one point Dylan picked up the strawberry on the edge of his plate by the stem and sliced Ariela's romantic heart wide open by offering it to her.

A startling yet pleasant thought flowed through her mind. He could be the *one*—if only he had a less dangerous occupation. She gave him a melting look—she couldn't help it.

"Would you like it?" His smile coaxed her to accept. "I saw how much you enjoyed yours."

Oh yes, she was definitely in trouble here. Reaching out, she picked the berry from between his fingers and took a dainty bite while he watched. It felt naughty, full of implications.

Stop it Ariela, you're being ridiculous. It was just a damn strawberry!

Except what was happening between them, while feeling deceptively casual, was intensely intimate. It was one of the strangest dates she'd ever been on, not that it had veered far from the norm. It hadn't. It just *felt* different.

Setting the stem aside, she dabbed her mouth with her napkin. "Thank you."

This was one time she actually wanted a man to dominate the conversation. She repeatedly opened up subjects only to be drawn back in when Dylan asked questions in return. It was impossible not to feel disappointed because he was so fascinating, his experiences wildly different from hers. She pictured him as the metaphorical canteen of water in the desert, an oasis, a cool, gratifying plunge into experiences both foreign and elemental. She wanted to drink deep, get her fill, but he smoothly turned the discussion back around, leaving her thirst for more unquenched.

For some inexplicable reason, he seemed to find her just as interesting. Imagine. They laughed like old friends, and sometimes her spontaneous trills of delight drew glances from other diners. Dylan wasn't the least bit bothered by it either, earning even more points in his favor. He was as lost in the moment as she was.

Picking up the thread of their earlier conversation before he could turn it back on her again, she asked, "And that's why you haven't settled down?"

"Not since Greece. Neither of us was ready for a commitment, especially Maria." Dylan shook his head and chuckled to himself. "I was in and out of her life so often, when I got back from Rome the last time I found she'd given away most of my clothes to her various boyfriends. I was lucky to get away with a few pairs of underwear."

Ariela covered her mouth, laughing into her hand. His anecdotes were some of the best she'd ever heard. "How could you stand her?"

"Well, she was gorgeous and uninhibited. That's a sexy combination for any guy."

"I'll bet," she said dryly, studying this charmer across the table. "Do you have your passport on you?"

"As a matter of fact, I do—habit."

"Can I see it?"

"Sure." He reached back and pulled it out. It was warm and curved from being in his pocket.

Ariela smothered another laugh when she saw it and went to work pressing it flat before opening it. She scanned all the stamps with interest. "Where's Tenerife?"

"It's an island off the northwest coast of Africa, part of the Canaries. Belongs to Spain. Very beautiful. You can climb the mountains and get lost in the clouds. Palm trees and miles of topless beaches."

"Topless beaches, hmm?" The corner of her mouth twitched when she glanced up at him before returning to the passport. "There on business?"

"She asked knowingly," he said with a twinkle in his eye. "No, I was doing a little research on my own time."

"I suspected as much." It was impossible to hold back her smile. "My mind is full of all kinds of possibilities."

Now he laughed outright and without apparent shame. "Au natural isn't all it's cracked up to be, I assure you. All it means is no matter what the age or physical condition of the bathers, anyone can go topless—and they do. So, for every opportunity to eyeball perky beauties, there's an even better chance you're going to find yourself experiencing a full-body shudder. Try and picture biting into the sourest lemon there is when you least expect it, and you'll understand the reaction I'm talking about here."

"I never realized public nudity could be so risky," she teased, returning the passport.

"You have no idea." He grinned and shifted to tuck it back into his pocket.

"I'm having such a nice time tonight."

The lines around his smile deepened. "Me too. What do you say we head out, maybe take a walk?"

"I'd like that."

"Would you mind if we picked up Max first? He'd never forgive me if word got around that I went for a walk without him. He's been known to hold a grudge."

"We wouldn't want that."

Dylan rose and came around the table to pull out her chair as Ariela set her napkin beside her empty plate. It thrilled her to finally find a true gentleman. When his hands brushed her shoulders, it was a struggle to ignore the tingles running down her spine. Unbidden, the image of her parents, so in love, flashed in her head. She pushed it away. This was only a date. No matter how charming, Dylan Bond wasn't the man for her. She could never allow herself to fall for a guy who made a career out of traipsing into treacherous situations.

Tara Mills

Four

Ariela waited in the car while Dylan jogged up the path to the side yard. He let himself into a chain link enclosure and disappeared. At the sound of desperate barking, she leaned across the center console and braced her hand on the driver's seat, trying to see what was happening out there. Unfortunately, the corner of the house blocked her view.

Without warning, Max blew through the chain-link gate and sent it crashing against the fence while he dragged his master behind him. Dylan's impossibly long strides seemed to defy the laws of nature. Every step was more like a leap, coming alarmingly close to actual splits. It looked both painful and comical. Then Max spotted Ariela. He ran around to the passenger side and jumped up, planting both front feet on her window and gave her a friendly woof. She was laughing when Dylan wrestled the dog to the back door.

"Get in the back, you irritating animal," he muttered.

Smothering her giggles, she instantly sobered when Max bounded into the back and stuck his head between the front seats. He moved up Ariela's arm, sniffing the entire way, before finally resting his chin on her shoulder. His hot, doggie breath steamed in her hair.

"Good dog, nice dog." She gave the top of his bony head an uneasy pat.

Dylan climbed into the car and reached around, shoving Max's muzzle back with one hand. It didn't take. The golden set his chin right back on her shoulder again.

"Sorry about that." Dylan tried once more with the same result. Grinning sheepishly, he said, "Don't worry. I have a trick up my sleeve."

Firing up the engine, he hit the power button on his door and opened the back window. All interest in Ariela evaporated and Max took up his position behind Dylan, facing into the wind as they pulled onto the street.

While inside, Dylan had put on a blazer. He reached into the left-hand pocket and pulled something out.

"Here, this is for you." He dropped it onto her lap.

Ariela picked up the lint roller, biting her lip with amusement.

"It's for your nice outfit," he explained.

"So I gathered. Did I mention how weird this date is?"

He shot her a playful grin. "Once or twice. Still a good thing?"

Ariela smiled. "It's a very good thing."

———

They parked along Scenic Lake. Even in the dying light of evening, there was a lot of activity. Families and singles were riding their bikes on the trails. The skateboard park was full of kids and the sounds carried over the hum of slow-cruising traffic. Baby strollers were still very much a part of the scene, yet soon the path lights would switch on.

Dylan carefully opened the back door, barely catching Max's leash before the retriever could take off without them. In the space of time it took him to lock the car, the dog must have felt the slack on the leash because he yanked his owner forward. Dylan made a desperate grab for Ariela's hand. She held on tight, stumbling after them.

Sparing her a quick glance, he apologized, "Didn't mean to startle you, but I don't want to get separated."

"Is that right?" She gave him a skeptical smile and left her hand where it was. "Your dog needs a little training."

"I agree." They both averted their eyes as the retriever lifted his leg on the first tree he came to. "We're still getting to know each other."

"Really?" Why did that surprise her? Dylan said he'd been out of the country. She was jerked out of her musings when Max hauled them to the next tree and sprinkled that one as well.

"Yes. He was my grandmother's dog, but he got too big for her to handle. I walked right into it when I came home. No one else was offering to take him, and since I have my own place with a fenced yard, it made sense." Dylan shrugged, his smile telling. "I don't really mind. I like the company."

His confession made her like him even more. "Looks like the feeling's mutual. What will you do with him while you're away?"

"The vet recommended a kennel. I stopped to check it out—it's pretty nice. Max is going to stay there. Aren't you, Maxi?" His mushy tone got the retriever all worked up. Dylan chuckled and continued. "When I get back at the end of the week, we'll look into obedience classes."

"You'll both probably get a lot out of it." Ariela smiled and skipped over a crack.

"Let's hope."

They crossed the grass to reach the lower path skirting the shoreline and Max slowed to a more comfortable lope.

"Look at that," murmured Ariela, admiring the moon coming up over the water. It cast a haunting, beautiful reflection.

He fell quiet, lost in thought for a moment while he studied it. "Next week, when I'm halfway around the world, I'll still be looking at that moon."

"But it's different."

Pondering what she said, he shook his head. "The distance and time zones, perhaps, but there are constants in this wide universe of ours that don't change. That's one of them."

They waited while Max sniffed around an over-grown bush and lifted his leg.

Dylan took that opportunity to ask, "Can I e-mail you while I'm gone?"

"Yes, I'll give you my address when you drop me off tonight."

Max pulled them back to the present and onto the path. They had to rein him in when he saw a couple with a pug coming from the opposite direction. The vicious little dog barked, straining to run at Max. The baffled retriever paused, his wagging tail frozen in midair as he looked at the other animal. Clearly, all he wanted to do was greet the little dog and share a friendly sniff. The man didn't allow it. He scooped up his snarling pet and gave Dylan and Ariela a curt nod before he and his wife strode away, noses in the air.

Turning in offense, Ariela stared after them. "That was frosty."

Dylan misunderstood her, assuming she meant the animal, not the couple. "Little dogs have more to prove, don't they, Maxi?" He playfully rubbed the golden's ears and Max pepped right up, the hostility already forgotten.

They were three quarters of the way around the lake when Ariela began to shiver.

Dylan noticed when she hugged herself. He tugged Max to a stop. "Here, take my coat."

"No. Then you'll be cold."

"I don't care."

"*I* do."

"Women." Shaking his head, he raised his arm, one eyebrow arched in challenge. "Then tuck in next to me."

Five seconds was all she gave herself to consider the offer before she snaked her arm under Dylan's blazer and around his waist. He pulled his jacket over her as best he could and snugged her against his warm side. It was a good fit.

"Better?" Based on his smile, he knew the answer.

"Much."

"I should have thought of it sooner."

"I wouldn't have accepted it sooner. My grandmother would not approve."

Nodding, he gave Ariela a squeeze. "Over dinner you mentioned you were raised by your grandmother. Do you want to tell me about it?"

"Maybe another time."

"Okay."

She liked that he backed off and didn't push her.

———

They drove Max home first then continued on to Ariela's. Pulling into the empty parking space behind the house, Dylan cut the engine. Would she ask him in? He hoped so.

She didn't disappoint. "Would you like to come up?"

"What about your roommate?"

"Jean's out tonight."

Sweet!

"Wait there." He hopped out of the car and came around to open her door.

Ariela graciously accepted his hand when she got out. Her

self–conscious laugh was cute as hell.

"I feel pampered. I'm not used to gallant gestures from my dates."

"It's a standard service when you sign on to the Dylan Bond plan." That earned another soft chuckle. He could get used to those.

The motion lights flashed on as they walked to the back stoop. Ariela fumbled with her keys in the lock, but then the door swung open and she stepped inside. He followed.

Dylan had no complaints as he climbed the stairs behind her. He had a perfect view of her tempting little ass. If anything, he was struggling with the urge to dive right into her, face first. There was something very appealing about getting up close and personal with a woman's derriere, pressing your lips against the sexy dimple that set off the top of her pretty bottom. Of course, it was best not to mention those kinds of impulses at the beginning of a relationship.

Ariela turned just inside her apartment door and flicked on the lights. "I think there's beer in the fridge. You interested?"

Loaded question. Better play it straight. "What kind?"

"Ron likes his Guinness."

"A Guinness would be great." *And who the hell is Ron?*

"Good. Sit down. I'll be right back." She dis-appeared into the kitchen.

Dylan sank onto the Jetsons' funky, teal sofa and waited.

"Do you want it in a glass?" she called.

"Please—but I'll pour it."

She returned, carrying two bottles and one glass. He smiled as she handed one to him, and he took his time pouring the stout. Noticing how amused she was by his careful technique, he explained, "You have to understand, this isn't just alcohol—

48

a six-pack to slam while you munch cheese puffs and watch the game—but rather the result of years of masterful devotion to a craft. Think of it as a fine wine, with many levels of enjoyment possible. You have the nose, the rich color, and finally the complex flavors on the tongue. It would be an insult to the brewer to drink it like swill."

Admiring the contents of his glass first, he savored the first swallow.

———

Being witness to that kind of pleasure felt downright indecent. Ariela could feel herself blushing all the way to her roots. She tipped back her bottle of juice, hiding behind it, but he noticed her embarrassment anyway. His smile was infectious and her lips spread against the mouth of her clear bottle.

"I love your blush," he told her. "Very cute. Come on." He patted the cushion next to him. "Have a seat."

Ariela lowered the bottle, but not the corners of her mouth, and sank slowly beside him.

He set his glass on the end table then turned with a request. "Forgive me?"

"For what?" she asked, mildly alarmed.

"For this."

He reached out and captured her face in his hands, then moved in. Ariela stopped breathing, held spellbound by how the intense blue of his eyes deepened even more as he closed the distance. When the brush of his lips came, it was so gentle, so right. They both smiled without disconnecting.

Ariela fumbled to put her juice on the floor without spilling it. Dylan helped her out. He took it and set it next to his glass.

"You know," he whispered, his voice low and rough. "I wouldn't be offended if you felt like touching me too," Then his hand was back, caressing her face, her cheek, tracing her jaw and throat. "If I touch you where it hurts, let me know, okay?" he murmured against her ear.

She shuddered at the heat of his breath on her sensitive skin, yet somehow managed to nod. She wanted to stretch under Dylan's hands like a cat, almost as much as she wanted to run hers all over him. Her hands made the decision for her, pressing against his chest and feeling the shape of him under his shirt. His nipples tightened beneath her palms and she pressed them with the heels of her hands. But there was more, so much more she needed to explore so she moved on, riding over his collarbone, curling over his shoulders, and sending her fingers into the silky hair at the nape of his neck. They moved together, their lips meeting and retreating, cautiously tasting until he finally stopped the nonsense. His next kiss was relentless—hungry and demanding. He coaxed her lips apart and thrust his tongue inside. Her head swimming, her body pliant, Ariela moaned, drunk on the subtle taste of Guinness on his breath.

Somehow Dylan managed to shed his jacket without breaking the kiss. When his hands found her body again, they were so hot they could have ironed cotton. She gripped his hair, her knuckles pressing against his scalp as she held on tight, drinking desperately from his lips as if he truly was that canteen she'd pictured during dinner.

Her prediction he'd be one hell of a kisser was dead accurate. He knew exactly where and how to touch a woman. When they broke apart, they were both panting for air, shaken, and stunned. The last thing Ariela expected to see were her own confused emotions flashing across Dylan's face.

"I think I'd better go." He wrenched away from her. "I want to leave you with a good opinion of me. That's not going to happen if I stay."

Nice to know she wasn't the only one impossibly aroused. She walked him to the door and they stared at each other, both still susceptible to the powerful pull, buzzing like electricity, between them.

"My e-mail," she reminded him, feeling as weak as she sounded.

"Tomorrow. Give it to me tomorrow. I really need to go— *now*—or I won't be able to leave. I'm sorry." He fled, pulling the door closed behind him.

Stunned, Ariela waited, listening as his car drove off. She'd been so wrapped up in the moment, she hadn't even recognized how dangerously close she'd come to tossing away her principles in a moment of sexual haze. It was good he'd left. She wasn't a casual-sex kind of person, and to her relief, neither was Dylan, apparently.

Five minutes later, her telephone rang. Ariela hurried out of the bathroom with her toothbrush in hand, a frothy mint rim circling her lips. She picked up, assuming it was Jean. It wasn't.

"I'm closing in on six months here," Dylan explained without preface.

Ariela blinked in surprise. "Pardon?"

"I haven't had sex in six months. My self-control was pretty strained when I bolted. I was ready to pin you to your couch like a butterfly in a bug collection." He caught his breath, as if he'd been running. "I just thought you should know. It's not a rejection, far from it."

Relieved, she smiled. "Thanks. I wondered. *Six months?*"

"Just about." There was a pause on his end before he added,

"There were opportunities. But they weren't offers I was willing to follow up on, if you get my drift. Besides, until recently, I've been on the fly for so long, relationship sex was out."

"I think I understand."

"Good. I just thought you should know."

"I can beat you by two months," she told him with a slow smile.

"Seriously? Eight months?"

"Much to my chagrin. I sort of lapsed back with an old boyfriend for convenience's sake, but after two days, I remembered why I found him so irritating in the first place."

He laughed. "I think we both need to work on this. Why don't we discuss it more tomorrow? I'll give you a call after eleven, if that's okay with you."

"I'll pencil you in."

His chuckle deepened her grin. "Sleep well, Ariela."

"Fat chance now." She hung up to the sound of his laughter.

Five

Ariela shuffled into the kitchen Saturday morning and found Jean already at the table having her morning toast and coffee.

She was just about to take a sip when she snorted at the sight of Ariela and had to set down her cup or spill. Looking up with a grin, she asked, "Rough night? That's some impressive bed hair. Should I get my camera?"

"Ha-ha. I'm a little rumpled. Get over it."

"How's your head?"

Ariela stifled a yawn. "Better. When did you get home?" She headed over to the stove and lifted the kettle, shaking it to gauge how much water was in it before turning on the burner.

"Two hours ago. Ron wanted to get to the garage early so he'd be done by four. We're going to a comedy club tonight— catch a little dinner first."

While Ariela set up her bowl of instant oatmeal, Jean returned for a refill on coffee. She kindly poured a cup for Ariela as well and slid it down the counter to her.

"Looks like you could use it."

"Thanks." Ariela let out a deep groan at her first swallow of the day.

Returning to her seat, Jean pointed to the plate on the table. "There's toast if you're interested."

"Now you're talking."

By Ariela's third bite, her brain had finally booted up. She stopped eating and frowned at Jean. "Why did you say you're home?"

"Ron wanted to get to work early, and I didn't want to hang around his place." The shrill whistle of the kettle made both women jump. Laughing at herself, Jean said, "Stay put. I've got it." A minute later she set the steaming bowl down in front of Ariela with the spoon already in it. "There you go. But you can stir your own oatmeal." Jean dropped back onto her chair and picked up her mug. "So, I never got to ask you about that guy yesterday. When I came back upstairs later you were zonked out."

Ariela felt her cheeks heat.

Jean's eyebrows shot up. "Oh yeah? What am I missing?"

"We went out to dinner last night."

"You did not!"

Her eyes cast down, Ariela licked her spoon clean. "Did too. He called and asked me out. He said he was going to call. I just didn't expect it so soon."

"And?"

"And…" said Ariela, slowly carving swirls into her cereal, "I had such a great time." Looking up, she made a scary and heartfelt confession. "I felt like Cinderella, you know—when she goes out, expecting to have a nice time, and she's still blown away?"

Jean's mouth dropped open. "No kidding?"

Ariela nodded. "He…is…something." Erasing the swirls with the back of her spoon, she started over. "Dylan has table manners too. You know how much I value those."

Jean sighed and rolled her hand impatiently, coaxing Ariela to go on.

"He's a journalist, so he's been everywhere. He had me laughing most of the time." Then Ariela's eyes went soft. "Oh Jean, he's so nice. I mean, so, so nice."

Jean stared at her, an expression of wonder on her face. "Wow."

"Is it crazy to be so hopeful about him already?"

Jean shrugged. "I don't know. Doesn't every date start hopefully?"

"Not the ones I've been on," Ariela reminded her.

"I'll give you that."

"I wish I knew. I feel like a tornado is cutting through my insides." Ariela looked bleakly at her friend. "Of course, his job is a big problem for me."

Jean cocked her head, a frown of confusion on her face. "He's a journalist."

"A journalist who's been covering war zones for years."

"For real?"

"I wish I were kidding."

Jean was understandably sympathetic, but there wasn't much she could offer as far as help went. She took another swallow of coffee and asked instead, "So what's on your agenda today?"

"I'm waiting for Dylan to call at eleven."

"You're going to bend your rules and see him again?"

Ariela threw up her hand, equally amazed. "I know. I'm insane. This makes no sense at all."

"Well, I suppose you know what you're doing," Jean said with obvious skepticism. "Now, if you'll excuse me, I need a nap. We didn't get much sleep last night." She set her cup in the sink and sauntered out.

"Sure, rub it in," Ariela called after her then sagged in her chair, suddenly worried she was losing her marbles over a gorgeous pair of eyes.

———

Ariela went down to the office to use the computer just

before ten. She wanted to create a card for Dylan, small enough to fit in his wallet, but with everything on it. Of course she realized she'd probably gone a bit overboard when she started playing with styles, fonts, colors, and various borders. It looked cramped—and needy.

"Geez, why don't I tell him my blood type while I'm at it?"

Huffing out a breath she tapped the backspace key until all evidence of her mailing address and business number were gone. Better. It was a waste of cardstock, but she didn't care once it came out of the printer looking fabulous.

Only now did she glance at the clock. She'd spent forty-five minutes on this so far? Oh well. Committed to the project, she trimmed it down and tossed the scraps into the recycling. Too bad she couldn't laminate it. As she stood there regretting the absence of a plastic sleeve for the card, she realized how insane it suddenly seemed. All told, she'd wasted an hour working on this. No way would she ever admit that to anyone—especially Dylan.

His call came right on time, something else to like about him. Dare she hope he'd been counting the minutes too?

"How are you feeling today?" he asked.

Smiling, she spun slowly back and forth in her office chair. "Much better."

"Feel like helping me with something?"

"That depends. If you're thinking about moving furniture, forget it."

He laughed. "No, Max needs a bath."

No kidding. He could use a toothbrush too.

"Ariela? You don't actually have to help. Really, I was just hoping you'd hang out with us today. I'll fire up the grill afterwards," he added, sweetening the deal.

She harrumphed, but she was smiling off into space when she did it. "Well, if you're going to twist my arm, okay. I have something for you anyway."

"How soon can I come get you?"

"I'm ready now."

"Cool. I'll be right over."

Ariela went back upstairs and swapped out her tennis shoes for sandals. If there was any chance her feet were going to get wet, the last thing she wanted to deal with later was uncomfortable shoes.

She saw Dylan's car coming down the alley from her bedroom window so she hurried out to meet him. With Jean home, and both of their cars already parked in back, there wasn't space for him. Anxious about blocking the alley, Ariela ran around to the passenger side and hopped in without fanfare. She played it casual when she handed over the little card as soon as she was buckled.

"Here, this is for you."

Dylan looked it over. "Very nice. It's going right in my wallet."

"That's the idea."

He was wearing a gray, zippered sweatshirt over an old, washed-out T-shirt. It was so beat up the detached collar hung around his throat like a necklace. His bare legs made quite an impression on her. He was wearing shorts and running shoes—no socks—so there was a nice, long stretch of manly leg showing. He had great legs. She kept stealing glances at them as they flexed and moved on the pedals. She couldn't help it.

Dylan pulled the car onto the concrete pavers embedded in his front lawn.

"You don't use the alley?" she asked.

"There's only one spot, and the upstairs tenant uses it."

"Oh, I thought you had the entire house."

"No, I just use the downstairs apartment. We go in through the side door. No one goes to the front."

Following him through the side gate, she asked, "Did you pick up for me?"

Dylan stopped and turned with a puzzled expression, then broke into a slow smile of comprehension. "Oh ...you mean did I get rid of the stuff I stashed in here from the car?"

"Uh-huh."

"It's put away, but you're not allowed to open any closets."

"I'll try to resist the urge."

He gave a snort of amusement. "It's for your own safety."

The guy could make her laugh. "Good to know."

Dylan reached for the unlocked door and pulled it open for her. She had one foot on the step when, out of nowhere, Max came charging, a dog with an escape plan, and knocked her legs right out from under her. Luckily Dylan's reflexes were just as fast. He caught her as she fell back and smoothly set her upright again. His swift intervention was most appreciated. She didn't need a second fall this weekend.

"Damn!" he swore at himself. "I'm sorry. I should have warned you that could happen."

"I'm cool. Do we need to catch him?"

"No, I closed the gate so he can run free in the yard."

They walked right into a cozy kitchen and Dylan nodded toward the small, wooden table and chairs along the wall. "You can hang your purse on a chair if you want."

Ariela did just that. Turning with a shrug, she said, "Okay, I'm here. Now what?"

"It isn't much, but come on. I'll give you a tour."

Dylan took her hand and towed her into the living room. The decorator in her resurfaced and decided the dull grays and blues were all wrong. They made the room feel smaller than it was. She felt genuine revulsion when she looked at his couch, hidden beneath the ugliest patchwork quilt she'd ever seen. At least the stylish easy chair facing the television was a step in the right direction. It just didn't go with the rest. Good thing too. There was a rack of TV trays standing against the wall, not two feet away from the television. She had a hunch Dylan rarely ate at his kitchen table.

"Do you know how long it's been since I saw TV trays?" she asked.

He smiled. "How long?"

Snickering with amusement, she walked over to them and followed the battered edge of one with her fingertip. "I must have been five or six at the most. They were down in my Grandma's basement. She'd let me drag one upstairs to use for my art projects. I think she was afraid I'd get crayon on her coffee table."

"So you're an artist too?"

"I'm a designer. Crayons, pencils, markers—they're all in my blood."

Her gaze returned to the sofa and she stared at it for a silent beat.

"The couch belongs to Max," Dylan explained, noting her reaction to the quilt.

She nodded. The room was unfashionably comfortable, smelled of dog, but on the plus side, it had very good lighting. She admired the handsome windows—nicely proportioned and in good condition. However, the glass itself needed a good washing. At least there was decent airflow. She turned to the walls again, interested in the framed pieces he'd hung. Where most people had artwork or family photos, Dylan had showcased news articles, dating all the way back to the Kennedy assassination and Nixon impeachment.

"And you're a political junkie," she said with a bemused smile.

Dylan grinned. "Guilty as charged."

There was a low shelf overfilled with books. Messy stacks sat on the floor in front of it, because there was no room to tuck anything more. A cardboard box was set beside the easy chair, and it was stacked high with old newspapers and magazines, the overflow begin-ning to crowd a tall, gooseneck reading lamp.

"Homey." Ariela smiled, all in all, approving his space.

He tugged her along. "And this is my room."

His bed was made. There was a heaped basket of dirty clothes on the floor beside the dresser, but otherwise it was tidy. His warning about his closets leaped to mind, and Ariela smiled again.

"And the bath," he said, drawing her away.

Ariela peeked through the door and went into shock. It was newly re-done, sleek and large, with an over-sized shower, huge mirror, and fantastic lighting. Even the towels looked plush. It blew her away. She wondered which of her competitors he'd used, because they'd done a terrific job.

Dylan laughed. "Let me explain. I've suffered through some pretty horrendous bathrooms. I can't even begin to describe some of them. If you're going to crave luxury when you get home, go with the room that matters most first."

"This is fabulous!"

"I felt an urge to splurge."

"Nice job."

"Maybe you can help me with the rest of the apartment—eventually."

"Possibly," she answered with a noncommittal shrug.

"It never mattered much before. I saw my place as just another motel room, or a temporary way station. But once I get this last trip over, I won't be able to leave it this way. It's just not conducive to good mental flow"

Big surprise. Ariela's eyes went to the desk tucked into a corner of the room, facing the wall. "Well, the first thing you should do is move your desk closer to a window or at least face it out into the room. No wonder this place blocks you."

"I usually take a walk to get the old juices flowing, but you raise a fair point."

She wandered over to the smaller side window and looked outside. Max was tossing a toy into the air and racing around with it, a low, playful growl slipping out occasionally. Without turning, she said, "It seems a shame he has to go to a kennel so soon."

Dylan joined her at the window. "It's the only option. Max is too strong for my grandmother." He pulled the curtain back to follow the dog along the fence. "I still don't know the whole truth about her fall, but that doesn't change the fact that she's too frail to keep him. She asked everyone else in the family before finally checking with me. Knowing my job, she didn't hold out much hope, but her timing was right. I was already thinking about making some changes. So she still gets to see him, and I have a dog again. It works out for all of us." Dylan smiled when Max rolled onto his back and worried the hell out of his toy before flinging it away. He leaped up and ran after it.

"That's nice—sweet." Ariela glanced over, and her eyes

took an unguarded tour down Dylan's body, finally settling on his legs again. She actually jumped when he chuckled, realizing, to her horror, she'd been busted.

He turned his right leg out slightly, offering her a better look. "Well, what do you think?"

Ariela laughed and chose the safest route open to her. "You're a fancy dresser, I'll give you that."

"I dress for the occasion."

"Aren't I an occasion?" She enjoyed how he brought out her playful side.

"That goes without saying, but I'd rather not deal with the dog in my Sunday best." He walked over to the kitchen and lifted the window above the sink. "Would you mind screwing a hose to the faucet when I pass it through?"

"And the value of having me around today begins to make sense." She smirked. "Sure. I think I can manage that."

Dylan went outside and removed the screen. He passed her the hose. "Careful not to pinch off the flow when you close the window," he said through the opening.

"No kidding." Her sarcasm came with an eye roll—a two-for-one special. "Anything else?"

"Yeah, come out and join me."

She attached the hose to the faucet before stretching to shut the window.

He ran back, calling out, "Wait! I forgot—you need to turn on the water. Make it warm, not hot."

"Warm, not hot," she mumbled. "How's this, good?"

"Perfect. Now come out."

She found Dylan holding Max by the collar. The dog looked perfectly happy standing in a plastic kiddie pool. She stayed well back while Dylan sprayed the animal down.

He glanced up. "This would go a lot faster if you helped me."

Seeing her squirm, his left eyebrow went up. "Haven't you ever washed a dog?"

She screwed up her face and shook her head. "No."

"Ever *have* a dog?"

"Never."

"I suppose you're a cat person."

Ariela shuddered and gave her head a violent shake. "No way."

Dylan stared at her. "Seriously? You've never had either?"

"My grandmother said they smelled bad and would make the house a mess. She was right."

"You poor kid." He went back to spraying Max.

"Au contraire. My friend Missy had a cat *and* a dog and their house was covered in fur. It looked clean, but it wasn't. I dropped a cupcake on their just-cleaned kitchen floor once, and when I picked it up, there was so much hair in the frosting I nearly gagged. They could never keep the cat off the table or the counters, either. That grossed me out even more, because all I could think about was the cat in his litter box."

"Cats clean themselves, you know."

"You'd have to dip him in bleach, and I still wouldn't be satisfied." She shuddered with horror. "After the cupcake incident, I never ate anything that wasn't right out of a sealed package when I was there."

"That's sad, but I understand." He ran his hand over Max as he continued to wet his back. "I once made friends with a kid just so I could play with his dog." He smiled at the memory.

"It isn't that I don't like animals, in theory. I just never wanted one."

"Well, I won't make you touch Max, but would you at least consider being my official hose handler?"

"Hose handler? You're joking."

"Garden hose." He innocently waved it in front of her, but his grin admitted more than he did. "You spray Max when he needs it, and I'll do all the dirty work. Deal?"

She couldn't hold back the little smile when she wandered over and held out her hand.

He slapped the nozzle into her palm. "He needs more under his belly."

Ariela crouched down and pointed upward, wetting not only Max, but nailing Dylan right in the face.

He jerked back in surprise. "Holy shit! You shot water up my nose." Dylan buried his face in the crook of his arm and dried himself on his sleeve while still managing to hold onto the dog who was wriggling just as wildly as if they were about to play a new game.

Ariela shook with laughter. "I'm sorry. I didn't mean it."

Dylan came up sputtering. "I'd be more convinced if you weren't laughing."

"I can't help it," she said, certain she didn't look remotely sorry.

He nudged her with his elbow, but he was grinning too. "Don't make me take that hose away from you."

"You'd have to fight me for it, and I'd win."

"You think so?"

"I know so. There's plenty more where that came from." Her thumb toyed with the molded trigger and she gave him a feisty look.

They both jumped when Max cut off their teasing with an impatient bark.

Ariela laughed. "Looks like he loves this."

"He's a water hound. If I don't close the door to the bathroom when I'm in the shower, he'll nose right in with me. Trust me—the last thing you want to feel is a wet dog against your leg when you're half asleep." He doused the dog, drenching him. "I think we're ready for the shampoo. Could you hand it to me?"

Ariela picked up the bottle, and just as she put it into Dylan's hand, he pulled back in alarm.

"Look out!" Max went into a full body shake, spattering them both. "Now, why would you do that?" Dylan asked the dog. "We're just going to have to wet you down again, stupid mutt."

Fifteen minutes later, freshly bathed, Max tore around the yard, rolling in the warm grass while Dylan bent down to grab one edge of the pool.

Ariela walked up behind him, admiring his muscular butt. "You sure know how to impress a girl. Need any help?"

"Sure."

Together, they tugged the pool over to the bushes and tipped the water out of it. Dylan took it from there, rolling the pool on its edge into a gap between the fence and the back of his garage.

He turned, wiping his hands on his wet shirt. "You hungry?"

"I could eat."

"Good. I'll light the grill then we can go in and wash up."

When they got inside, Dylan paused to open a bottle of wine to let it breathe. Ariela looked at the glasses he set out, then at him. "Don't assume you're getting lucky tonight." Her tone was teasing, but the message wasn't.

He reeled back dramatically, as if she'd struck him. "Well, fine. What's the point then? I'll just get my keys and take you home."

Ariela was staring at him, stunned, when he spun back with a chuckle. For a second there, she thought he was serious. Making a face, she said sarcastically, "Very amusing."

Shifting into host mode, Dylan opened the refrigerator. He whipped around a second later, a wild look in his eyes. "Tell me you like steak!"

"I like steak."

He patted his chest. "Whew."

"You're very strange." Ariela gave him a big smile. "What can I do?"

Dylan put her to work slicing potatoes and onions while he shucked corn.

"Potatoes go on first," he said, grabbing the foil packet she'd made and heading for the door. "Why don't you bring the wine and join me? I'm not comfortable leaving Max out there with a hot grill."

Of course, Max didn't go anywhere near the grill, but it was nice to be outside. Ariela grabbed one of the lawn chairs and dumped dried seeds out of it before sitting down. Dylan opened a second chair and dropped into it. Even slouching, the guy was sexy.

She watched him as he closed his eyes and inhaled, clearly appreciating the bouquet of the wine in his glass. Then he took a slow, contemplative sip. His lashes swept up and their eyes locked. Ariela couldn't blink, couldn't look away. His quiet gaze pulled at her, made her want to get up and go to him. The urge was almost irresistible. He broke their connection first to glance at the grill. Sitting forward he set his glass down on the patio next to his chair.

"Would you protect my wine from Max in case he comes

over to investigate? I should rotate the potatoes."

"Sure."

Over the course of the next half hour, Dylan was up and out of his chair more often than an anxious mother. Ariela offered to help, but he waved her off. "Just be comfortable."

It was hard to follow that advice when he was running around all the time, even taking the time to top off her wine.

During a momentary lull, he dropped into his chair, stretched his long legs into the warm sunshine, and said with a sigh of complete sincerity, "Isn't this relaxing?"

Ariela burst out laughing. "For me? Yes."

He chuckled and hopped up again to turn the steaks and rotate the potatoes one last time. "Well, I'm having a ball."

"You're not normal," she reminded him gravely.

He looked pleased that she thought so, wiggling his eyebrows playfully before taking another sip of wine. Dylan rolled his neck and shoulders, and she watched his head fall back for a moment. That throat was made to be kissed. "I'm looking forward to a shower after this," he admitted with a low groan.

"Why don't you go take one? I can watch things for ten minutes."

"But you're doing the dishes."

"Am I?"

"Yep. Do you want to know why?"

"I guess I do." This she had to hear.

"Because I knew you'd insist. I'm just ahead of the game."

She snorted when she laughed. "You think you're so smart."

"Am I wrong?"

"No," she admitted, crinkling her nose at him.

Dylan grinned. "Don't do that."

"Do what?"

"Crinkle your nose at me."

"Why not?"

"Because it makes me want to jump you, and I don't think that chair will support both of us."

Ariela's heart skipped and fluttered excitedly at the thought, but she played it cool. Looking down at the cheap aluminum frame and slatted seat beneath her, she nodded. "You're probably right. You'd better stay right where you are."

"Not so easy when you look so damn appealing."

Ariela laughed and swept her flyaway hair back from her face. "Need I remind you this is not a date?"

He sputtered on his next sip of wine. "It isn't?"

"No. I told you I can't date you right now."

"Then what is this?"

"Heck if I know. Hanging out?"

"So definitely no sex."

"Most definitely."

"Hmm. Then I guess we might as well eat." Dylan shot to his feet.

That was way too easy. Did he somehow know all he'd have to do is crook his finger and she'd come? What was she doing? This was madness—like putting a cigarette and a lighter in front of someone who's trying to quit. She was going to have the shakes if she didn't figure a way out of this before she did something reckless and stupid.

He picked up the plate beside the grill and pulled the meat off the coals and stacked the potatoes on top. With a tip of his head, he pointed her toward the door. "Come on. We're eating inside."

Ariela picked up the bottle and raced around him to reach

the door first. She pulled it open with a grand bow. "Allow me."

He chuckled. "Thank you."

Following him inside, Ariela came to a dead stop and got hit in the butt by the door when it swung closed. She was too shocked to care. When the hell had Dylan found the time to set the table?

"Pick a chair." He headed to the counter to organize their plates.

In no time, he set a plate in front of her then claimed the other chair. Before she knew it, they were sharing another meal, this time at his intimate little table.

She found herself watching him while she ate, taking everything in. It was unusual for her to feel so comfortable with anyone this fast, even more unusual to hear her private thoughts about them escape between bites. "Do you know what I really like about you?"

He gave her a slow grin. "My culinary expertise?"

"No, I'm talking on a purely superficial level here." She reached for her glass, unsure why she'd raised the subject. It was obvious he wasn't going to let it drop now. "Your eyes." Looking down with a mild case of embarrassment, she stabbed a potato with her fork.

Dylan straightened in his chair. "Oh, is that what you meant?"

Venturing a peek at him she asked, "What are you talking about?"

"When you were lying on the sidewalk, you looked up at me and said, 'wow' before you fainted. I had no idea what to make of it."

"Oh god." Ariela bit her lower lip. "I suffer from honesty under duress."

"My eyes, huh?" His unmistakably bashful smile was endearing. Then he had to go and ruin it with his next question. "Don't you think it's a little early to decide?"

His wink exasperated her. "Why do all guys think their penises are their best features?"

"Interesting that you immediately jumped to that conclusion. Very interesting." He raised his glass to her and chuckled.

Ariela snorted. "Like you weren't implying it."

Dylan stopped baiting her. "Since you started the confessions, do you want to know what I find appealing about you?"

Ariela's fork hung suspended in midair.

"Everything. I have to admit, when you went all *damsel in distress* on me, old-fashioned chivalry kicked in, hard. It didn't hurt that you're so damn pretty. There's something irresistible about a helpless woman. I needed to be there for you. Unconscious and defenseless, you were lovely. Aware and playful, you're downright powerful."

Her eyebrows shot up. "Powerful? No one's ever called me powerful before. Wow, and here I thought you held all the good cards at the table."

His smile was warm and oh so right. "Not a chance."

After they finished eating, Dylan put their scraps into Max's dish then went to let the mostly-dry retriever inside while they cleaned up. As soon as the sink was filled with hot soapy water, Ariela grabbed Dylan by the shoulders and steered him out of the kitchen.

"Don't you have a shower to take?" she asked.

Glancing over his shoulder, he gave her a cocky grin. "I do. Wanna scrub my back?"

"Nice try." She left him in the living room.

Max parked himself next to her, hoping for more tidbits. Twice, she told him everything was gone, but just looking at the dog got him all worked up. *Kind of like his master.* Amused at the thought, she decided it was probably best to ignore the retriever. Not until she was drying her hands on the towel did he lope off to curl up on the sofa.

Ariela wandered over to Dylan's stack of maga-zines, but she'd barely had a moment to shift them before he walked out of the bathroom. A rush of heat shot through her. From bored to aroused in one startling second. His aftershave wasn't making it any easier. At the first heady whiff, she inhaled his scent deep into her lungs and sighed. He noticed.

Smiling at how she was looking at him, he said, "I dressed for Max earlier. Now I'm dressed for you."

Fanning her face, she grinned. "And I appreciate it." A truer statement was never spoken.

"Can I interest you in a w-a-l-k?"

She shrugged. "S-u-r-e. Why are we spelling?"

Dylan's eyes danced. "Watch." He looked over at the dog. "Want to go for a walk?"

Max shot like a bullet off the couch and shifted excitedly from foot to foot at the door.

"He knows the word *walk*?" Just speaking the word prompted a desperate whimper from Max. She giggled. "Cool."

Clipping the leash to the dog's collar, Dylan opened the door, and Max threw himself down the steps, dragging his master with him. Dylan yanked him to a stop and turned. "Yesterday, I didn't stand a chance. He took off before I was ready. All I could do was try to keep up. Damn dog can set a wicked pace when you're not paying attention."

Reminded of Dylan's gravity defying balletic leaps the night before, she laughed. "I'm convinced."

———

Max watered many things along the way: trees, flowers, a mailbox, a stone wall, and a hydrant.

"I haven't actually walked this way before," Ariela admitted.

"But you've driven through here, haven't you?"

She thought about it. "I don't think I have."

Up ahead, there was a pretty, little house, well-tended. As cute as the old neighborhood was in general, this unassuming home stood head and shoulders above its neighbors because it enjoyed obviously devoted maintenance. Even the landscaping made a statement.

"That house is beautiful," she said with a sigh as they walked past.

"It is."

"Do you know who lives there?" She could hardly tear her eyes away.

"Not by name. They're an older couple."

"I figured that." She looked longingly at the property. "Do you ever want to see the inside of a house?"

His eyebrows inched up. "I never really thought about it."

"Even when I was a kid, I liked to look at houses. Riding in the car or on the school bus, I'd fall in love with some of them. I'd try so hard to see inside. The best ones had big picture windows that allowed me to see right through them and into the backyards. I really wanted to explore those."

Dylan reached out and casually draped his arm across her shoulders. "You were a born interior decorator, huh?"

"Pretty much. I wasn't even ten when I discovered floor plans and blueprints. I'd draw my own on the sidewalk and on the driveway with my big chalk. The librarians used to give me the strangest looks when I brought my stacks of books up to the desk. I didn't care." She laughed and confided, "When I was about thirteen, a friend and I actually got kicked out of a store in the mall for rearranging their furniture department. Up until then, I'd been a model kid, never in any trouble, but I couldn't stay away from faux marble lamps and coffee tables. It was a blow to my grandmother."

He shook with laughter. "Are you serious?"

"Dead serious, but since then I've channeled my impulses into something more constructive. I haven't been kicked out of a furniture store since. I admit it's still hard to drag me away from paint displays, but at least I'm allowed to take samples."

"Where did you come from?" Dylan stopped and turned, his arms going around her. His smile was cockeyed, but it sorted itself out when he moved in to kiss her.

Max tugged against the leash, but to no avail. Giving up, he plopped down on the pavement to wait.

The scent of Dylan's aftershave mingled seductively with the soft feel of his lips pressed against hers. The combination tipped Ariela into an honest-to-god swoon. If he weren't holding her, she would have ended up as a puddle at his feet.

"I really want to cuddle with you on the couch, but I don't think Max will make room for us. Is your place free?" he asked against her ear, his warm breath doing a little stroking of its own.

Feeling a bit warm all of a sudden, Ariela nodded. "Jean and Ron are going out."

Dylan's smile grew. He kissed her temple and sent her pulse

into orbit. "So my thoughts aren't out of line?" he asked.

Ariela's eyes rolled closed, and she swayed against him. "God, no."

He grinned. "Good, let's cut through here. We'll take Max home the back way."

Six

Dylan never stopped touching Ariela in the car on the way to her house. It started simply enough, a gentle stroke up her arm that ended under her hair. His fingers began kneading her neck muscles, and her eyes shuttered closed, and her head fell back against the headrest. She bolted up with a yelp.

Dylan shot her a look of concern. "You okay?"

"I was terrific until I forgot about my lump."

He chuckled and drew his hand out, caressing her cheek before returning it to the wheel and signaling his turn.

Ariela had described the unsettled feeling Dylan gave her as a tornado, but now she wasn't sure that was the right comparison. A tornado was loud and violent, certainly, but after careful consideration, that seemed too dry. No, this was closer to a tsunami or hurricane churning through her insides because there was moisture, a great deal of very unmistakable moisture to go along with the roaring in her ears and the rumbling in her chest.

As they climbed the staircase, her footsteps felt springy, buoyant on the treads. It was as if her legs were pogo sticks. Did he feel any of this? Could he tell she was lost in a maelstrom he'd set off?

Inside the apartment, Dylan allowed her just enough time to hang up her purse before he caught her around the waist and turned her in his arms. There was something in his eyes, those luscious, lapis blue eyes, that sent tension vibrating along her spine. For a fraction of a second, he simply looked at her with just a hint of a smile. Then he moved on her, decisively, closing the space between them.

Ariela looped her arms behind his neck and held on, perfectly ready and willing to be plundered. Her feet left the floor at the same time their lips connected and suddenly they were collapsing on the couch. Dylan's hand protected her head down to the cushions. That simple, thoughtful act undid her. Ariela kissed him long and hard, rewarding his consideration.

Finally coming up for air, she nuzzled along his jaw. "You smell fantastic."

"So do you," he growled, diving at her throat.

"My perfume wore off hours ago."

"I know."

That was it—she was his if he wanted her. What an easy conquest she'd turned out to be. She couldn't even summon up disappointment in herself. The reality was, she'd never wanted anything, anyone more, and it was no use fighting it.

Dylan pulled his head back, his lust for her unmistakable in his smoldering eyes. "Are we on the same page here?"

She cracked a little smile. "God, I hope so."

With a groan, he crushed his lips to hers and Ariela felt a slight sting against her teeth. Then his tongue ventured out and soothed the pain away. Now his kiss mellowed from one of heated urgency to a calmer, solid claim. He had a right to be here, to possess her, because she'd granted it. Ariela wanted to feel Dylan's hard body against hers, but she realized he wasn't a guy to take without invitation. Even now, if she changed her mind and asked him to stop, he'd do it, no matter how difficult it was to pull back. Confidence in that made her want him even more. This would be an utter surrender, an open agreement with an occupying force.

She fumbled with the buttons on his shirt while he held himself over her, working her top up with one hand.

He looked down, grinning at her impatience. "Just clarifying something here. You're not interested in me?"

"How many times do I have to tell you? At this time, you're on my banned substances list." Ariela swept his shirt apart and ran her hands over his chest, squeezing his yummy pecs.

Dylan backed off to give her room. "I think you need to sit up."

Ariela pulled her top over her head and tossed it to the floor while he unbuttoned his cuffs and slipped out of his shirt, dropping it aside. Finally, both of them bared above the waist they took a minute to truly appreciate what they saw. Ariela broke the spell first by reaching for him. Dylan rode her body down to the cushions.

"I don't want to crush you." He shifted onto his side and pulled Ariela in, kissing her while his fingers followed the outer curve of her breast. The kiss deepened as his hand closed around it and Ariela felt herself slipping into an exquisite stupor, her brain function receding even more with every gentle squeeze, every stroke of his tongue along hers.

Then reality intruded.

Ariela covered the hand massaging her breast and stopped him, breaking the kiss at the same time. "This is probably the last chance to ask this before we completely lose our heads, so I have to mention it." Dylan eased back and looked at her. "Are you safe?" she asked.

"Safe?"

"As in free of infections, STDs . You know."

"Definitely. I've been very careful. Clean bill of health. How about you?"

She combed the hair back at his temples and smiled. "No worries. I have written proof, if you're interested."

Dylan rolled forward and kissed her. "I don't think that'll be necessary." He nuzzled between Ariela's breasts then shifted to suck a nipple to a hard point. She groaned with disappointment when he stopped.

"Birth control?" he asked.

"I'm on the pill."

He sighed with relief, no doubt glad he didn't have to go foraging for a condom. "Where do you want to go, Ariela?" He swirled his tongue lazily around her areola, watching her suggestively as he did it. Those eyes owned her, no question.

Ariela hesitated. "You've been more places than I have. How about you suggest something, be my tour guide?"

Dylan's grin was as slow as the Cheshire cat's. "I think I know a few destinations guaranteed to put a smile on your face." He pressed his pelvis against her and the solid, unmistakable promise of what she felt sent a jolt of lust screaming right through her.

"Take me," Ariela whispered.

Dylan drew her down to the floor, and together they removed her slacks. With her stretched out naked before him, all Dylan could do was kneel in gratitude and gaze at her for a moment. Then he reached out, his hands floating lightly above her, following her contours like a delicate whisper. Ariela broke out in goose bumps, her skin instantly chilled. He smiled when her nipples puckered tight, drawing her areolas into the action. Bending down, he took them into his warm mouth, one at a time.

She shivered. "I'm cold."

"I think I can help."

Dylan moved between her legs and kissed and stroked down her torso, across her stomach, before finally bringing his kisses where she needed him, wanted him most. Her knees fell open like butterfly wings on either side of him, and he slid an arm under her hips and dipped his head, tasting her with a careful tongue.

Ariela's lashes dropped closed, though she never stopped brushing through his hair. Slowly, steadily, Dylan brought warmth back to her body. Every lap, every flick, and every thrust of his tongue intensified the heat spreading through her. The hand that had stroked his head just minutes ago now gripped him by the hair. No way was she letting him go now. He shifted to slide a finger inside of her, and she groaned with relief. When he added another and brought his mouth back to her, she couldn't stop herself from meeting the motions of his hand. Her climax hit her hard and fast, but it wasn't enough, not nearly enough.

"Now—please, I can't wait," she cried.

Her urgency was so great she didn't allow him time to kick out of his pants before he pressed into her. Ariela's muscles went weak with incalculable relief.

"Yes," she said with a low moan.

Ariela rose to meet his kiss, their lips and loins locked.

Sex with Dylan felt shockingly different. There was a profound sense of intimacy, completion even. It overwhelmed and unnerved her.

Like when this was over he was going to take back something important, vital even, and leave her grieving the loss.

Thrown by the idea, she clamped down around him, feeling unusually possessive all of a sudden.

"Where are you Ariela?" he asked softly, searching her face. She brought him into focus and was moved by the tenderness and concern in his eyes.

"Wherever you are," she told him and held him tighter.

But he stiffened on top of her, and not in a good way. Had she done something wrong? Accidentally hurt him somehow?

"Dylan?"

But he'd looked up. She turned her head in the same direction and screamed in startled horror at seeing Jean and Rob standing in the open door, their mouths wide with shock.

Dylan rolled to his side, shielding them both with his back.

Give us a minute, all right?" he ground out, his frustration loud and clear.

"Done," said Rob and the next thing they knew, the door slammed closed. They could hear rapid footsteps retreating down the back stairs.

"I'm so stupid." Ariela groaned and clutched her head. "I should have suggested we take this into my room. This is embarrassing."

Dylan sighed against her shoulder and raked his hair back. The mood had definitely shifted.

Poor guy. He'd just had what amounted to a bucket of ice water thrown on him. *Coitus interruptus.*

"I'm so sorry," she whispered, seeking his forgive-ness.

"Why are you apologizing?" He frowned at her in confusion.

"Major mood killer. At least I got to come." She gave his cheek an apologetic caress.

"I'll survive." Then he muttered, "I can't believe I didn't hear them."

"*I* didn't hear them, either."

"But I'm used to watching my back. It matters in the field."

Dylan pushed up from the floor. He took a second to tuck himself back and zip his pants before he reached down to help

Ariela to her feet.

"How much time before they come back?" he asked with a glance at the door.

"I suspect they'll stay away for hours now. It's been a long time since I had to think about hanging a tie on the doorknob. I completely forgot to do it."

"That your signal?"

"Since college." She sighed and flapped her arms helplessly at her sides. "Excuse me."

Ariela went into her room. When she returned she was wearing her sky blue bathrobe.

"Does this break your six-month celibacy streak or not?" She tried to suppress her little smile, but it was no good.

Dylan looked up from buttoning his shirt and chuckled. "I think I broke up with myself tonight. What can I say? The relationship had grown stale and predictable. The passion just wasn't there anymore."

Ariela laughed softly. "Will I see you tomorrow?"

His face fell. "I wish, but I don't think I can swing it. I have to drop in on my grandma for a visit with Max in the morning, after my jog. By the time we finally get home, I'll have a lot of organizing to do for my trip. But I'll call if I can."

He held open his arms, and she walked into them and snuggled close. "This is your last trip over there, right?"

"Unless I hear something different from my editor, that's where things stand."

"Good." Ariela pulled back to look up at him. "Because until you get back for good, this—whatever this is between us—can't happen."

He stroked the back of her hair, careful to avoid her lump. "I'll call you when I get home. We have unfinished business between us now."

———

The next morning, Ariela was fixing herself scrambled eggs and toast for breakfast when Jean wandered in, wearing the big, bunny slippers Ron had given her on her last birthday. Ariela stiffened, feeling as uncomfortable as Jean looked.

They both spoke at once then broke off just as abruptly.

Jean took a deep breath and started again. "I'm so sorry—"

"It was my fault. I should have taken him to my bedroom, or remembered the damn tie."

"But I saw his car. It didn't even register. We didn't mean to walk in on you like that."

"Stop." Ariela held up a hand and gave Jean a pleading look. "I would feel a million times better if we pretended nothing happened last night, okay? You didn't bust us. Just put it out of your mind."

"I should have—," Jean said, clearly desperate to explain.

Ariela cut her off. "You're not hearing me."

"—knocked," Jean finished.

"All right. We're both sorry. We're both embarrassed. Can we move on now?" asked Ariela.

Please shut up.

"Yes." Jean came over and looked at what Ariela was cooking. "Can you leave the pan on? I think I'll have eggs too."

"I need to keep busy. Why don't you take these? I'll make more."

"You sure?"

"Yes. Sit down." Ariela slid the eggs onto a plate and handed it over.

Jean grabbed the salt and pepper and headed to the table.

Quickly beating two more eggs, Ariela was just pouring them into the pan when she heard something odd behind her. She turned and caught Jean shaking with the giggles so hard she was having trouble keeping egg on her fork.

Ariela scowled. "What the hell is up with you?"

Jean waved off the question and looked down, avoiding Ariela's eyes, but her shoulders were bouncing violently when she succumbed to another fit of giggles.

"You're really mean sometimes. Do you know that?" Ariela snapped.

"I can't help it." Jean said, apologetically, if not necessarily sincerely. "I think I need a napkin."

Ariela thrust a paper towel at her. "Tell me what's so flipping funny."

"All of us." Jean seemed to be fighting to get herself under control. "It was like slow motion." She dabbed at the corners of her eyes. "Were you able to finish?"

"Are you *insane*? You guys standing there in the doorway, staring, was a real mood killer. Dylan went home right after you left."

"I'm sorry." Finally—she looked it.

"Well, you didn't screw up my climax, but poor Dylan was another story. I think it was pretty tough on him."

"I can imagine."

"Please don't."

"That's not what I meant."

"Sorry."

"So, you obviously like him." Jean was blatantly trolling for more details. Best friends were entitled.

Ariela turned off the pan and got a fresh plate out of the cabinet. "It's worse than that," she admitted with a heavy sigh.

"I'm actually starting to care about Dylan already. I'm out of my element here. No one has ever invaded my mental and physical space like he has. I can't get him out of my head. This trip of his is going to be torture when all I can think about is being with him again. It's good he's leaving. I need to step back and get my emotions under control."

Dropping into her chair, Ariela stared at her plate. She could feel Jean silently studying her for a moment before she got up, squeezed Ariela's shoulder, and went to pour two glasses of orange juice. She set Ariela's in front of her then returned to her own place at the table.

"Thanks," Ariela said softly.

Jean allowed her to eat for a few minutes before her impatience burst. "Well? Are you going to tell me how good the sex was or not?"

Ariela looked up. "I didn't know you expected me to."

Jean kicked the leg of Ariela's chair.

Holding up her hands in surrender, Ariela laughed. "Okay, okay." She could feel her face flare. "It was so good, so right. We connected." She looked at her friend expressively. "Really connected, on every level imaginable. It felt right—incredibly, deliciously right."

"Oh my god! You're falling for him." Jean stared, wide-eyed.

Ariela's stomach gave a sickening lurch and she set down her fork and slid the plate away. "Hardly," she lied, hoping denial made it true. "No. I'm willing to admit I have a very intense crush on Dylan, but that's it."

Jean shook her slice of toast at her. "A crush? You're not thirteen anymore, Ariela."

She picked up her juice, holding the glass in front of her

heart like a shield. "That's my point. I'm not going to confuse my feelings for something else, something more now. That stupid trusting kid is long gone."

They looked at each other, both remembering how it felt to rush headlong into emotional confessions prematurely. It hurt, deeper than expected, when it didn't turn out the way they'd hoped. Caution was a hard lesson to learn, even as a teen. It stayed with you.

Taking a much needed swallow, Ariela set her glass down harder than intended. "Why am I driving myself crazy over him right now anyway? He's going back to Iraq tomorrow morning. Nothing, I'm serious, nothing is happening between us until he's stateside for good. I'm not going to put myself through that."

Jean glanced up from spreading jelly on her toast with the back of a spoon. "And he's okay with your terms?"

"He said this is his last trip."

"Then what are you so worried about?"

"I wish I knew."

Seven

Ariela didn't expect Dylan to call her Sunday. He'd told her he'd be busy. Still, when he didn't phone, she moped around the apartment. She'd never felt so unsettled, so restless and conflicted in her life. What was wrong with her? They'd seen each other twice! Three times if she stretched it to include the accident. Where was her backbone? Had she taken complete leave of her senses when she slept with him yesterday? That wasn't her! She'd thrown all caution to the wind. Not good.

Deep in her gut, she knew it was wise to keep him at a distance. At least until he was working stateside permanently. He'd been so cavalier about wearing flak jackets and dodging bullets when he'd talked about his job. Bullets! That conversation, right there, should have been his elimination round. Instead, she was depressed because he hadn't called.

The funk of misery and self-pity hung heavy in the apartment. Jean suggested they go out to lunch—her treat. Ariela declined then sulked over her peanut butter and jelly sandwich. That was apparently the last straw for Jean. She left.

When Ariela finally went to bed, earlier than usual, she kept her phone close on the off chance that Dylan might still call. She lay there, staring at the dark ceiling, arguing with herself. Of course, she knew she could have called him, but then she would have looked ridiculous. You can't tell a guy he doesn't have a shot with you then pursue him anyway!

Besides, there was something distasteful about chasing him, not to mention her grandmother's old rules died hard. Ariela wasn't about to make a spectacle of herself. She wanted Dylan to miss her enough to make the effort. It would be incredibly reassuring if he did. If he didn't, well, then she'd know where she stood so she could adjust her expectations accordingly.

It was surprising how exhausting disappointment could be. When Ariela finally gave in to the pull of sleep—and she'd fought it hard—it was so deep, she might have been drugged.

Ariela slogged her way back to consciousness hours later, her phone pressed against her cheek. It was the soft yet persistent sound coming out if it that finally roused her. She cracked an eye open and saw the clock. A quarter to six in the morning? Shifting the phone to her ear, she mumbled incoherently.

"Ariela, are you there yet? Come on, honey. Wake up." There was chuckling on the other end of the line.

"Dylan?" she croaked, her first word of the day.

"Yeah, it's me. I realize there are a lot better ways to wake a woman from a sound sleep, but this will have to do for now. I couldn't leave without hearing your voice again."

"Where are you?"

"At the airport. I'm just about to board. Since this is the last chance I get to talk to you before international charges apply, I wanted to seize it."

"I waited all yesterday for a call," she whispered.

Dylan's tone softened with regret. "I'm sorry. I thought calling would be a mistake. I wanted to believe it was a good idea to slow things down a little, take a step back, and give us both time to breathe. It should have been easier not to call."

"It wasn't?"

"No."

She smiled sleepily and hugged her extra pillow to her chest. "Good."

"Listen, they're kicking the doorstops out of the way, so I

have to go. I'll send you an e-mail. Watch for it, if not late tomorrow, the next day."

"Okay. Be safe."

The phone went silent in her hand. Ariela set it on the bedside table and drifted back to sleep, feeling better now that they'd talked. Her relief didn't last. Less than ten minutes later she jerked awake with a cry of anguish, her heart hammering in her chest. She'd dreamed Dylan's plane was hit by rocket fire and sent into a dizzying spin before it crashed into the runway at the Baghdad International Airport.

Sitting up against the headboard, she pulled the covers close and hugged herself. It was no good. All she could think about were the daily reports of gunfire and suicide bombings wherever people gathered. She couldn't stop herself from picturing Dylan waiting to be cleared through the busy checkpoints outside the International Green Zone when a bomber struck. She imagined him riding in a car en-route from the airport when another vehicle pulls alongside and gunmen open fire.

Weeping and rocking, she berated herself for her imagination, for her weakness where Dylan was concerned, and most of all, for not following her own rules. Idiot! This is why she'd sworn never to care for a man in a perilous occupation. Once was enough for one lifetime.

———

Down in their design studio several hours later, Jean closed the front door behind the deliveryman and hurried over to Ariela's desk waving a large express envelope in the air. "Look, look. Our new software is here. Should we install it now?"

Ariela set her paperwork aside. "Let's see what's involved first."

Jean pulled the strip off the edge and shook the contents onto her desk. She picked up a plastic-wrapped disk and pamphlet.

"Do you know what this means?" asked Ariela.

Jean looked up from her reading. "What does *what* mean? What have you got there?"

"Nothing. I just had a horrible thought. Mrs. Corley is going to want to revamp her kitchen yet again when she finds out what we can do with that."

"Don't tell her," Jean said, scanning the pamphlet in her hands.

"There's a thought. She doesn't have to know, does she? Ugh, I've got to lock her down on something. She's driving me crazy."

"And we have bills to pay."

"There's that too."

Jean looked up again and caught Ariela pressing her thumbs into her temples. "Headache?" she asked.

"No, just crampy and crabby. I'm just not into working today."

"That's right. Dylan left this morning."

"Yeah."

The way Ariela drooped back in her chair and met Jean's eyes spoke volumes. Her unmistakable unhappiness brought on a rush of sympathy in her friend. "Why don't you take a field trip?" Jean suggested.

"A field trip?"

"You need something to take your mind off Dylan, for a little while, anyway. How about running to the office-supply store for us? We've got quite a list."

"Can't I just mope instead?" Ariela dropped her cheek onto her hand.

Jean shook her head and smiled. "No. You moped all yesterday. Now you need to pull it together."

Ariela groaned, but it didn't change Jean's mind.

"Fine," Ariela moodily agreed. "Where's the list?" She rolled her chair back and stood, throwing out her limp arm. Jean stretched across her desk and slapped the notepad into Ariela's open hand.

With her purse slung over her shoulder, Ariela headed for the door, though she turned on her way out to say, "I'm going to kill a lot of time—a *lot* of time."

"I hope so. Don't come back with that dark cloud hanging over your head."

———

Ariela managed to squander two hours before the guilt got to her. She decided to bring back a peace offering.

Jean peeked in the first bag and looked up at her. "Rum?"

"And strawberries, and limes, and ice."

"Oh my. I see daiquiris in your future." Jean pretended to read an imaginary crystal ball.

"I was hoping in *our* future. Sorry I've been such a pill."

Jean came around the desk and threw her arm across Ariela's shoulders, giving her a squeeze. "I understand. Trust me. I understand."

"I'm not coping with this very well and it makes no sense at all." Ariela dropped her head onto Jean's shoulder and sighed as her friend rubbed her back.

"The rest of our afternoon is free. Why don't we drag the groceries upstairs and dig out the blender?"

Ariela lifted her head and nodded. "That sounds really good to me."

"Me too."

An hour later, they were half in the bag when Ron tapped on the door and walked in with two bags of fast food.

"Hey, babe," Jean purred.

He grinned, then caught Ariela's eye and looked away, clearly uncomfortable about walking in on her and Dylan the other night. Ariela found his deep blush hysterically funny. In all the years she'd known Ron, this was a first. Of course, had she been sober, there was no way she could have managed this face-off with such aplomb, but leave it to alcohol to relieve an awkward situation.

"Daiquiri, Ron?" she asked, offering her glass.

"I'd rather have a beer." He set the bags on the coffee table and slipped into the kitchen.

Jean watched him go with a devious smile. "Will you excuse me a minute?"

"Sure."

Jean went after him while Ariela leaned forward to snoop through the bags. She grabbed a sandwich and was searching for sauce when a loud slap made her look up. Jean's hands were firmly planted on Ron's ass. She gave him a good squeeze as they enjoyed a long kiss. Ariela smiled wistfully and turned away. Ron was obviously spending the night.

They watched a little television while they ate. Afterwards, Ariela excused herself and ran down to the office to check the computer. Unfortunately, there was no message from Dylan yet. It was obviously too soon.

It was doubly depressing to go back upstairs and find that the television was off and Jean's bedroom door was closed.

With nothing else to do, Ariela locked the door for the night and shut off the lights.

Sometime later, while she was reading quietly in bed, the pounding started. It took just a minute more before the entire house started shaking. The nightstand on her right began to creep across the hardwood floor, and the lamp sitting on top of it slowly rotated away from her, shining toward the closet.

"Damn it." Ariela reached out and turned the lamp back around.

Jean's waterbed had to go. Their poor old house couldn't take the abuse. Honestly, just the weight of the damn thing was enough to worry Ariela, but when those two got the major wave action going, it was downright terrifying. Houses weren't meant to be pounded sideways. Sometimes she pictured the entire structure collapsing on the lawn. Just folding up like a paper bag. How many studs had they cracked? How many nails had worked loose? Pretty tough to put those things out of your mind while watching your furniture parade around your room.

"Wrap it up, already!" she yelled, pitching her book at the wall.

When she heard them laughing softly together, Ariela wasn't prepared for the wave of melancholy that swept through her. She loved them and envied them. Jean and Rob had each other and what did she have? A ridiculous crush on a guy she shouldn't even be considering. She knew better and yet, she still missed Dylan. That realization, right there, frightened her more than the house collapsing in around her.

———

Her mood did not improve the next morning when she walked into the kitchen and found the refrigerator standing in the center of the room. Now she was even more adamant that the damn bed had to go. This wasn't the first time the appliance had crept across the floor, propelled along by the violent fucking on the other side of the wall. It was high time she had a chat with Jean.

One thing was certain—it was ridiculous to feel embarrassed about being caught in the act after this. At least she'd never moved major appliances to the very ends of their cords.

Because Ariela took the time to start a pot of coffee first, Ron beat her to the bathroom. That left her only enough time for an abbreviated shower. She had to forgo washing her hair and pulled it into a simple ponytail instead.

When she came out of the bathroom, Jean was standing in the kitchen wearing her short, terry robe and studying the refrigerator with amused detachment.

"Come on, together," Ariela said. "You push low. I'll push high."

After they maneuvered the appliance back against the wall, Ariela broached the subject. Not surprising, her roommate balked.

"Beds are expensive," Jean countered.

Ariela threw her arm up at their refrigerator. "And the whole house coming down around us wouldn't be?"

Jean laughed. "Don't you think you're being just a little paranoid?"

"Not when you're moving furniture and major appliances."

Jean's eyes narrowed skeptically. "What furniture?"

"My nightstand for starters. I had to give up on reading because the lamp wouldn't stay still."

"Seriously?"

"Uh, yeah." Ariela nodded.

"Huh." Jean gradually smiled. "Ron's kind of an animal."

"I'm happy for you," said Ariela flatly, not budging on this. "Maybe you could head over to Burbank's a little early today and work something out with Lyle, since you're going there to look at sofas for the Dreyer job anyway."

Jean's smile dissolved. "What's gotten into you lately? You're either pissy or mopey. I can't stand it."

Ariela stared at the empty doorway after Jean stomped out, feeling more miserable than ever. She knew exactly what had gotten into her—Dylan.

———

There was an e-mail waiting for Ariela on Tuesday morning when she got down to the office. Her hand was shaking and her heart was racing when she opened it.

Knock it off, Ariela! You're putting too much importance on something so innocent.

TO: arielap@
SUBJECT: Checking in
MESSAGE: Well, I'm in Amman at the moment. I'm waiting to hook up with Jim, my friend and photographer. He won't be here for a few hours yet, so I have a little time to catch a few winks. I nearly missed my connecting flight from London. There wasn't much time to run from one gate to the next. Luckily I'm carrying everything. I have to. We'll be in Baghdad tomorrow. It's already one hundred and five degrees, and it's not even eleven in the morning. I need to power up while I can, so I'd better sign off and look for

an outlet. I can't get you out of my mind. Why didn't I bring your picture with me? We'll have to do something about that. Dylan

The buttons above his message caught her eye. Only one interested her. *Reply*? Hell yes, she wanted to reply.

TO: dylanbond@
SUBJECT: Hey there
MESSAGE: Just read your e-mail. Hope everything's still going okay. You want a picture of me? I suppose we can work something out, but I'll expect one of you in return. I haven't been the best company since you left. I actually used alcohol to cope last night, but I don't think that's a practical long-term solution. I'm open to better suggestions. Feel free to make a few. The best that I can come up with is seeing you home, safe and sound. Please be careful. Ariela

That didn't sound presumptuous or emotional, did it? She read it again, worrying over all the ways her words could be interpreted, or misinterpreted, then hit send. It was out there now, on its way to his computer. Of course, doubts hit as soon as she'd committed to the message.

She was giving the poor guy mixed signals. One minute she says he's un-datable. The next, she's boinking him on her living room floor. Now she'd just confessed, in writing, that it took alcohol to help her cope after he left? If he was confused, and he had to be, she was even more confused. She'd already decided to ease away from Dylan after her nightmare, but just seeing he'd sent an e-mail made her euphoric. She hadn't felt this good since Saturday night. That reminder made her blood pressure spike.

As incredible as it seemed for a woman typically reserved about sex, she still couldn't condemn herself for sleeping with him so soon. They'd connected in so many ways. No one had ever made her feel so comfortable, yet exhilarated, in her life. She'd never experienced an attraction quite like this before. Dylan was beyond appealing, inside and out. Ariela had sensed he'd be a considerate and attentive lover. He didn't disappoint. Recalling how his eyes had transitioned from gorgeous to downright devastating when aroused was enough to break her out in a sweat. Even half a world away, he managed to get to her.

Regret was impossible when she'd do the same thing all over again, without hesitation. She just wanted the chance. It was unfair that they'd been interrupted. Next time would be different. Next time, it would be her bed put to the test, her walls that failed to completely muffle the sounds they made during lovemaking.

———

The hot glare of the desert sunshine was killer, and the talc-like sand was already working its way into his crevices when Dylan stepped off the Rhino bus, the armored transport used to shuttle people between the Baghdad airport and the International Green Zone.

"Bond, you bastard." An officer wearing the standard tan, camouflage uniform walked over sporting a big grin. "I thought I'd seen the last of you."

Dylan grinned back. "Couldn't stay away, Paul." They shook hands like old friends.

Jim joined them, offering his hand next. "How's it hanging,

Paul?"

"Loose, but loaded, and ready to fire, my friend."

Jim laughed. The one thing these two had in common was a taste for double entendre.

Dylan broke in. "Are you off duty, Barnes?"

"Just. You want to head over to the Country Club?"

"We need to stop at the CPIC first. Why don't we meet you there after we check in and get our press badges?"

"Sounds good. I'll snag us a table."

———

Dylan and Jim joined the end of a small line outside the Baghdad Country Club and waited while soldiers, both men and women, checked their weapons at the door before heading in. When they were finally waved through, they found Paul sitting alone in a corner. Someone had taken the fourth chair, and it looked like he'd had to fight to keep the remaining two for them. The place was hopping.

"Beer?" a server called over heads as they headed over to their table.

"Two." Dylan held up two fingers just in case she couldn't hear him over the noise.

Paul nodded to them. "Sorry, the patio filled up early."

"This is fine." Dylan pulled out a chair and sat down.

"Seriously, I thought I'd seen the last of you." Paul leaned in, shaking his head at Dylan.

"We're just ahead of a campaign stop."

"Ah." Paul kicked back and groaned. "Another high-profile visit."

Jim shrugged. "Tricks of the trade. They'd probably be kissing Iraqi babies if they could get close enough."

"Hey, I saw Amir the other day," Paul told Dylan.

"Did you? How's he doing?"

"He hooked up with a couple of Dutch freelancers. He's still going."

The server brought their drinks, and a second for Barnes.

"I hope they're treating him right. He's fantastic."

"The guy knows what he's doing, no question." Paul studied Dylan thoughtfully. "That's what got to you, isn't it?"

"What do you mean?"

"Sending stringers out in your place. It must have killed you not to be out there with them."

Dylan blew out a deep breath. "Yeah. I felt like a goddamned baby in a highchair, waiting to be fed information. But it beats the hell out of losing a good friend."

Jim turned on him, perturbed. "Why do you do that to yourself? You aren't responsible for Khalid's death. He could have been shot anywhere, at any time."

Dylan toyed idly with his bottle. "He was working for me."

Now Jim glared. "You had no choice. It got too damn dangerous, and you know it. If you'd gone out, you would have put more people at risk. Not just the ones working with you either, but civilians caught in the middle had you been spotted by the wrong people."

Paul nodded, in total agreement with the photographer. "Jim's right. You can go without shaving, tan yourself nice and dark, but nothing's going to fool these guys once they get a load of your baby blues. Face it, Bond, this isn't Bosnia. You can't go native here like you did there."

"That's why I put in for a transfer."

Paul was sympathetic. "What are you doing now?"

Dylan gave him a slow smile. "I'm working on holding

some pretty big feet to the fire."

Paul's eyebrows rose with interest. "Really? Care to share?"

"Can't. Not yet. But I'll send you the article once it's written."

"I'll watch for it." Paul took a swig of beer and chuckled. "You always took your fourth-estate responsibilities seriously. That's why I trust you."

"Me too," Jim added, and they saluted Dylan with their brews.

———

After waking much too early on Wednesday morning only to toss and turn when she couldn't fall back to sleep, Ariela gave up and snuck downstairs to check her computer. Looking at the clock she tried to figure out Dylan's local time. Nine A.M.?

A jolt of excitement shot through her chest when she saw another message waiting. She needed to take a moment to mentally shore up the sandbags around her heart before opening it. To her surprise, she found herself smiling as soon as she started reading. Dylan's tone was comfortable, playful, and sexy. This she could handle. Keep emotion out of it and just have fun. She could play along.

TO: arielap@
SUBJECT: Thinking of you
MESSAGE: Since you asked, masturbation is helping me handle the distance between us. When I close my eyes I can see you, feel and smell you, all over again. You should consider it, as a healthier alternative to alcohol. Maybe we should think about getting you a

little toy for those lonely nights, if you don't already have one. It should take the edge off a little until I can take care of your needs personally. Damn, now I wish I was alone instead of hanging around in a big rec room with a bunch of off-duty soldiers. The two senators should be arriving within the hour. I love how you taste. Dylan

She stared at the computer screen, reread the message, and let out a quiet chirp of glee. Time for a reply.

TO: dylanbond@
SUBJECT: I suppose I asked for it
MESSAGE: How am I supposed to concentrate on hardwood floors now? Just so I'm not the only one at a disadvantage, you should know that your kisses are so good, you could cause long-term brain damage. What do you think of that? Ha! I do have a power tool in my drawer but, well, I'm not going to say why, it's on temporary leave. If you don't get back soon, conscription is definitely in its future. Weather's lovely here. Ariela

She was stunned and elated when her in-box blinked back with a new message from him right away. *He's on right now, half a world away? Far out!*

TO: arielap@
SUBJECT: My kisses huh?
MESSAGE: It's nice to know I can rattle your bones from here. I'm not entirely indifferent to your kisses, either. Why the hell didn't I take a picture of you with my phone? Dumb. You could send me a picture. Something sexy would be nice. Attach it to your next

message. The politicians were here and gone in a matter of hours. I should be able to hop a ride out of here first thing tomorrow, if all goes well. I'll keep you posted. In the meantime, I need to write my column, so I have to sign off. Watching for that naked picture—
Dylan

She was upstairs and back in five minutes, scanning a favorite photo onto her computer for him.

TO: dylanbond@
SUBJECT: Pic
MESSAGE: This is what I have, so it's gonna have to suffice. Sorry, but I wouldn't even feel comfortable asking Jean to take a picture of me naked. How, by the way, did a request for a sexy picture become a naked picture? I like your chest, almost as much as I like your firm, gorgeous ass. Sorry, my mind is wandering here. I'm so glad you'll be back soon. Come over when you can. Ariela

To her delight, he was still there and got right back to her.

TO: arielap@
SUBJECT: That was quick
MESSAGE: Nice picture. This will do. Don't expect to see me until late Friday. I'm just on my way out to meet with an Iraqi interpreter. He comes highly recommended and he'll be a good contact to have for any residual work I might get in the future. The job is impossible without the right local help. Until I see your pretty smile in person, I'll make do with your image. Missing you more each day—Dylan

Ariela stared at the last line of his message. He missed her? Did he just admit this could be more than sex for him too? Now what was she supposed to do? Nothing. There was nothing she could do until she saw him again. Only then would she know if they were heading toward a relationship. If he was hinting at more with that closing line, it could only mean one thing—he was through taking dangerous assignments. She couldn't have stopped the rush of optimism when it engulfed her, even if she'd wanted to.

Tara Mills

Eight

When it became obvious on Friday morning that Ariela would be utterly useless all day, Jean decided to handle their afternoon meeting with a potential client herself and leave her partner to manage the office on her own. It was no use. Ariela lacked focus. She started out working with the new software, familiarizing herself with its features, but even that, something she loved, failed to hold her attention. She ended up playing solitaire instead.

Time slowed. Ariela was conscious of every tick of the second hand as it circled the clock. After two hours had passed without a single phone call, it was time to give up. She shut down her computer and went to turn off the big printer. Dylan walked in just as she straightened up.

Damn, he looked good, so good. His warm tan enhanced his brilliant blue eyes, giving them the intensity of lasers targeted on her. His smile, well, his smile was slow, warm, and loaded with promise. They stood motionless, gazing at each other without words. Ariela moved first, going over to the copier to shut it off without turning from him.

Then Dylan headed right for her, and she waited, watching every determined step with a pounding heart.

She half expected him to smell like the beach, warm sunshine and coconut oil. The idea lured her in. The reality was even better. He was simply clean, unadulterated Dylan. She leaned into him, and he caught her tight in his arms. She almost sobbed when his mouth covered hers. Their skin flared with heat everywhere they touched as they fed from each other.

Slowly, Dylan eased back. "You're done here right?" Even

foggy from the kiss, she understood it was a courtesy question. What he really meant was, "You're done here."

She smiled, swaying against him when he nuzzled into her neck. "I'm done."

He relaxed his hold, but didn't let go. "My car's out front. Do you need anything tonight?"

"Where are we going?"

"My place. You're spending the night. I'm not putting up with a stand-in for you anymore."

She laughed. "An overnight bag might be nice."

"Just hurry." He gave her another quick peck and let her go.

Ariela ran to the front door, flipped the sign, and shot the dead bolt home. Dylan was already holding the back door open for her when she turned. They raced up the stairs, Dylan's hands roving impatiently over her body as she led the way.

While she tossed a few things into a bag, Dylan was dispatched to the kitchen to grab her birth-control pills. When he got back and tossed them onto her bed, he was even more impatient.

"Are you ready yet?"

She looked over in disbelief. "I thought you didn't want to stick me like a bug in a case?"

The reminder made him grin. "I'm over it."

Ariela laughed. "Is that right? Well, I don't think I'm going to mind being impaled, either."

He shot her a look of desperation. "If you talk like that we'll never get out of here. Have a heart."

———

The first thing that Ariela noticed when they exploded into his kitchen was the absence of Max.

"You didn't stop at the kennel?" she asked, turning to Dylan.

"No. He's not my first priority at the moment. Besides, they expected to have him through tomorrow." He pulled Ariela's bag out of her hand and dropped it on the floor, then drew her purse off her shoulder and dropped that too.

"Something on your mind?" she asked, helping him with the buttons on her blouse.

"How about a shower?" he asked with a low rumble, pressing suggestively against her.

"Now, there's an idea."

Ariela's shirt gaped open as he pulled her by the hand to the bathroom. They stopped in front of the mirror and Dylan turned her toward it. He pressed against her back and kissed her neck, his eyes locked on hers while his hands came up to unhook the front of her bra. He swept it apart and scooped her breasts into his hands, massaging them rhythmically while they watched.

Ariela groaned and reached behind her head to touch Dylan's hair, but he moved out of reach and dipped slightly to slide his hands down her torso, stopping at the fly of her slacks. He pressed a kiss into the curve of her back as he eased the zipper down and exposed her lace panties.

"I couldn't get you out of my mind," he said huskily, scraping his cheek along her shoulder blade, making her shudder at the sensation.

Dylan kissed his way back to her neck while his hand slid down inside the front of her underwear. Ariela held her breath as he explored, his touch so tantalizing she moved helplessly into it. He cupped her, his fingers playing over and in her as he pressed the heel of his hand against her mound, massaging her in a circular motion. It was delicious torture. Ariela dissolved, draping back against him like a loose garment. He moved fast, wrapping his free arm around her waist to support her.

"Ariela," he murmured.

She forced her heavy eyelids open, and in the mirror, Dylan flashed the sexiest smile she'd ever seen in her life.

"Did you miss me?" He pressed little kisses along her shoulder, his eyes locked on her.

Ariela bit her lower lip, but she couldn't stop the smile that gave her away. "Maybe a little."

He chuckled and moved his hands up to her breasts. Thank god he was holding her up. She needed his support.

Ariela's head rolled back and forth against his shoulder. "I don't think there's any blood left in my brain now."

"Good. Strip," he ordered, then went into the shower to turn on the faucet. He tested the water and stepped back out again.

Without bothering with his buttons first, Dylan whipped his shirt up over his head and dropped it inside-out onto the floor.

They watched each other silently, intensely as they slid their pants down, exposing thigh, knee, finally calf, at the same time. Dylan's solid erection sprang out at her, pointing to what it wanted in very explicit terms.

Ariela couldn't resist this man. She ran her hands down his body and combed her fingers through the trail of hair bisecting Dylan's chest, his torso, and his lean stomach. Her progress stalled at the top of his pubic area, and she stared at his jutting erection, fascinated and just a little nervous, yet unable to pull back or look away.

Woof! There wasn't a single thing wrong with him from what she could see. Then Ariela laughed at herself and looked up, finally noticing his curious expression.

"Should I be worried about the laugh?" he asked.

Chuckling now, she shook her head. "I stand corrected. You

were right. I *was* being hasty when I said your eyes are your best feature."

Dylan's deep rich laugh mingled with hers, and he held open the shower door for her. "Get in there."

Ariela stepped under the spray and turned, completely unprepared for how fast he moved on her. He pressed her up against the cool, tile wall, her body suddenly a living buffer between two temperature extremes.

The feel of Dylan's chest hair brushing over her breasts made Ariela's nipples contract even tighter. Tantalized by the sensation, she mashed herself against him, craving full-body contact. She scuffed her chest and stomach rosy on him. His right leg invaded the space between her thighs, and she rode it slowly, brushing her calf across his coarser leg, like a cat, every point of contact making her skin more sensitive.

Dylan pinned her hands out flat against the wall and held her there. Now she was immobile, dangling over his thigh, her toes just brushing the tiles.

Could this be what the word ravish means?

It was unbelievably hot, thrilling. Ariela's heart thumped wildly as Dylan made slow, deliberate love to her mouth. His tongue swept over everything, tasting, teasing, and stroking her in ways she never knew were possible. She'd never been kissed like this. Then he drew her tongue into his mouth and performed a guided tour there. It was the most erotic moment of her life—so far.

Ever so gradually, Dylan eased back and admired Ariela, still immobilized beneath the spray. She tried to imagine how she looked to him right then, her lips red and swollen, her eyes glazed with passion.

"You...are...stunning," he told her, then used his upper thigh to nuzzle between her legs. He smiled at the breathless gasp it produced.

Of course, the washing that followed was merely a pretense to touch and stroke one another, and it only exacerbated the already unstable situation. They kissed again as water rained over their faces, seeking narrow passages between their bodies.

At one point, Dylan bent Ariela forward, his hands covering hers on the tile, and slipped inside her from behind. Their groans of pleasure echoed in the enclosed space.

Ariela cried out in protest when he withdrew. "Why are you stopping?"

"The water's getting cold." He reached around her and shut it off.

Still dripping, they raced to his bedroom, and Dylan threw back the covers of the imperfectly made bed. "This can't happen soon enough for me."

"Tell me about it." Ariela gave him an eager stroke then dropped backward onto the bed, her arms wide in invitation.

Her knees came up around him as Dylan sank on top of her, and their bodies merged instantaneously. There was no fumbling, no positioning, and no manual guidance. He simply penetrated her, tongue and cock.

The hunger, the need to ferociously collide was palpable, but to Ariela's surprise, she found herself tearing up when Dylan chose a more tender approach.

What started out so reckless, so wild had turned in on itself, smothering out the ungodly need and leaving something entirely different in its place. Ariela had expected Dylan to drive into her quick and hard and hurtle them over their first climax as fast as possible. Once he'd taken down that hard edge, they would enjoy each other at a more leisurely pace.

She'd never known anyone more unpredictable.

Dylan nuzzled into Ariela's neck. "You smell so good." Drawing back, he smiled and visually traced around her head. "There's a damp halo radiating out from your wet hair on the sheet. The way it frames your face is startlingly beautiful. I have to kiss you again."

Touched and amazed, Ariela brushed the hair back from his temple. He turned into her hand, kissing the inside of her wrist.

That simple gesture frightened her. There was more happening between them than simply sex and companionship. She was in real danger of falling fast and hard for Dylan. Ariela was afraid of needing him, longing for him, but recognized she was well on her way already. Is this what she'd always protected herself against? Not just hero types but men in general? Was fear of men and the vulnerability they brought out in her the reason she habitually sabotaged her relationships? Was she going to be as weak as her mother in the end, because she never allowed herself to be tested? Where were her calluses? Where were her scrapes and bruises? All in her head, that's where. She was owed a day of reckoning for sidestepping true emotional entanglements for so long.

Ariela looked up at Dylan and returned his smile, clinging to his shoulders as they moved together. She knew she wasn't going to get out of it so easy this time. He was the embodiment of everything she'd run from. He was idealistic, warm, funny, smart, interesting, and intense. She was halfway in love with him already, and that wasn't even taking his most excellent chassis into consideration. Nope, her bare ass was hanging out there now, and she had no clue what was going to come up and bite it.

Dylan hooked Ariela's legs back with his arms and surged

over her giving her even more to think about.

Immobilized, she could only take what he gave her, which turned out to be plenty. He was still taking his time, but his thrusts were more powerful now, more purposeful. Dylan held nothing back, and she was, oh, so grateful.

———

Dylan loved how Ariela touched him, how her soft fingertips traced his areolas, how she lightly pinched his hard nipples. She liked to squeeze his earlobes too, and run her nails lightly down the sides of his neck and up into his hair. He didn't mind the bite of her fingernails on his arms or shoulders, either. He especially loved the silky touch of her ass and thighs against him, how her eyelashes fluttered and she gasped softly whenever he rotated deep inside her. He could feel her swelling around him, tightening, and he coaxed her along, every thrust heightening her color. Heat seemed to radiate from her glowing skin.

"Dylan." Her voice was shaky, her eyes wide.

"Let go, Ariela. I'll follow."

There it was. With a sudden cry, she seized, and her fingers dug into his arms. She clenched around him in release, her head thrown back, and her mouth open in a silent scream of ecstasy. Two more forceful drives and Dylan locked hips with her and groaned as his body jerked. He felt his energy drain away with every involuntary spasm. Collapsing with exhaustion, they clung to each other and trembled for several silent minutes, their lungs gasping for air.

Dylan was shaken, stunned. *What the hell just happened here?* He'd been sexually active since age sixteen, had even thought he was in love a couple of times, and yet, this felt different. No way. He didn't want this. It was too damn soon. They were still trying each other on for size, for Christ's sake. He didn't believe in falling head over heels or whirlwind romances. He'd silently scorned and ridiculed guys who claimed it happened that way for them—*saps*. He'd listened to their anecdotes with skepticism, unable to accept the possibility. Well, this was a kick in the ass. Finding himself in the same situation was the perfect way to prove him wrong. Irony loved giving life lessons.

It was a full five minutes before either spoke. They lay together, Ariela snuggled close in his arms. Dylan dipped his head and pressed a soft kiss to her temple, having finally come to terms with the startling discovery of his deepening feelings. Call it whatever he liked, he was becoming emotionally involved.

"How are you doing? Okay?" he asked.

She laughed. "Okay? I'm fantastic, but still recovering. God, that was so necessary."

He chuckled. "No kidding. I've been saving up."

"I appreciate it."

Dylan toyed with her hair. He liked how it looked spilling around her face and across his chest. It gave him an idea.

"Wait here." He leaped up and ran out of the room.

———

Ariela tugged the sheet up around herself and snuggled into the nearest pillow, pushing her irrational fear of the future aside in favor of happiness now.

He was holding his phone when he came back.

"This is the perfect time to snap a few. Any objections?" He gave her a hopeful smile.

Ariela considered the question then shook her head. "Just promise me you'll keep these to yourself."

"I promise."

He had her sit up then he draped the sheet in a suggestive way. He wanted one breast exposed. After careful deliberation about which breast, he posed her and snapped his picture.

"Take a look." He showed her. "That is one sexy picture."

"That's not bad," she admitted with surprise. "And no one else gets to see this—ever."

"I agree." Dylan took the phone back. "Do a few more?"

"What did you have in mind?"

"I think it's time to lose the sheet." Before she could stop him, he snatched it away and stepped up onto the mattress, straddling her legs as he looked down on her. "I'll call this one *Afterglow*."

Playing up to the camera, she informed him, "You're hard again."

He leered back at her. "What do you expect?"

"I expect you to show me a little more of the world. Someplace hot and exotic might be nice."

He grinned and sank to his knees, reaching over to set the phone on the nightstand. With a growl that sent Ariela's heart rate into an excited gallop, he dropped on top of her and they rolled across the mattress.

———

Dylan couldn't get enough of Ariela that night. He would have felt bad about robbing her of a decent sleep if she hadn't reached for him just as often until exhaustion finally took its toll. When he eventually woke, he found he was still pinned beneath her. It didn't look like she'd moved after collapsing on top of him the last time.

He glanced over at the clock. It was half past eleven, closing in on noon. The morning sunshine had already retreated while they slept, moving off the bed. The light was indirect now, unlike earlier when he'd woken to full, radiant heat and planted himself between her thighs with a luxurious moan. He was astonished at how much he wanted her. The craving never abated, no matter how many times they fed the carnal beast.

Dipping his chin, he kissed the top of Ariela's head. She smiled and shifted, her hand traveling automatically to his groin. He thought she was going to stroke him back to life again, but her fingernails went to his balls instead and worked lazily through the hairs. Now he really groaned.

"You know the saying that the way to a man's heart is through his stomach?" he asked.

She released a sexy sigh. "Um hum." Flexing her fingers, she drew her nails across his sack from underneath.

God that felt good.

"They lied." He gave her back a grateful rub. "A good ball scratch will do the trick."

Ariela jiggled with laughter on top of him. "I'll remember that."

He gave her a squeeze. "Please do."

Ariela's smile was warmer than the sunshine when she turned her head to look at him.

He smiled back. "How are you feeling? I've put you through your paces." Reaching down, he stopped her hand before she could scratch him raw.

She answered with a playful wriggle and a musical laugh. "I've never felt better."

"Thank you for last night." He chuckled, lightly tugging a

lock of her hair. "And this morning."

"Any regrets?" She pushed herself up and straddled him. When the sheet slid to her waist, Dylan cupped her breasts. He stared at her as if she were crazy. "Hell, no. You?"

"That's another big no." Ariela dipped down for a quick kiss then bounded out of bed. "I get the bathroom first," she called, rounding the doorway.

Dylan sat up and kicked free of the remaining covers, rubbing his eyes and face. He was in trouble, deep, scary trouble. However, his anxiety blew out like a candle when Ariela, all wonderfully curvy and naked, waltzed back into the bedroom.

Her eyebrows arched up at the look in his eyes. She smiled. "You're awfully appealing all rumpled in the morning."

He chuckled. "I was thinking the same thing about you." Dylan rose to his feet and enjoyed a long stretch. Coming back to ease, he grabbed his keys and phone from the bedside table. "I need water, coffee, breakfast, and juice, in that order. Come on. Let's get dressed. I'm buying."

Nine

After a late breakfast, they stopped at the kennel and collected Max. The dog was so wound up Dylan needed Ariela's help to wrestle him into the car. They decided to take the golden retriever to the lake nearby so he could burn off his excess energy.

Dylan took a Frisbee out of his trunk and man and dog played fetch for twenty minutes while Ariela twisted back and forth on a nearby swing, content just to watch them. She laughed at their tug of war, loving how they both growled and frisked around.

How many ways was this man going to win her over? Did she ever stand a chance with him? Probably not. So who was he really—the serious journalist, the daring flirt, the pet owner with a heart of gold, or the incredibly giving lover? Or were those qualifiers merely facets of the whole irresistible gem? How could she protect herself when she was already dazzled?

She guessed their game of fetch was over when she saw Dylan rub his shoulder after his last throw. When Max trotted back, Frisbee in his mouth, his master caught him by the collar and clipped on the leash.

"You ready?" he called to her.

Nodding, Ariela untangled herself from the twisted chain and bounded up to join them on their walk.

Her heart melted when Dylan held out his hand to her. She reached for it and they wandered the paths again, circling the lake. Their stroll was companion-able, silent. She didn't feel compelled, and it seemed neither did Dylan, to ruin the peace with unnecessary chatter.

When Max tugged them to the water, Dylan eased up to allow him to drink. Of course, as soon as Dylan bent to kiss Ariela, Max took advantage of their inattention to wade in deeper. They managed to haul him back before he completely immersed himself, but the dog was wet enough now to make the drive home unpleasant. He was far from dry when they got back to the parked car. Leaping onto the backseat, Max left dark doggie prints all over the upholstery. The smell of wet dog was so pungent, Ariela was glad when Dylan suggested they roll the windows down for the drive.

Twenty minutes later, Dylan pulled into the parking space in front of his house and killed the engine. Turning to her with wide eyes, he said, "Sorry, I just assumed you were coming back here with me. I guess I should have checked first. Are you okay with this or would you prefer something else?"

Smiling, Ariela reached out and gave his cheek a playful little pat. "This is fine. I believe I booked you for the entire weekend."

He laughed. "Is that right? Well, I'd better not disappoint or it'll be my head."

"Satisfaction guaranteed?"

His eyes were twinkling now. "That's a motto to live by. How am I doing so far?"

"Be sure to leave a customer comment card on the nightstand. You might just see a raise in your future."

Dylan leaned in and kissed her on the forehead. "I kinda like you."

Ariela kissed the tip of his nose. "You're growing on me too."

A piercing bark nearly burst their eardrums.

"Max!" Dylan yelled back. "You want to give me a heart

attack?" He turned to Ariela. "I think that's our cue."

Climbing out of the car, Dylan lifted the handle on the rear door and was thrown backward three steps when Max blasted through it.

He looked stunned when he shut the door and met Ariela's eyes over the roof of the car. "Here I thought he'd mellow out after the park."

"I'll get him." Ariela ran to the gate and waved Max through. He seemed more than happy to run around the yard, sniffing and raising his leg on all his favorite spots. "I think he's just glad to be home. I'll bet he settles down now." She closed the gate behind Dylan.

Once inside, Max headed straight for his bowls in the kitchen. He took a long, noisy drink before making himself comfortable on the sofa.

Dylan looked at Ariela and shrugged. "So, what should we do? Feel like playing a little back-gammon?"

She perked up. "Backgammon? Wow, it's been years. Sure, I could whip your butt."

He cracked a skeptical smile. "We'll see." Dylan went to his bedroom and came back with a handsome, wooden, inlaid board that he opened on the table.

His left eyebrow twitched in an intriguing way. "I think we need cocktails."

Ariela looked up from placing her pieces. "Maybe. What do you have?"

"I'm not sure. Let's scrounge."

She followed him to the cabinets where they did a thorough search. She even checked the refrigerator and freezer. You never know. Dylan cheered when he pulled a few assorted bottles out of his forgotten liquor stash.

They settled on lemonade and rum then returned to the table with their glasses.

"Are you ready to lose?" Dylan asked with a cocky grin.

She stared boldly back at him. "Are you?"

He nodded at the dice. "Roll."

Dylan easily won the first few games. He was an aggressive player, always willing to attack where Ariela was more conservative and held back. A few times, she got burned because she couldn't roll herself back into the game until he'd already taken the majority of his pieces off the board. After that Ariela switched to a running game, racing for the safety of home. It worked, reversing her fortunes. Dylan was forced to revise his strategy, and though he never won again, their games were closer.

"So, you haven't talked much about this past week." Ariela tossed her dice.

"Because it wasn't very interesting." He made his move, narrowly missing one of her vulnerable pieces. "You're lucky," he said, pointing to it.

"Just remember the word retribution, my friend."

Dylan laughed. "You're talking to a writer here. Are you sure you want to take me on in vocabulary too?"

Ariela smiled as she considered it. She was pleased Dylan seemed to enjoy the more spirited games best too, especially when neither could tell how they'd end. It was the intensity of those particular matches that brought out their playful sides, and they taunted and teased each other constantly. Time and time again, to Ariela's complete surprise, considering how competitive Dylan had begun, he would encourage her to take out one of his pieces, rather than make the kinder move. It always worked in her favor, yet he congratulated her just the same.

After yet another defeat, Dylan tucked his dice away and took hers out of her hand.

Startled, she looked up at him. "Are we finished?"

"Depends on what you mean by finished."

The guy could write a book on innuendo.

Snorting, Ariela smiled. "Backgammon."

"Ah. Then, yes, we're finished." Dylan grabbed Ariela's hand and drew her up and around the table. He slid his chair back and pulled her down on his lap, caressing her cheek.

She felt the brush of his thumb across her ear and pressed into his hand even as she sank into his kiss, humming low in her throat. Driving her fingers into his hair, she gripped his head and let herself go.

Her brain was fogged, in a good way, when she slowly drew back. "Mm, you have the softest hair."

"Do I?" he asked absently, his attention on her torso.

His hand slid under her shirt and cupped her breast. The heat of his palm surrounded her. There was a slight pinch on her furling nipple. Responding to it, she turned into him. When their lips connected again, she drew him in, sucking on his tongue.

His eyes were all pupil when he eased back. "What do you think?" It was the tone of the question, deep and seductive, that thrilled her, not necessarily the words. The teasing kiss to the corner of her mouth had already wiped her head blank of everything else.

"Was that a proposition? You've got me so stirred up I didn't catch it. How much blood do you think is left in my head just now?"

Dylan chuckled. "Enough."

She stretched up and kissed him on the forehead. "We still have things to talk about."

He tweaked her neglected nipple through her bra. "Such as?"

Ariela stood so she could straddle him, leaving her feet to hang down the outsides of his calves. Open this way, the bulge of his erection was hard against her. She rolled her hips a few times, rubbing herself on him with a groan. What was she doing?

Biting her lip, she finally asked, "Is this just sex? If it is, I'd like to know."

Dylan smiled. "My pants aren't even unzipped."

"Don't make me hurt you."

He wrapped his arms around her waist and gave her a squeeze. "If all I wanted was sex, I wouldn't have called you again, or e-mailed you, or kidnapped you from your office when I got home. I'm willing to spend some serious investigative time on you—see how it plays out. Then I'll know how to write this story and predict an ending. Can you live with that for the time being?"

"I was just wondering."

"So you're saying I'm an acceptable candidate now?" he asked with a disarming grin.

"Now that you're not ducking bullets and mortar fire? Yeah, I'm willing to revise your status."

"I appreciate it." His eyes rolled closed as she ground against his swollen fly again. "So we're in the exploratory stage then, right?" he asked, a gruff catch in his voice.

Ariela nodded. "That's right, oh, very right." She enjoyed what his hands were doing on her breasts and the way his lips moved along her neck and shoulder.

"Good, because there's a lot more of you I want to explore." Dylan lifted her right off his lap and set her on her feet. Talk about a turn-on. Ariela gave him a saucy smile and whipped up her shirt, flashing him. Then she took off running, Dylan right behind her. He caught her just outside the bedroom. Scooping her up, Dylan carried her to the bed and dropped her into the center of it.

———

They stripped at record speed, their clothes flying in all directions then Dylan crawled over the top of her and settled down, teasing her with his lips while his impatient erection poked her in the thigh.

Ariela pulled him hard against her and asked, "Will I ever get enough?"

"I hope not."

Dylan nuzzled and licked along Ariela's neck and throat, then backed off so he could get to her nipples, smiling when they puckered for him.

"Time to test the waters." His hand wandered down her ribcage, slowed over her belly, flared out to trace her pelvic bone, then curled between her legs. She was definitely ready for him. Ariela's hips left the mattress, straining for more when he slid a finger inside of her and used his thumb to tease her further.

"It's not enough. I need you!" she growled with aggravation.

Was there anything more flattering to the male ego than a statement like that? Smiling, he withdrew his hand, and she sank back with a ragged breath.

"What if I do this?" He rose up and grabbed her ankles, pressing her legs back and spreading them wide.

"Yes!" she cried, urging him on.

It moved him, more than he expected, and for a moment, all he could do was gaze at her. She was offering herself to him— every luscious inch, his to enjoy. But he wanted something deeper. He hadn't realized just how badly he wanted more from a woman until Ariela. He'd been alone, and yes, lonely, for so long. He had close friendships, contacts, but actual physical and emotional intimacy? No. He'd been adrift in a rudderless boat, blown wherever the winds of war and conflict carried him. Forming new attachments only to lose them, sometimes violently, time and time again. Oh, how he craved stability and security. He wanted the ceaseless tension to leave his body. What wouldn't he give to know how it felt to be completely relaxed and unguarded? When he was with Ariela, he sensed he was closer than he'd ever come to finding what he so desperately craved.

Watching him with a frown of concern, she asked, "Dylan?"

He let go of her ankle so he could caress her face, her neck, her breast. When she touched him back, he turned into her hand. It was sad, yet funny, how you could miss the gift of touch without ever knowing it.

Dylan slowly dropped to kiss her, their eyes locked. She rose to meet him and their simple kiss became far more poignant than either probably expected.

"Everything okay?" Fussing with his hair, her question was little more than a nervous whisper.

Dylan leaned in and kissed just below her ear. "Better than okay."

Ariela smiled with relief and wrapped her legs around him, drawing him in. He let her take him, conscious of her bare heels pressing into his buttocks, the first intimate brush of their sexes, and finally, that exquisite moment when she closed around him and he was lost in her warm embrace.

Then Dylan took over, his movements slow, sinuous. Suddenly hypersensitive to sensation, he was fully aware of how her body enveloped him. He watched her eyes fall closed, and tried to visualize how it felt for her. Reading her fleeting expressions, he gathered every inward stroke was a tantalizing promise, every retreat a heavy disappointment. She fought to hold him deep, clenching her muscles around him, yet he drew away, creating exquisite ripples in his wake. It was the sweetest torture.

He looked with wonder at the lovely face mere inches from his. When she opened her eyes, he saw they were glazed with passion. He didn't think he could grow tired of looking at Ariela, gazing on her, especially now that he'd seen her face lit during climax. That radiance alone, flaring for him, brought on by him, spurred him on. He wanted to see it again. His drives grew fevered, relentless. Ariela absorbed them eagerly, straining to take and wring everything she could out of them.

Then she began to tremble in his arms, her muscles taut with tension. Ariela grabbed his hips and pulled him into her body. Dylan groaned as he went along, ramming into her so hard he drove her across the bed on her back. Her shaky smile reassured him she couldn't be happier with what he was doing. Then her face, her breasts, her chest, all flared like sunset, and she threw back her head and let out a piercing wail that transformed into a wild, ecstatic laugh.

Emotions commingled with pleasure and ripped through Dylan so forcefully he was swept away in a violent rush seconds later.

Only when he'd regained control of his body did he drop to

his side next to her, his chest heaving. "Wow."

"No kidding," Ariela agreed, equally breathless. "Thank god I'm on birth control."

He slid his arm around her waist and shuddered. "Let's not even go there."

But he couldn't help it now. Dylan found himself imagining all the combinations they could come up with for their offspring—his eyes and her hair, her nose and his chin, her smile and his hands. The height would be somewhere in the middle for girls, for boys, he'd be looking them in the eye one day. Maybe looking up at them. It was a sobering thought.

Ariela gave him a congratulatory smile. "Well, you knocked that one right out of the box."

He chuckled. "I think you mean park."

Her eyes were sparkling when she reached over and toyed with his ear. "Not this time. I meant box."

"Ah." Dylan smiled and, banding his arms around her, rolled to his back, taking Ariela with him. "I didn't hurt you, did I?"

No answer was required. Ariela smiled and pushed herself up to straddle his hips. He stroked his hands lightly along her sides, across her lower ribs, and finally to her breasts. Lifting them both from underneath, he brought a nipple to his mouth. He swirled his tongue around the tight tip before drawing on it. Ariela groaned as he inflated under her. She rose up and slid down over him, taking him into her body once more.

There was no urgency this time, they'd spent that energy already, but it didn't mean they were finished with each other. Dylan rubbed her legs, her hips, and her torso as she moved on him. His contented smile was all for her, because of her, and he felt a strange peace settle in his chest.

Peace, what a novel concept. He could get used to this.

Reaching up, he hooked the hands gripping his shoulders, meshed his fingers with hers and brought her knuckles to his lips, kissing them.

———

Ariela stared back at him, captivated by his beautiful blue gaze, his smile, and the unexpected tenderness that was as much a part of him as his playful side. She wasn't just wiping her sexual dry spell off the books with Dylan. She was sweeping every unsatisfying relationship preceding him right out the door. The thought made her laugh, as if released from a weight she didn't know she was carrying. He smiled back.

Their next kiss was unhurried. They took their time tasting, exploring, and savoring the sensations they created together. But her movements had noticeably slowed.

He mentioned it. "You're getting tired."

"I am."

Dylan dug his heels into the mattress and thrust up, taking over as her energy waned. She was already trembling when his thumb nuzzled between her legs. Ariela shattered like glass in an earthquake and continued to shake as tremors rolled through her. Then he seized with a groan and she collapsed on top of him, utterly drained as his body gradually relaxed.

Not only could she hear his heart pounding under her ear, she could feel it. As he slowly returned to normal, she felt herself drifting off. His heartbeat was better than a lullaby. He made it even better when he clasped his hands behind her, his elbows loose at her sides. She shifted slightly so they'd both be more comfortable then settled back down with a contented sigh. He gave her a squeeze, letting her know he was in complete agreement.

She wasn't sure how much time had passed, it may have been minutes or a half-hour or more, but when Dylan stiffened under her, Ariela's eyes popped open in alarm. She was so startled to see Max sitting right against the edge of the bed, watching them, she dove for the sheets. Dylan turned on his side, screening her while she wondered how long the dog had been sitting there. Had he watched them do the mattress mambo?

"I think it's our destiny to be caught," he said with a rueful chuckle and pulled the sheet over them both. "Get out, Max. Go on."

Max wagged his tail against the floor and looked at his master, immovable.

Dylan sighed. "I'll bet you need to go outside."

That got the dog up. Patting Ariela's naked hip, Dylan got out of bed. "Be right back."

Without putting on a stitch of clothing, he padded through the house with the dog frisking at his side. The man seemed so casual about nudity. She'd never been that confident, that comfortable with her body. Obviously—she'd hidden from his dog! Embarrassing.

He stopped just inside the bedroom door and looked at her with a tired smile. "Are you hungry?"

She eyed him up and down. He was framed so perfectly, not posing or on display. He was simply there, unapologetic in all his masculine glory. She loved it.

"Starving," she said wickedly.

He laughed. "You know what I mean. We managed to kill a few more hours. Now I could really go for some Chinese food."

She loved Chinese. "I was just thinking the same thing!"

Dylan bent down and picked up her shirt, tossing it to her.

"Come on. I have a monster craving for egg rolls."

———

It was late Sunday morning when Ariela stretched and snaked her hand between the sheets to touch Dylan. His side of the bed was cool and empty. Before she even had a chance to pout, she heard excitement in his voice in the next room. She rolled out of bed and stooped to picked up his discarded shirt and slipped it on, rubbing the fabric against her bare skin. Dipping her nose inside the collar, she inhaled his scent and felt an inconvenient rush of lust.

She found Dylan pacing in the kitchen, around the living room, and back into the kitchen again, the telephone to his ear, an eager look on his handsome face.

"No, we can't risk it. Are you familiar with Scenic Lake?" Dylan paused, listening. "Right. There's a tree straight down from where Colgate runs into Scenic Drive. Cut across to the lower walking path, and you'll find a pretty distinctive tree, looks like the Headless Horseman looming up at you, with his arms outstretched." Dylan laughed at what he heard. "Trust me—you'll know it when you see it. On the backside of that tree, you'll find a deep depression in the bark...Uh-huh. It's about four feet up. Tuck the flash drive right in there, just far enough so it isn't obvious. But be sure you don't wedge it. Right, I don't think you'd get another crack at this...Yeah."

He turned and gave Ariela a sexy smile when she walked over. She returned the favor, fully appreciating how his faded blue jeans hung low on his hips, leaving his tongue-worthy navel exposed. Her gaze fell to his bare toes flexing into the carpet and she laughed softly. Playfully raising his eyebrows, Dylan held out his arm in invitation. Ariela moved against him, wrapping her arms around his waist. She nuzzled his chest and sighed as his hand rode up under her hair and lightly scratched her scalp, mimicking his toes in the rug. She did a little stroking, a little scratching, of her own, finally ending at his scrumptious ass. Life couldn't get any better.

"How soon can you get there?" He pressed a kiss to the top of Ariela's head then flexed his butt, giving her more to grab. Delighted, she gave him a deeper squeeze. "Mmm, sounds good. Give me a week to go over everything and double-check what I find...I know. I hear ya. Keep your head down and don't try to contact me unless it's important...You bet. Good luck and hey...Thanks."

Dylan shut his phone and she leaned back to look at him, her eyebrows raised in question.

"My mole," he explained, sliding the phone into his front pocket. "Do you want to join me when I take Max for a w.a.l.k. or would you rather go home instead?"

"Either way, you're going to end up working afterwards, aren't you?"

He smiled. "Yep."

"And I can see you're excited," she said, amused and resigned.

"Sorry. This could be golden. I'm getting a full flash drive!"

"You might as well take me home. I don't have any clean clothes, and I'm out of underwear."

"You can always go without."

She rose up on her toes and gave him a light kiss. "Yes, but how long can a woman go like that?"

"You're asking me?" He grinned. "Indefinitely."

"There's a surprise." She rolled of her eyes, but secretly cheered his answer. "I think we'd better get dressed."

"One second." He tugged her back against him and gently brought her chin up.

She decided he could have all the time he wanted.

Tara Mills

Ten

Dylan clipped the leash to Max's collar and opened his car door. The dog leaped across the driver's seat and hit the ground right behind him.

"A little impatient?" he asked the dog with a chuckle. "Come on."

They headed across the street and cut over to the upper bike path, headed for the walking trail skirting the shoreline. Being Sunday, the park was full of people and dogs, but it was pleasant. The temperature hovered around eighty degrees. Big, billowy clouds lumbered across the deep blue sky. He watched three kayakers on the water while Max lifted his leg on an overgrown bush. When they continued, Dylan toyed with the idea of taking up kayaking himself, now that he was home. He wondered if Ariela would consider doing it with him.

Did she even swim? Huh. There were still so many things to learn about her. He was just taking notes on her food preferences, her sleeping habits, how she preferred her coffee in the morning, and how many cups she allowed herself.

He flat out liked the woman, a lot. He liked the look of her, the smell of her, and the taste of her went right to his dick, instantly making him rock hard. Ariela was a calm person, and frankly, after everything he'd been through and seen, a little calm in the chaos was a good thing. He could relax around her. It didn't feel like he was auditioning for something, nor was there an underlying need to prove anything.

Dylan wondered when she'd open up to him about her history. He knew she was raised by her grandmother. When she'd shied away from the circumstances, he hadn't pressed.

He'd simply be there for her. He'd learned long ago when people were ready to talk, they usually sought him out, and it was worth the wait. He wasn't going to push her because that would ruin the comfort level they'd found together.

Seeing his tree coming up, he scanned the area, assuring himself no one was in the immediate vicinity. Feeling safe to proceed, he coaxed Max over to the tree. While the dog lifted his leg, Dylan slid his fingers into the crevice in the bark and extracted the flash drive. Casually pocketing it, he drew Max back to the path.

Now they were cooking with gas.

———

Ariela was zonked out on the couch with a romantic comedy on the television when Jean got home. She sat up with a yawn and rubbed her eyes.

"What are you doing here?" Jean asked, swinging her purse by the strap onto the chair. She kicked out of her shoes and left them by the door.

"Dylan had to work, so he brought me back." Ariela stretched and groaned. "I can't believe I fell asleep. And this is my favorite movie too."

Jean smiled. "Catching up?"

"Must be." Ariela gave another big yawn and stood. "Where've you been?"

"At Ron's parents' place. It was his uncle's birthday. There was cake and mind-numbing conversation. Your couch is looking good to me about now."

Ariela turned on her way to the kitchen to ask, "You trying to earn points with his family?"

"No need. They love me."

"You're good together." Ariela shuffled into the kitchen to stare into the refrigerator. "You hungry?"

"No. But I wouldn't mind something to drink."

"I'm grabbing a root beer. Want one?"

"Sure."

Ariela grabbed two and closed the door with a rattle of bottles and jars. She handed one to her friend. They both sagged against the counter and popped the tops on their cans.

When Jean came up for air, she asked, "So how's Dylan? The luster off those sapphire eyes of his yet?"

Ariela cracked a smile. "Actually, he's better than ever, with only one flaw."

Jean's eyebrows rose. "Oh yeah?"

"His dog."

It was a good thing Jean had swallowed or she would have spewed root beer all over Ariela when she lost it.

Shaking with the giggles, she double-checked what she just heard. "His *dog*?"

"Max isn't a bad animal. He's just there. All. The. Time. It's creepy."

"Like a doggie stalker?" Jean teased.

Ariela toasted the idea. "Exactly."

Jean scoffed at her. "I don't think you dislike animals as much as you claim."

"Don't be so sure."

"I know you," Jean said firmly. "You'd be devastated if you accidentally hit a dog or cat with your car. You'd do everything in your power to help them."

"That's because I object to anything suffering."

"See? That's what I mean. You, my dear, doth protest too strongly."

"Believe what you want," Ariela said carelessly, but hid her smile behind the rim of her can.

———

Dylan and Max turned up at the office on Monday, just before noon. He was back to wearing his worn jeans, a T-shirt, and his dark blue hoodie, and yet, it didn't hurt him in the least.

"What are you doing here?" Ariela asked, pleasantly surprised when he walked in.

Max made a beeline for her, straining at the leash, much to Jean's amusement. Ariela was forced to pat the dog's head when it landed in her lap and he snuffled at her.

"Good boy, go away," she said, shoving him back.

Dylan laughed and tugged him out of the way by the collar so he could take a crack at her himself. He bent down and gave her a soft, lingering kiss. "Hi," he murmured before straightening. "We dropped by to have lunch with you, if that's okay." He shot a warm smile at Jean.

"Oh, that's nice." Ariela came out of her chair and gave him a squeeze. "But we usually just eat sandwiches out back."

Dylan pulled a crumpled, brown bag out of his pocket and waved it at her. "I came prepared."

Then he noticed Max's head, deep in Ariela's trash can. "What are you after?"

"I think he smells the banana peel in there," Ariela said.

Dylan wrestled the dog away from the bin, and set it on top of her desk, safely out of reach.

"We're officially on lunch break. The answering machine is on." Jean pushed back from her desk and stood. "Dylan, I'm going upstairs to grab my lunch. Can I bring you a beer?"

"Sure. Thanks." He maneuvered the dog out the back door.

"We'll meet you ladies outside."

Ariela turned to Jean, her eyebrows raised.

Jean grinned back. "Nice surprise."

It was the first of many casual lunch dates to follow. Whenever Ariela heard Max's toenails scrabbling up the front steps, she'd grab her waste basket and set it up high before Max even cleared the door. It saved time. Of course, once Jean bought a box of dog biscuits for Max—that was it. He always went directly to her.

Rising from her office chair the following Thursday, Ariela went to greet Dylan and collect her kiss. The dog broke toward Jean and she gave his ears a vigorous rub while he tried to climb into her lap for more love.

"Down." Laughing, she shoved Max off and brushed helplessly at her skirt. Giving up with a heavy sigh, she looked at Dylan. "I know you've got one."

He grinned and dug into his jacket pocket, giving the lint roller an underhanded toss. "Yes!" Jean cried when she caught it.

Ariela laughed at her. "I warned you about buying those dog treats." Then she turned back to Dylan. "How's your reading coming along? Are your eyes crossed yet?"

He chuckled. "Almost. This thing is a lot bigger than just Senator Norton. You wouldn't believe the money involved. It's incredible."

"This is all from that single flash drive?" asked Jean, glancing up as she peeled the used sticky paper off the roll.

"That was just the tip of the iceberg. We're beyond that now. I'm trying to set up an interview with someone who was there that October. He saw quite a bit. From what I've heard, he walked out in disgust. He's not ready to talk yet, but I think he will."

"Good luck with that," said Jean. Doubt tinged her tone. "Heads up." She tossed the roller back to him and Dylan returned it to his pocket.

Ariela ducked under her desk for her abandoned shoes. Wiggling into the pumps, she looked up at both of them and asked, "Are we having lunch or not?"

Outside, Jean chose to sit on the old redwood bench, leaving the back steps to Dylan and Ariela. He was one step up from her, his left leg stretched out beside her. She studied his worn-out, grass stained, running shoe and noticed the wear in the heel. She could tell he walked on the outside of his foot. Not an important fact in the scheme of things, but it interested her.

As he tossed scraps to Max, she wondered if Dylan was satisfied to be back. Did he find the work fulfilling enough after what he'd been doing? He was spending an awful lot of time reading. This paper trail he was following was important, no doubt, but how long before he grew bored with the work? With her? Her news that they got the Bitterstock contract and would be designing their new offices could hardly compete with political protests, clashes with militants, roadside bombings, and a country trying to rebuild itself out of the ashes. She felt like she was living on borrowed time.

Dylan tossed the last bit of crust to Max. The dog snapped it up, swallowing it whole.

"Has he ever missed?" Ariela asked.

"Not very often." Dylan looked at the dog and held up his empty hands. "That's it. All gone."

Max settled down on the grass, his chin between his front paws, and a miserable, suffering look in his eyes. They all laughed at him.

"What a baby. You'd think you were starving him or something," said Jean.

"And I gave him half my sandwich too," Ariela reminded them, feeling grumpy about it all of a sudden.

Dylan gave her a tap with the outside of his leg. "I told you not to bother."

"Yeah, yeah."

"She's crazy about dogs," Jean told him, grinning at Ariela.

"I am not," Ariela insisted.

Dylan dropped his arms around her shoulders and pulled her back, kissing the top of her head. "She really is," he agreed with Jean.

"I know."

"So…" Dylan looked over at Jean. "Any chance I can steal her away now?"

Ariela turned to scowl at him. "Why don't you ask me?"

He chuckled. "Because this is more fun. I knew I'd get a rise out of you."

"Don't you have more reading to do?"

"Yes. But I'm taking the rest of the day off. Play hooky with me."

It was pretty tough to withstand the look in his eyes. Ariela turned to Jean. "What do you think? Can you manage by yourself for the rest of the day?"

"I don't have any off-site appointments, so yeah, I can hold down the fort."

Dylan gave Ariela a squeeze. "Yes! Go pack a bag." He boosted her to her feet.

Ariela grinned, shaking her head at Jean. "See what I have to put up with?"

Jean laughed. "You poor thing."

———

From that day on, the only reason Ariela went back to her apartment was to change out her wardrobe. Dylan had taken to washing her laundry with his, and he'd given up a drawer for her underwear.

When Ariela returned to Dylan's after work the following Friday, he was on the phone, as usual. He was always on the phone.

She stopped to give him a quick peck then walked to the bedroom, unbuttoning her blouse on the way.

He grinned when he heard her say, "Don't get up," to Max on her way by, her voice dripping with sarcasm. The dog never budged from his lazy sprawl on the couch.

Dylan followed her to the bedroom, barely two minutes later. Stopping right inside the open door, he leaned against the jamb and watched Ariela step out of her skirt. She laid it on the bed.

He gave her a warm smile. "I'm glad you're home. Max missed you."

She laughed. "Yeah, I saw that. Any thoughts on dinner tonight?" She rolled her thigh-high hose down her legs, taking her time because she liked teasing him. He was definitely into watching.

"I'm getting a few ideas," he said, eying the bed behind her.

Toying with him a little more she wriggled out of her panties next. "I'm thinking of the immediate future."

"So am I. Can I join you in the shower?"

"You have to ask?" She shot her panties at him. He snatched them out of the air. They were still warm. He knew if he brought her underwear to his face, they'd never leave this room.

"It's a courtesy question."

"Yeah, you like those." She brushed by him and turned to throw an invitation over her shoulder, crooking a finger at him. He followed.

Dylan went to turn on the shower and strip, knowing he was about to use sex to delay raising a tense subject for a little while longer. If she stormed out on him tonight, at least they'd had this first.

Tara Mills

Eleven

Dylan gave good shower. His hands flowed like warm water down Ariela's naked curves as he dropped to his knees before her. Nudging her feet apart, he held her firmly by the hips and moved in for a taste, then stayed for the meal.

Ariela gripped his hair and felt her blood heat to scalding. Looking down, she watched droplets bead on his thick lashes and fall from his nose. When she wiped his wet brow his murmur of appreciation rumbled through her very core like a deep echo. His thumbs rubbed and spread her for the fingers that followed. She gasped as he lifted her off her heels with every long thrust. His tongue was relentless and carried Ariela over the edge of pleasure. She cried out, her body buffeted by forces beyond her control, then collapsed in front of him. Dylan drew her close and held her as the water rained down over them both.

Still feeling buzzed and shaky, Ariela thought it best if she stayed on her knees a little longer, but there was no reason Dylan had to. Her hand followed his thigh to his erection. She took hold of him and stroked slowly, loving how solid, how silky he felt.

Nuzzling against his neck and shoulder, she made a suggestion. "Why don't you stand?"

He looked surprised then kissed her and rose to his feet. She didn't want to rush this. In her eyes, Dylan was the living embodiment of masculine beauty, every inch of him. He deserved some admiration. Following along his shaft with the sensitive pads of her fingers, her heartbeat spiked with excitement when it jumped as she reached the end.

"I take it you like this?" She cupped him with her other hand, knowing she was in control.

"Yes." His eyes slowly closed and a deep rumble of pleasure escaped him. Water splashed off his shoulders and coursed down his chest and torso in rivulets.

Ariela leaned forward and kissed him, just the tip. When she looked up, he was watching her, every muscle in his body locked with tension. Emboldened, she gave him a little lick next. His flavor was so faint she could barely taste him. There was a quiet, desperate look in his eyes when she glanced up now. She'd toyed with him long enough. This time she didn't tease, she didn't retreat. When her mouth closed around him, Dylan's fingers burrowed into her hair. He cupped her head, his breathing labored, audible in the enclosed shower.

She knew he was close when his arms shot out. He planted his hands on either side of the shower for support as he shuddered and shook.

Feeling pleased with herself, Ariela gave him one final kiss then rose to her feet. Dylan wrapped his arms around her, stroking her back, her bottom. Ariela stretched to shut off the water and he kissed her neck, her jaw, and finally her mouth.

"Thank you." His eyes were dark with emotion.

"My pleasure. You've been so good to me. I thought it was time I returned the favor."

"I'll never push the issue, but I appreciate that you offered."

Ariela pressed herself against him and her smile wavered when she realized she'd just expressed her love for him for the first time. That act, freely given, spoke volumes even if she refused to voice the words. It wasn't clear if Dylan was aware of the fact. Doubtful. But she felt better, lighter now, because at least she was ready to acknowledge the truth to herself. She'd fallen for the guy, hard, and there was nothing she wouldn't do for him.

"Come on," said Dylan, breaking into her thoughts. "We really should put something in our stomachs. I'm sure Max is looking for food too."

While Dylan called for pizza delivery, Ariela went into the bedroom and pulled on his discarded shirt. She loved the scent of him and wanted to wrap herself up in it. However, that was all she put on.

Dylan turned when she walked out. He raked his fingers through his damp hair and gave her a flicker of a smile. "Ariela, I've got news."

Sensing his uneasiness, she took a deep breath. "I'm...I guess I'm waiting."

"I'm going back to Iraq."

Her eyes went wide with alarm. "You're what?" she asked sharply.

"I got a call I never thought would come."

Her eyes narrowed. "How long have you known?"

"I was on the phone when you came in," he admitted quietly.

"And you didn't *say* anything?" She was hurt and angry.

He threw up his arms, looking wretched. "Because I knew how you'd take it. Can you blame me for wanting to put off a fight?"

"Yes! Yes, I can blame you. You lied, Dylan. You led me to believe you were through covering conflicts like Iraq."

"I didn't lie. To my knowledge, I was done. The possibility that I might be pulled back in was remote. It wasn't worth mentioning."

"Withholding information like that is the same as lying from where I'm standing."

"Ariela, please, you need to hear something. Then you'll understand why I have to go. Would you listen? Please?" He reached for her, but she pulled away.

"Don't touch me." Ariela crossed her arms and glared at him. "I'll listen, but I don't know if I'll ever be able to trust you again."

"Just hear me out then decide. Maybe you should sit down."

He gestured toward his desk chair and she backed up to it and spun it around, slowly lowering herself onto the seat.

He began to pace, his hand squeezing the back of his neck. Tension radiated off of him like heat.

"When I went to Baghdad in 2003, a colleague introduced me to Khalid Gouda. He was fresh out of engineering school, with a young wife, and a new baby. He needed to work and I needed a translator. We hit it off right away. Working so intimately with someone like that, day in and day out, you grow really close to them. I shared many meals with Khalid and Hanna. I played with their son."

Then Dylan stopped and turned, his face haggard. "Five months ago, he'd smuggled someone to me at my hotel. The interview went long. After taking the man back, Khalid was hurrying home, trying to beat the curfew, when he came upon a random checkpoint. They saw his speed—he probably didn't know if it was even safe to stop—and they shot him through the windshield before he could reach them. Everyone's grown jumpy after so many bombings. Just one more regrettable incident among hundreds."

Ariela sniffled, holding herself back from going to him, even though she yearned to comfort Dylan for having to experience the grief all over again.

"What do you know about honor killings?" His question

surprised her.

She frowned. "Nothing."

"A law was passed when Saddam was in power, outlawing the practice. That didn't mean it stopped entirely, but it happened less frequently. But since Saddam was overthrown, there's been a huge jump in honor killings. Women can be condemned without proof of sexual impropriety. Just the suspicion she's had sex before marriage, or outside her marriage, can be a death sentence."

"What does this have to do with you? With your friend?"

"Hanna's in hiding."

Ariela stared at him, horrified. "Why?"

"A good friend of Khalid's visited her after his death and left money for their son. Hanna's family immediately assumed he'd paid her for services rendered."

"How could they?" Ariela's temper flared at the indignity and injustice.

"You don't know the culture. They believe she dishonored the family so she fled with the boy. Friends have been sheltering her for two months."

"I still don't understand how this involves you."

"Hanna knew I was trying to write a story on this very thing when Khalid was killed. She wants to tell it. But she'll only talk to me."

"Won't she be in more danger if she meets with you?"

"We're taking precautions to minimize the risk to all of us. Hanna's in danger every day of her life now. Maybe there's something I can do to help her. I have to try."

Ariela stood. It was time he understood where she was coming from. "My turn."

———

Dylan didn't know what to expect when she squared her shoulders and looked back at him, her eyes as haunted as his probably were. He knew that look. He'd seen it a million times already, in a million different faces. Pain was universal.

"When I was twelve, I came home from school and there were cars in front of our house, in our driveway. Two of them were squad cars. I saw my grandma's car and I remember peeking in the backseat. I wondered if she'd brought me anything."

Her eyes were glittering when they met his and she covered her mouth for a second, as if holding back a sob. He took a step toward her, but she shook her head and waved him back.

"Don't. Not yet."

Dylan nodded. "Okay."

"Everyone was in the living room when I went inside. My mom looked white. I'd never seen her like that. My dad's partner, Ryan, was sitting on the coffee table with his elbows on his knees. He was leaning over, holding my mom's hands. He was crying, Dylan. He was crying. It terrified me. I couldn't hear what he was saying, but I could tell my mom wasn't hearing it either. She was in shock."

Now Ariela's tears flowed, one after another, and he watched, feeling helpless because she wouldn't let him any closer.

"There are tissues behind you, on the desk," he reminded her.

"Thank you." She turned and yanked a few out of the box. "That's when my grandma finally noticed me. She tried to steer me away from the living room, but I wouldn't move. I fought her. She had to pick me up and carry me to my room. It was too late. I knew what had happened. I'd seen my mom's face. It was like a bowling ball fell right through my chest. It wasn't until the funeral that I learned the whole story. A stupid gas-station robbery. My dad pulled a woman out of harm's way, just in time…for her. He took the bullet. They called it an honorable death." She snorted. "As if that's supposed to make us happy and proud. It didn't, not really. All we knew was suddenly there was this gaping black hole in the very center of our lives."

She blotted her eyes and sniffled into the wad of tissues. "I couldn't go up to the casket. I could barely make it through the service. My older cousin took me out and we played jacks in the lobby of the funeral home. She let me keep them afterwards." She gave Dylan a bleak smile. "My mom never recovered. She didn't want to. She was barely a shadow of herself. I never heard her laugh again. Never saw her smile. I had to remind her to eat, to get out of bed, to bathe. She cried—all the time. I was so grateful when the doctor prescribed sleeping pills. I couldn't handle her grief. I thought she'd get better. I never dreamed she'd take all those pills at once after I left for school. She simply couldn't face life without him."

Turning to grab two more dry tissues, she was blinking back fresh tears when she faced him again. "My grandma picked me up later that day and took me to live with her. I lost my dad, my mom, my home, my friends, and had to start over in a new school where no one understood why I was so quiet. No one understood me."

Dylan was crying when he pulled Ariela close and held her tight. "I understand."

He closed his eyes in relief when she grabbed him around

the waist, holding onto him just as hard.

"I don't want to lose you," she whispered into his shirt.

"That's the last thing I want too."

"And I'm still pissed at you, but I understand a little better now. I feel so selfish. I hate it."

"Give me seven days, ten tops. I've got someone already on the ground setting things up before I even get there."

"And you'll be careful?"

He stroked Ariela's hair, needing to commit everything about her to memory. "I'm always careful. I don't take stupid risks."

There was no reason to mention calculated risks.

———

Ariela agreed to stay with Max at Dylan's this time. He'd probably handle Dylan's absence better if he weren't uprooted too. Naturally, Ariela refrained from mentioning she'd most likely cope better if she were here with Max as well. It might prove more comforting if she could sense Dylan around her, smell him on the sheets in the bedroom.

Then Dylan was back on the phone, checking his flights and arranging a rendezvous with his friend Jim, who was covering political demonstrations in Adana. They would hook up in Amman and hopefully catch a flight across to Baghdad. They didn't want to face a fifteen hour, high speed race across the dangerous desert if security precautions temporarily closed Baghdad International Airport again. If that happened, there would be no way he'd be done and back in a week's time. Ali Hadad, their new translator, would meet up with them in Baghdad.

Ariela stood helplessly by while Dylan packed his carryall.

He made sure to include extra batteries and blank tapes for his small recorder. Afterwards, he gave Max ten minutes of all-out play on the carpet, wrestling with the dog and rolling around like a big kid. Watching them, her heart melted even more.

Climbing to his feet, Dylan bent over his desk and jotted something down for her. "This is my satphone number. Cell coverage is spotty in some areas, non-existent in others. I don't know the details of where I'll be once I get there so I can't make any guarantees, but I should be able to send an e-mail regardless. As long as I can lock onto a satellite signal. This number is for emergencies only. I have to conserve the battery, so it won't be on unless I'm looking for a link."

Then it was time to go. They took Dylan's car. He was clearly surprised when she asked him to park instead of pull along the loading and unloading curb.

"You don't have to come in with me," he told her.

"I know. But I want to."

He gave her the keys as they walked inside together.

Ariela wondered how her world-record happiness had spun off course so fast. There was no way she was bringing Dylan down after their talk had supposedly settled everything, yet she couldn't get her emotions under control.

One week, all he asked was one stinking week, and she felt like a woman in mourning. If she could be strong through this last assignment, she would prove to herself she wasn't a mess of anxiety and show him she wasn't going to be an obstacle in his career. She wanted to be supportive, but she'd rather see Dylan heading off to Washington for a few days instead of picturing him ducking bullets. Last time, last time, last time, she chanted in her head like a mantra. It helped her put on a sunny smile for his benefit.

She walked Dylan to the airport-security checkpoint, and they kissed good-bye outside the cordoned area. Ariela remained behind, watching as he worked his way forward in the line. Cleared through the metal detector, he grabbed the strap of his bag on the other side. Sliding his feet back into his shoes and his wallet into his pocket, he looked over and found her. She smiled when he nodded to her.

"I'm shooting for Saturday, maybe Sunday," he called. "I'll get a message to you somehow and let you know if that changes. Watch for it so you'll know when I'm due in. I expect you to pick me up. You have my car."

They both laughed—though hers was bittersweet.

"I'll be here," she promised.

He gave her a final wave before being swept away in a sea of travelers. Seeing no reason to linger, Ariela turned and made her way out. She opened her phone as she walked and dialed Jean.

"Hello?"

"Jean?" Ariela's voice broke with emotion.

"Ariela? My god, what's wrong?"

"I'm in love and I'm flipping scared, that's what's wrong." She broke into tears, ignoring the curious looks she was drawing as she walked out into the night.

"Come home." Jean was balm on a burn.

"Okay," Ariela mumbled then shut her phone with a sniffle.

———

Back at their apartment, Jean set a brand new box of tissues on the table between them and the friends clasped hands. Ariela felt lost in a jumble of emotion as Jean looked on with sympathy.

"This has to do with your dad, doesn't it?"

Ariela dabbed at her tears. "Probably. It's all related now."

"I think you're afraid of losing anyone else. I think you're even more afraid to identify with your mom."

Ariela shivered and remembered the blank stare of grief she'd come to associate with her mother before she took her own life. "I'm not my mom."

"You're right; you're not. Remember that. And Dylan's not your dad."

"I couldn't protect myself from him. I had a rule, but I guess I wanted *him* more. How stupid is that? Maybe if he'd told me there was a chance he'd wind up putting himself at risk again, I might have stood my ground. Oh, who am I kidding? Shit!" she pounded the table. "I would have done the same damn thing. I just…I just couldn't seem to help myself."

"And now you've fallen in love with him."

"I should have avoided Dylan like the plague."

Jean dropped her cheek into her palm and sighed. "But even if he just sticks to flying all over the country and into Europe, are you telling me you'd be fine?"

Ariela nodded.

"Bull," Jean said flatly. "You would have gotten all freaked out about airplane crashes or something else. You look for reasons to close yourself off, but honey," she squeezed Ariela's hand, "there are no guarantees in life, period. You just have to leap at chances when they come along, and savor every moment you can. You said yourself your parents were happy."

"They were," Ariela whispered. "Very happy."

"Maybe opening yourself up to what your parents had wouldn't be such a bad thing. That kind of happiness is a rare and precious gift."

"Need I remind you my mom killed herself after my dad was shot? She took pills and left me too, barely two months later. I lost both parents! What if I find out I can't cope, either? What if I grow to love Dylan so much I can't face life without him?"

Jean looked her in the eye, steady as a rock. "You've already coped with loss, and you survived. Would you rather not have known your parents at all?"

Ariela blotted her eyes and sniffled. "No, I loved them."

Her mind drifted back to that tragic morning again. Her dad's arms were wrapped around her mom as she rinsed their dishes in the sink. He swayed with her from side to side, kissing her neck until she laughed. Ariela could still hear it, her mother's very last laugh. She'd been a byproduct of all the love they'd felt for each other. There was so much of it that it spilled over onto her. She'd never felt shortchanged.

Ariela came back to herself when Jean reached out and hooked a stray tendril of hair behind her ear. "Are you okay? You were a million miles away just now."

Ariela sighed miserably. "I wish I wasn't behaving like this. At least Dylan didn't see it. I'd be so ashamed."

"Have you told him any of this so he'll under-stand?"

"Yes. A lot of good that did me."

Jean smiled despite the mood. "He deserved to know."

Ariela nodded, sulking.

"Where are you sleeping tonight?" Jean asked.

"At his place. Max is waiting for me. I just wish it was Dylan instead."

———

Dylan walked through the Queen Alia International Airport, searching for a familiar face. He almost missed his friend because Jim's features were hidden behind a pita sandwich, which appeared to be getting away from him. Dylan smiled and walked over to him.

"Halley," he said with a chuckle. "Eating again, I see."

"I've gotta do something to keep weight on down here. It's supposed to be lamb, but I beg to differ. This is definitely mutton," said his Aussie friend.

"You hope. You're about to lose a tomato there." Dylan pointed to a sliding globule.

Jim shot out his tongue to catch it. "Messy as hell." Creamy cucumber sauce leaked over and between his fingers. Only a quick flip of his hand and an emergency lick kept the sauce from spilling onto his white shirt. Dylan patted his pockets, searching for something Jim could wipe with. He found a napkin in his jacket.

"Here." Dylan thrust it at his friend and watched the comical motions ensue as Jim tried not to lose what control he had over his shawarma. It was hopeless.

"Oh, fuck it. I'm done here." Disgusted, Jim strode over to the nearest canister. "I need the men's room. I'll be right back."

Dylan waited while his surprisingly lanky partner wandered off in search of a sink. He wondered whether it was genes, the ability to stretch the calories throughout his frame, or simply hollow legs that allowed Jim to eat like he did, yet still appear starvation thin.

Jim seemed cheerier by the time he strolled back from the restroom. "So, you sorry to be back so soon?"

Dylan shrugged. "Mixed emotions. I've always loved this city."

"I'll second that."

They strolled out of the building and into the night. There

was no waiting for a taxi.

The car pulled up in front of the small hotel where Jim had spent the last three nights. They climbed the stairs to his room. When the door swung open, Dylan raised his eyebrows as he took in the only bed, undersized and sagging in the center, covered by an obnoxious, pea green spread.

"Screw you," Jim said, chafing at Dylan's silence. "It's clean and cheap. I don't get reimbursed as fast as you do."

Dylan grinned and held up his hand, forestalling further argument. "I didn't say anything."

"Yeah, yeah."

Jim's surly manner didn't bother Dylan. He'd known him long enough to understand Jim was all piss, no shit. It was a persona he'd developed to come across tougher than he actually was—a survival technique. Dylan just happened to be in on it.

He swung his bag off of his shoulder, set it down on the small table, and pulled out his computer. Jim flopped backwards onto the bed.

"Bitch about the room all you want, but you owe me a little thanks for insisting on a south facing window for your damn satphone. Remember that when you're finally online."

Dylan placed the satphone on the sill and connected it to his computer. Then he turned back with a little grin. "Thank you."

"Don't mention it." Their eyes connected and they both chuckled.

Since he had to wait for everything to boot up anyway, Dylan grabbed his toiletry kit and headed for the bathroom.

"How's the water?" he asked.

"Use the bottled when you brush your teeth, otherwise you'll swear you just ate bloody pussy."

Dylan stopped mid-stride and shot a disgusted look at Jim.

"Do you have to be so crude when we're alone? Christ."

"Sorry. Bottled water is on the back of the commode. Hey, it's not the Grand Hyatt or the Radisson, but there's no chance in hell anyone's gonna bomb this place next."

It was hard to deny his friend's logic.

Jim rolled over and saw Ariela's picture staring back at him from the computer screen. He craned his neck to get a better look then called to Dylan. He didn't catch it.

Stepping into the open doorway with his toothbrush sticking out of his mouth, Dylan gave his friend a questioning look. Jim pointed at the computer. "Is that your Sleeping Beauty?" he repeated.

"Yep." Dylan's mouth stretched into a big smile, despite the toothbrush. "That's Ariela."

"She looks sweet. Pretty." Jim rolled onto his back and looked up at the ceiling. "Very girl-next-door."

Dylan chuckled and turned back to the sink.

"Looks like you're connected," called Jim.

Dylan gave one more swish and spit, turning on the faucet to rinse the sink. He could smell the iron in the water.

Going right for the table, Dylan pulled the chair up behind him and sat in front of the screen.

"So, what's she like?" Jim asked, his head resting on his arm, his ankles comfortably crossed, but extending over the end of the bed.

"She's just right."

"You're leaving a lot to the imagination here."

Dylan ignored him.

Jim grinned. "Yep, I might just have to swing by, check her out myself. I'll give her a dose of the old Halley charm."

That turned Dylan's head, but he was grinning. "I can't

imagine you'd remember where you left it. Now, be quiet; I'm sending her a message."

"Can I read it?"

"Absolutely not."

Jim laughed and kicked off his shoes.

TO: arielap@
SUBJECT: Checking in
MESSAGE: Well I made it without any hassles. I'll be spending the next few hours on what looks like the world's most uncomfortable mattress beside an over-sized blanket hog with sharp elbows and even sharper toenails. The only thing Jim has going for him, from where I'll be, is fresh breath. Everyone's obsessive about something, I guess.

Good news. We'll be able to catch the flight to Baghdad tomorrow. Ali will pick us up at the airport, so that's working out. We won't be staying at the Hamra Hotel right away. Ali found us a safe house close to where we'll be meeting with Hanna, early the following morning. Considering I don't know what might crop up over the next couple of days, my messages will probably be sporadic at best. Electricity is going to be a factor, but I'll make sure I keep you posted on the important stuff.

You don't know how incredibly hard it was to walk away and leave you in the airport. We need to replace that memory with a better one. You waiting for me should do the trick. Pet Max for me—hell, pet yourself for me while you're at it. I'll imagine it from here. I'll be in touch. I miss you already—Dylan

Twelve

Ariela was tempted to bring Max to work with her, but she didn't know what to expect from him around the office, and their yard wasn't fenced. She opted to leave him at home with his toys and his couch. At least it would be familiar.

Hours later, she realized she should have taken him to work. He'd been in the garbage and now it was strewn all over the apartment. Max had taken the choicest morsels up on the couch and worked on them there, making a serious mess. Only now did Ariela fully appreciate the merits of the hideous blanket Dylan had covering the sofa cushions.

Banishing Max to the yard, she went looking for a broom and dustpan, then set to work, sweeping up most of the loose debris first. Once the large stuff was out of the way she was ready to vacuum the little bits out of the rug. Ariela hoped she could get the coffee grounds up without staining, but she had her doubts. Unfortunately, after a lengthy search, she was forced to conclude Dylan didn't own a vacuum.

Ariela grabbed the basket of dirty clothes from the bedroom and dropped the used bathroom towels on top. Even though the mere sight of the dog's blanket practically set off her gag reflex, she nabbed it on her way out anyway. It had to be washed.

She opened the door that led to the shared front entry and threw open the basement door, leaving it wide open. Ariela hated this basement, but she didn't want to haul the laundry over to her place and put this disgusting blanket in her machine. Clopping downstairs, the damp, earthy smell made her skin crawl almost as much as the rough, irregular walls. It reminded her of a dungeon. The inadequate lighting made it even worse. She avoided looking around so she wouldn't see any mice scurrying around in the shadows or spy anything dead in one of the traps Dylan had set out. Yuck.

He might not own a vacuum, but at least his washer and dryer were relatively new and pretty nice. A large, commercial-style florescent fixture hung from the bare rafters above them. She flew to the nearby switch, and voila, there was light. She looked around again, anxiously trying to spot, well, hoping not to spot actually, anything scary or disgusting down there with her. She didn't want to step on anything.

A well-stocked shelf stood next to the washer. The detergent and other related sundries might belong to the upstairs tenant, but Ariela wasn't going to sweat that little detail. She wanted to get the load started and hightail it back upstairs before she had a close encounter of the eight-legged kind

She might have broken a speed record, fastest laundress in the west, well, technically the east. Forget separating colors from whites. Who cares if there are shirts and socks inside out? In it all went, in one irregular dump. She smoothed it out because she had to, not because she wanted to. It beat the heck out of running down here to deal with an unbalanced washer later.

Max was stretched out on the grass, gnawing on a large dirty bone, when Ariela pulled the kitchen door closed behind her. There was no way she was leaving him alone in the house again without the blanket back on the sofa. She'd seen what he was capable of.

"Come on," she called to him, resigned. He hurried over, and she clipped on his leash and worked him over to the car. He was extremely pleased about taking a ride.

When they got to her house, she had to shove Max back when she got out because there was no way she wanted to wrestle him and a vacuum cleaner into the car at the same time.

"No, just me. You wait here."

Jean was following her step-aerobics video when Ariela walked in.

She looked up, breathing hard. "What's up?"

"I need our vacuum. Dylan doesn't have one, and the dog made a huge mess today." She dragged the machine out of the closet and shut the door. "I don't have this pet thing down yet, but I'm learning."

Jean laughed as the door closed. "See ya."

Max seemed disappointed when they didn't actually go for a walk, but he was ready enough to get over it when she unclipped his leash and let him have the yard to himself again.

Ten minutes later, the carpet looked much better, not great, but much better. She wound the cord and ran down to throw the wash into the dryer, then sprinted back upstairs with her heart pumping.

Feeling guilty for banishing the dog outside all this time, Ariela grabbed one of Dylan's books off the packed shelf and took it outside to read in the sun. So much had happened between her and Dylan since she first sat in this lawn chair on that fateful Saturday. She'd given him her heart and received so much in return. Yes, she was worried about him. Dylan was heading back into danger, but she had to trust him, trust that he knew how to protect himself, and trust that he would come back to her again. Anything else was just too terrifying to contemplate. They still had so much ahead of them.

Only after the ugly quilt came out of the dryer, clean and relatively free of dog hair, was Max allowed back inside. He eyed the vacuum warily, hating it on sight as it sat by the door. He growled and shot it suspicious looks. Ariela found it highly amusing—until he sniffed and raised his leg. She put the vacuum back in the car.

When she returned, Ariela checked to see if there was an e-mail from Dylan yet. To her relief, he'd made it to Amman. A wave of loneliness and longing swept through her as she pictured him turning in for the night with Jim, the blanket hog. She couldn't catch her laugh when it escaped. She really missed him. The man brought her up, he brought her down. Was there anything more bizarre or emotionally charged than suddenly finding you're in a relationship? She pulled the keyboard toward her.

TO: dylanbond@

SUBJECT:

MESSAGE: I'm lending comfort and aid to my enemy. Translation—I'm learning how to deal with Max. I didn't realize he could be so destructive, but don't worry, it was only the garbage. I'm onto him now. I'm going to lock the trash in the bathroom before I leave. I watered your plants, did the laundry, and noticed you don't have a vacuum. You didn't tell me if Max is allowed on your bed. I wasn't going to let him up there, but I think we're both missing you a lot so, well, you've been temporarily replaced. Let me know if this isn't okay. I can shut the door.

I can't get over how much I miss you. So much, I'm sleeping in your shirt. It's the one thing I intentionally didn't wash. Keep your head down, help Hanna, and hurry back. If you die over there, I'll kill you. Ariela

———

Ali Hadad was twenty-four, a handsome kid, whose college education had been cut short first by the American's drive into Baghdad, then again when it got too dangerous for the professors to hold classes and the students to reach the university to attend them. Just having a book on the bus was a deadly gamble.

Ali's father was part of the university faculty, a professor of mathematics, but he'd been forced to flee when several of his peers were rounded up and taken away. A few were found executed. The others simply vanished, leaving a gaping hole in their households. Professor Hadad had taken refuge in Canada, where he worked to bring his family, one by one, to safety. In the meantime, Ali sought any means available to help support his remaining family, which meant working for the occupying forces and offering his services to journalists as an interpreter.

The kid was a natural at the job. Competent, smart, and resourceful, he was careful to keep his involvement with the Westerners a secret.

Jim and Dylan both climbed into the back of their young driver's car. The kid had a pistol on the seat next to him, just in case. Dylan lifted the blanket off the floor so Jim could shift his long legs and a second gun dropped out of it. Dylan reached down to pick it up.

"Loaded?" Jim asked.

Dylan checked. "Yep."

"I only shoot pictures. That thing's your responsibility."

"I figured."

They both hunkered down so they wouldn't be seen from the outside. Kidnappings were a very real threat. Westerners were specifically targeted, so it was extremely risky to venture out without good cause.

"Remind me to stop and pick up some perfume for Ariela when we get back to Jordan."

Only after he said that did it strike Dylan as comical, considering he was holding a gun in his lap at the time.

Now all they had to worry about was getting through the clogged streets of Baghdad without incident.

Ali shifted his mirror, looking to catch Dylan's eyes. As soon as he had his attention, he turned it back. "I will be coming for you in a police vehicle tomorrow. Don't be alarmed."

Dylan's eyebrows shot up. "How did you arrange that?"

He gave his head an imperceptible shake. "I can't say, but we'll only have a short time to use it, if we aren't going to get caught. Trust me, it is the best way." Dylan didn't doubt it for a second.

———

Debris littered the street in this neighborhood and a huge crater remained from an earlier bomb blast. They cut wide around the shell of the burned-out car. Even though they didn't see a soul outside, that didn't mean there weren't eyes watching. They had to be very careful.

A radio under Ali's leg broke the tense silence. He asked a question and quietly acknowledged the reply. Speaking to Dylan and Jim in an undertone, he asked, "Are you ready? We're almost there. I'll let you out as close as I can, but you must hurry inside because I can't delay or we'll be noticed. The front door is unlocked. Take the gun."

Dylan slid his shoulder strap up his arm and saw Jim doing the same thing.

Ali alerted them right before he stopped and Jim dove out the door first, immediately followed by Dylan. He carefully pressed the door closed behind him, just enough so it would latch, then hurried inside. Their driver was already pulling away.

They knew there was food and water waiting in the abandoned house. Ali had warned them, vigorously, to be quiet and stay hidden. From the little he saw on his way in, Dylan hated to think of Hanna forced to take refuge in a neighborhood like this. He wanted to get her out, now more than ever. Was it possible?

The house was easily seen from the street, so they made their silent way to a back room, away from windows, to camp out for the night. It would be safest. Jim stretched out on the hard floor and used his duffle bag for a pillow while Dylan settled his back against the wall, every sense he had on alert. He had the gun—first watch fell to him.

Thirteen

Waking up alone was unsettling, given the circumstances. Dylan looked around the cold, vacant room and rotated his aching shoulder. He'd slept with his arm pinned beneath him and had cut off the circulation to both. Turning onto his back, he squeezed his arm all the way down, trying to bring it back to life.

It was time to go in search of his photographer.

Jim was sitting on the floor in the empty front room, out of the line-of-sight from the outside, his back to the wall, a game of solitaire set out in front of him. The gun was on his right. Dylan was proud of him.

"Better light in here," Jim said quietly, answering the question before it was asked. He nodded toward the empty window sill and the broken glass beneath it.

"This place has seen better days," Dylan whispered, avoiding chunks of concrete as he made his way over, dust clinging to his shoes. The house had clearly been abandoned. Or so he thought. More likely, it had been stripped.

Jim placed a card then looked up, keeping his voice low. "Keep to this side of the room, so you aren't seen through the window."

Dylan was picking his way over the concrete rubble, trying to make as little noise as possible, when he suddenly drew back from the wall and hissed, "What the hell is that?"

"You know what it is," said Jim without looking up. "I've been trying to ignore the damn wall for over an hour. I've almost reached the indifferent stage so don't screw with me."

Dylan eased away from the brown-stained, bullet-riddled

wall, then dropped to the floor beside his friend and watched him place another card. "Well, now we know why the house is empty."

Jim grunted and shifted a card.

"I think I prefer the Sheraton," Dylan muttered.

"I *know* I prefer the Sheraton." Jim sorted through his remaining cards, gave up with a muted curse, swept all of them back into a pile again, and started shuffling.

"Where are the facilities?" Dylan looked around.

"Back the way you came in. It's not much, but you'll be more comfortable afterwards. Oh, and the only water is what Ali left with us."

"I figured."

Dylan worked himself stiffly back up and turned away from the wall of violence as he went out. After answering the pressing call of nature, he went searching through the metal footlocker Ali had left in the room where they'd spent the night. He'd included a large jug of bottled water. Dylan poured a little over his fingers to wash, but was forced to dry his hands on his pants. Thirsty, he tipped the bottle back and took a swig. It soothed his parched throat.

His most pressing needs met, now he was ready to rummage through the box for breakfast. There were two apples, two oranges, dates, pistachio nuts, and pita bread, with the popular white, feta-like cheese called Jibneh Arabieh. Dylan used the bottom of his shirt as an improvised sling and loaded it up with an assortment of food, then caught the handle of the water jug on his way out.

Jim glanced up, apparently knowing intuitively food that was coming. The man was as bad as Max. "Excellent, what do you have there?"

Dylan crossed his ankles and sank down beside him and spread what he brought out on his lap.

Jim frowned. "No jerky?"

"There's jerky?"

"Yes. For all I know, it might be seasoned goat, but who cares? It's pretty tasty. Heavy on the cumin, but I can deal with it."

"Sorry, I didn't see it. Do you have your knife on you?"

"Always."

"How about cutting up this apple? There's only two, so we might want to save the other one."

"Sure." Jim pulled out his knife and folded the blade out, putting it to work.

Dylan peeled the orange and began sectioning his half, eating the first of his succulent segments.

"Here's your apple." Jim dropped the rough-cut fruit on his lap. "I'll take a few of those dates."

Dylan passed him a handful along with a little bread as well. They ate in silence, the jug of water between them.

"You know," Jim finally said, wiping his mouth with the back of his hand after taking a good, long swig of water. "I'm thinking of making a change too. I've gotta get out of here. It's too damn hot. I'm thinking Helsinki."

"Helsinki? Yeah, that'd be a big change, but it's pretty expensive. I don't think you could afford it, doing what you're doing, without sacrificing your autonomy." Dylan popped his last date into his mouth. "I know you. I don't think you can work inside the system."

Jim dropped his head against the wall and rocked it back and forth, his Adam's apple thrust out. "Damn it. You're right. Money might be sporadic, but at least when I get it, I can make it stretch farther here. Unfortunately, I have to *be* here to spend it." He glanced over and asked, "Do you know what I can't stop thinking about lately, what I miss most?"

"What's that?"

"Short skirts and long legs," he murmured dreamily. "I've been away so bloody long I've almost forgotten what a pair of heels can do for a nice ankle and a shapely calf. That's a shame, it really is, a goddamned, crying shame. I'm a man in my prime." Jim struck himself in the chest. "I shouldn't be surviving on memories already."

"You need to get out more."

"I need to get home more."

It was hard to argue with that.

Dylan sighed. "I'm hoping we can wrap this up by tomorrow—Friday at the latest." He took a drink and set the water between them again. "Ariela didn't take the news I was heading back here very well. I don't blame her. She told me from the start she wouldn't get involved with me if I kept putting my neck on the line. Now I know her reasons. The thing is, I never even blinked when I said I was done. I believed it at the time. Now I look like a liar. This article will be the last one I write on Iraq, at least from here, anyway."

Jim snorted skeptically. "Right. You said that the last time."

"No, I mean it. I won't be sucked back again. There's no way I'm going to sacrifice my shot at a personal life with Ariela by making the wrong professional choice. That's what this is Jim, a choice. I've done my tour of duty, willingly, I might add, but now I'm ready to settle in at home. I'm going crazy just thinking about the woman I care about sleeping alone in my bed."

"You've almost convinced me." Jim grunted as he worked

his way up to a stand. "My feet are going to sleep. I need to walk it off."

Dylan smirked as his partner tiptoed miserably into the next room.

Jim turned back and said under his breath, "I'm gonna get some of that jerky. Do you want some?"

"No thanks." Dylan pulled his telephone out of his pocket and checked the battery level. It was down and he'd grabbed the wrong charger, not that he could have charged here anyway, or made a phone call for that matter. It was time to conserve what he had for emergencies. He looked at his pictures of Ariela one last time before he shut off the phone and snapped it closed.

Dylan was just tucking it away when Jim came back, tearing a stick of dried meat with his teeth.

"What time is it, anyway?" he asked Dylan.

Dylan checked his watch, converting the numbers to local time. "It's twenty to nine."

"What time did the kid say he'd be here?"

"Early."

"Then where the hell is he?"

"I wish I knew. Something is definitely off."

———

Ariela was just turning on the copier when Jean strolled into the office, stifling a big yawn.

"You're here early. Anything wrong?" Jean asked.

"Max needed to go out." Ariela dropped into her chair and rolled up to her desk, reaching to turn on the computer. She glanced up from logging in. "You know something? Having to deal with a pet really impresses on a person how much more work a kid would be. I don't think I'll be rushing into that anytime soon. I like my life as it is, especially when Dylan's around to share it with me."

Jean looked over the top of her computer screen. "Have you heard from him again?"

Ariela held up her hand, signaling Jean to give her a second. "No." She sagged back with a disappointed sigh. "Nothing since he got to Amman."

Jean squeezed Ariela's shoulder on her way to her own desk. "Well, he did warn you."

"I know." Ariela reread the old message, needing to feel their connection.

"Can I see it?"

"Sure."

Jean came around Ariela's desk to take a peek, leaning over her shoulder while she read. When she finished, she returned the mouse and straightened up. She was unusually quiet as she switched on her desk lamp and turned off the answering machine.

"Is something wrong?" Ariela asked.

Turning back, Jean gave a listless shrug, her attempt at a smile failing. "Nothing's wrong per se. I just envy you a little right now." Seeing Ariela's confusion, she explained. "My relationship with Ron isn't like yours. Sure, we love each other, we talk, we hang out and fool around, but he's never once written me. It's another layer of intimacy I might like to have, that's all. He gives me cards for my birthday and Valentine's Day, but all he does is sign them. A personal message might be nice once in a while."

Ariela closed out of her e-mail and went to unlock the door and turn on their open sign. Coming back, she asked, "Do you think Ron's the one? Can you see yourself married to him?"

Jean gave her a bashful smile and looked away. "I've been paging through bridal magazines when I'm shopping, but I don't have the nerve to buy one." Then her eyes returned to Ariela's and she nodded. "Yes, I'd marry him, if he asked."

Ariela was glad to hear it. "He'll ask. Ron loves you."

"Yeah, I know. I'm just getting impatient. It's been three years now."

"I think a heart-to-heart is overdue between the two of you. Maybe you should fix him a nice dinner and speak to him. This week would be perfect since I'm out of the way. As scary as it sounds, you need to let Ron know what you want. Tell him where you'd like to see this relationship go and when."

"Terrifying."

"No one said emotional exposure is easy."

Jean looked up in surprise. "When did you become the relationship expert?"

Ariela snorted. "Hardly an expert, but I think I understand both of you. This is the next logical step. To be honest, I've been expecting it for a while. Some guys just need a little prodding to get the ball rolling."

Jean rubbed her temples and groaned. "Everyone's an expert when it comes to someone else's love life." She held up her hands in surrender. "You just happen to be right in this case."

———

Mrs. Corley phoned later that morning, actually giving Ariela the first good news she'd ever delivered to her. She'd made her final decisions for her kitchen and accepted Ariela's enthusiastic flattery for her wonderful taste with delight. As far as Ariela was concerned, laying it on a little thick was worth it if it kept the woman from second-guessing herself.

For the balance of the day, Ariela was on the phone ordering cabinets, tile, fixtures, flooring, wallpaper, lining up contractors, and trying to schedule the jobs in order of priority.

With her work finally cleared away, she double checked her messages. Nothing. If only she knew something. Where was he? She'd memorized his earlier messages so she knew them by heart, but that didn't tame the wild anxiety she felt when there was no word at all. Even a two-word message would be appreciated right about now—a simple, *I'm okay*. Was that too much to ask?

—

Dylan sat on the bare floor of the abandoned house with his back against the wall and his spiral notebook resting on his knee as he made notes to himself, recording impressions of his trip the old-fashioned way. Satisfied so far, he rapped the pad with his pen a couple of times before flipping the tablet closed. He set it aside then shifted so he could reach into his pocket. Knowing he shouldn't didn't stop him from pulling out his phone and thumbing it open. Moments later, he brought up his photos of Ariela again. Resting his wrist on his knee, he studied her image, a tender smile on his face. He scrolled to the second photo and brought it closer, trying to see her in more detail.

His smile deepened as he gazed at Ariela's playful expression, her pose reminiscent of a pin-up girl from the forties, except she was nude, freshly tumbled, and luxuriously displayed on his sheets. Dylan loved the curve of her hip and the sweep of sexy thigh. To him, she was exquisite, inside and out. Just looking at Ariela's picture was making him hard. He tapped his head against the wall several times before shutting off the phone to conserve power.

When Ali didn't appear by eleven a.m., Dylan and Jim began to pace like caged animals. Something was wrong. They tossed disastrous scenarios back and forth, which only made their mounting anxiety worse.

Jim chewed off his fingernails one at a time, spitting them out as he rounded their improvised cell. "Do we call Paul yet and get a patrol out here to pick us up?"

Dylan scowled at him. "Get serious. Paul would shoot us personally for putting his men at risk. Just calm down. If we'd been compromised, we'd be dead by now. I say we give Ali whatever time he needs to work things out. Obviously he's run into a snag. We have to trust him."

"Doesn't look like you'll be out of here as early as Friday."

"You might be right."

Jim snorted and dropped down in a slump against the wall. "I'm going to rest my eyes for a while."

"Fine," he said, adding a soft, "And I'll just picture my relationship with Ariela imploding when I don't come back as soon as I'd hoped."

———

An hour later, Jim hurried into the back where Dylan had gone to brood. The photographer roused him with his foot. "Ali's coming."

Jim had spent their time apart spying on the neighborhood through his camera lens, his position at the bottom corner of the broken window obscured by overgrown shrubs outside.

Dylan climbed to his feet and stretched his stiff muscles. They'd spent a long, hard stretch in this desolate house, worrying about gunmen breaking in on them, yet unable to leave. Another night on this cold hard floor would have been intolerable. With their ration of water gone, they were facing dehydration and sanitation issues no one should have to face, and yet, millions of Iraqi citizens were in the exact same situation. He didn't envy them.

A car horn blew at the end of the street, and a moment later, Ali slipped in through the front door, pulling it closed behind him.

"Where the hell have you been?" Jim hissed before Dylan could stop him.

Ali didn't look offended. He looked sorrowful. Dylan knew it was bad.

"Hanna Gouda is dead. She disappeared late yesterday. I finally found her in the morgue. She'd been stabbed, many times, and her left hand was gone. I'm so sorry."

Dylan felt sick, nauseous. He grabbed hold of the wall just to remain standing. Ironic, he'd seen death, hundreds of times, and been able to handle it because it was part of the job. He'd learned how to insulate himself from the trauma, but this, this was personal. It hit him hard. His loyalty to Khalid and Hanna was the reason he'd put his relationship with Ariela in jeopardy to begin with.

"What about their son?"

"I heard he's with Hanna's uncle, but her brother and cousin are missing."

Most likely hidden by other family members to avoid punishment, Dylan presumed. They'd be celebrated inside the family and protected. She'll be forgotten. He wanted to weep, for his dead friends and for the little boy who would never know his wonderful, loving parents. It left him shaken and sick with misery.

Jim grabbed his arm. "Hey, are you all right?"

"No. No, I'm not. I'm pissed. I'm fucking pissed!" he shot back under his breath, still conscious of the need to remain undetected. "How can people do that? Just murder a member of their own family over an unfounded suspicion?" He laughed at himself, bitterly, remembering his reply to Ariela when she asked the same question. "You don't understand the culture," he murmured to himself and felt another wave of grief swell inside his chest. Oh god, it hurt.

"Dylan." Jim gave his arm another squeeze, finally breaking through the pain. Deep blue eyes locked with cool gray and brought a semblance of calm to the raging storm inside of him.

Dylan shook himself. They had decisions to make. "What happened with the police car?"

Ali's pain was as palpable as Dylan's. "My friend, Mo, never brought the truck, and I can't reach him. It would be much too dangerous for him and his family, if I try. I fear his time has run out. He walked the sharpened edge of the knife for three years. It was risky. I can't get a police vehicle without him."

Dylan understood what Ali wasn't saying. The radio would have helped them avoid checkpoints. Without it, they were subject to stops and searches. They could blunder into anything.

"I'm sorry about your friend," Jim told him.

"Are *you* safe?" Dylan didn't want anyone else at risk for his sake.

"Thank you, yes. I had to be sure I wasn't leading danger to you." Ali nodded sadly. "A police vehicle would have been better. People see them and are afraid. They don't want trouble, so they try to avoid being noticed and move away if possible, look away when it isn't. It's dangerous to meet the eyes of the men inside. It would have made it much easier to get you through the city. But I'm afraid there's more," said Ali gravely.

"How bad?" Dylan asked.

"The other women you were planning to interview, Noora and her sister, they've fled the city with their children. I went to their home. A different family is living there now."

Jim's head jerked back at the news. "What?"

"That fast?" Dylan asked, equally shocked.

Ali rubbed his temples, an apologetic look on his face. "It's not a good time to be Sunni in a Shia neighborhood, or Shia in a Sunni area. They are separating by sect, often violently. I just hope Noora and her family are safe. I have no way to find out."

"This is why we're in this bombed out, bullet-riddled house," said Jim. "The family who lived here were driven out."

Dylan groaned, seeing his Pulitzer disappear in a puff of smoke. He'd failed. He'd failed everyone; Khalid, Hanna, their little boy, Noora, and her sister, Amira, Jim, Ali, but most especially, Ariela. He'd sacrificed so much, and for what, to run up against a dead end? Hell no!

Hanna wanted this story told. So did Noora and Amira. They might have been silenced, but damn it, they still mattered. With the rights and status of women in this transforming country under discussion, they needed to be heard, silenced or not. He would speak for them. He would be their voice.

How? All three of his interviews just evaporated. They were going to be the safe conduits to other women. He couldn't arrange any others, not without endangering more sources. That was something he wouldn't consider.

Jim looked at Dylan. "Why don't you call your friends at the Baghdad bureau? They just might have to help. Otherwise, I don't see this happening."

"There's nothing they can do."

Ali broke in. "It would be very dangerous for me to go there now. If Mo talked, I'm already under suspicion. I can't be seen anywhere near the Americans or the Europeans. I wouldn't like to try."

Jim spun toward their interpreter in frustration. "Well, what do you suggest?" he asked.

Ali gave it some thought. "It might not be the interview you wanted, but my grandmother and aunts are willing to speak with you. I could take you safely there. My car wouldn't raise suspicions in front of our family home. You would have to keep out of sight and enter through the back and under cover, but it's an option."

Dylan considered the alternative carefully. "I have a deadline, but I don't want to do anything if it endangers your family."

Ali nodded gravely. "They are very strong women, very wise. You'll get an interview. I think we should leave now. Just let me signal my friend, Ram."

He brought a small radio out of his pocket. Before he pressed the button on the side, he said, "Collect your things before I call him. When he creates a distraction, we need to hurry."

Dylan and Jim left to get their bags from the back room. They would not be coming back here tonight. There was no reason now, and it would be too dangerous.

Jim stood up, slipping the strap of his pack over his shoulder. "Ready?"

Dylan zipped his tablet and pen away and gave a quick nod.

Ali's face was set when he met their eyes and raised the

radio. He spoke a curt word into it, and within seconds, they heard a loud boom at the end of the street. Then Ali was moving, running at a crouch to the car, with Jim and Dylan on his heels.

Jim reached the back door first and yanked it open, crawling inside, Dylan right behind him. He pulled the back door closed against his feet. Ali leaped into the front seat, and a second later, the engine roared to life. The kid threw the car into gear, spun the wheel, and made a tight U-turn. They headed off, away from the blast at a normal speed to avoid attention.

As they bounced along the rough roads without encountering trouble, Dylan's tension slowly eased a little. He was finally able to grin at Jim's bony butt.

"Think you can turn that out of my face now?"

Fourteen

Keeping Max under control when he was deter-mined to run free was a struggle. He strained against the leash so hard Ariela's shoulder hurt and the hard knot in her right calf threatened to drop her to the ground at any minute. She tugged the dog over to an empty bench and tied him there so she could take a break and stretch her leg before the cramp hit.

It amazed her to see how many people needed reassurance Max wasn't going to hurt them when they walked by. How could they be so blind to his ecstatic tail wagging and his happy-go-lucky grin, and with that lolling tongue hanging out? What were they afraid of, that he might lick them to death? Yes, he frisked and yipped, but it was in an eager-greeting kind of way, not a roll-up-your-pant-leg-because-that-leg-is-mine style. Max simply loved people, *and* other dogs—even the obnoxious little nippers. Honestly, she'd never met a dog with more obvious intentions. Still, the poor thing wasn't making many friends.

Feeling for him, she leaned down to untie his leash and pat his head. "Your dad should take you to obedience school." He turned and kissed her, a big, wet, sloppy kiss. She laughed and shoved him away. "Save those for your master. You know I'm immune."

Max looked at her as if he didn't buy it. Ariela wondered if maybe the dog had a point. She was collapsing under the weight of his charm.

They returned to the car, and she opened the back door so he could leap inside. His entire body wriggled with eagerness to get going. She shook her head, perplexed at how excited he was around the car—let me in, let me out, let me in, let me out! Bizarre.

Back at Dylan's place, Ariela let Max run loose in the yard while she went in to phone Jean. A little human interaction was exactly what she needed. Well, barring what she actually had in mind, her best friend would have to do in a pinch. Heck, she'd even extend the invite to Ron.

"Not tonight," was Jean's response. "Ron's coming over for dinner. You know, *the* dinner."

"No kidding?"

"I'm not sure I'm ready for this."

"Of course you are. Don't chicken out."

"What would you say to a woman who told you she wanted to marry you?"

"I'd say, I don't think it's legal in this state yet."

"Ha. This time pretend you're Ron."

"Sorry, not the time for levity, I guess. Jean, this is the next, natural step. One of you has to make it. Why can't it be you?"

"You're right. Why can't it be me?"

"There you go."

"Wish me luck."

"I wish you love."

Ariela hung up the phone and filled Max's dish, then went to call him in.

"It's just you and me tonight, kiddo. There's a good movie on cable. What do you say?"

Max snorted into his bowl, but at least his tail wagged a few times. Ariela decided to take that as a yes.

She made a bowl of popcorn then settled on the couch with the dog. They snacked together while the television flashed light and color into the otherwise dark room. She might even have stroked the dog's fur from time to time, though it was unconsciously done.

———

Dylan's cheek rested against the edge of the backseat, his body curled awkwardly on the floor. For safety's sake, there was no conversation in the car. When the vehicle came to a stop, he looked at Jim. They both visibly tensed, unsure if they'd run into a checkpoint or some other hazard. Ali cut the engine.

"We're here," he whispered. "Stay where you are until I come back for you."

He climbed out of the car, leaving the two men to shift uncomfortably in the small, unforgiving depressions of the floor. In a matter of minutes, he was back, this time with a woman. Ali went and opened the trunk to further block them as she beckoned with a gesture to Jim and Dylan. They hustled after her at a crouching run as she led them down a narrow corridor between the house and a tall, concrete wall.

Leaving their shoes in the kitchen, they were shown into a curtained sitting room. Ali came in through the front door, locking it behind him. Two women were already waiting. Dylan was surprised they'd left their heads uncovered in front of him. Perhaps they were Christian or, riskier still, nothing at all. Their escort from the car removed her black hijab and, with a graceful wave, invited them to sit.

Jim walked over to one of the chairs, straightening his tall frame as he went. They all heard the audible cracking of his bones. Dylan was delighted to see he wasn't the only one fighting back a smile at the unexpected concert.

Ali's grandmother was a tiny woman, but she had presence,

an undeniable strength. She didn't appear uncomfortable until Jim took out his camera. She and Ali exchanged a rapid flow of words while the other two women gravely watched Jim. He froze, silent, waiting for a verdict from their hostess.

Ali nodded, agreeing with something his grandmother said and held up his hand in appeasement. Then he turned to Jim. "I apologize, but we must insist you not take their pictures. It would be extremely dangerous if their images were published, even in an American article. The world is small since the Web. They continue here at the sufferance of others, as it is."

Dylan and Jim looked at each other.

Taken aback, Dylan asked, "What do you mean?"

Ali explained. "My grandfather was an educated man, like my father. He studied in England when he was young, then went on to travel the west before eventually coming home to settle and teach. Because of that, he was both accepted and distrusted by many. In order to keep his position at the university, he had to refrain from introducing radical ideas to his students. Still, he circulated articles challenging many of our customs and assumptions—under a pseudonym, of course. He was careful, but suspected nonetheless. World politics and history were his fields of study, so it was difficult, if not impossible, for him to remain completely silent." Ali smiled at his grandmother, sitting serenely at his side. "My family is less trusted by association."

Dylan raised his eyebrows at Jim and saw his resignation. Jim capped his lens.

The woman seated on the other side of the old woman spoke to her mother. Ali looked over at her and they exchanged a few words too. He nodded and turned back to Jim.

"If you'd care to follow my aunt, she would like to show

you something. You'll be permitted to bring your camera, but you cannot include her in any pictures you take."

Jim revived before their eyes. Standing up, he towered over the woman as she led him from the room. Dylan retrieved his notebook and recorder and flipped the pad open to check his questions, scanning down the list for something relevant to ask during this impromptu interview. The questions he'd prepared for Hanna no longer applied. He didn't know what they were going to discuss or where this would go.

Ali spoke with the old woman, nodding to her. "My grandmother would like me to offer you refreshments."

Dylan smiled at her. "I'd be grateful."

Ali conferred with his other aunt and she departed. While they waited for her return, Dylan looked around. One wall was full of shelves, oddly empty shelves. He wondered what the story was there.

Ali's aunt came back with a tray of finger foods and cups of tea. Once everyone was comfortable, she returned to her chair and spoke to Ali. He seemed to reassure her.

"My aunt apologizes for the modest offering, but that's my fault. I didn't give them time to prepare."

"This is very nice. Please thank them for their hospitality." Dylan appreciated their kindness, especially when everything was expensive and scarce. He took a sip of tea and smiled again, sincerely, at the two women, hoping they understood. Their smiles in response reassured him. Helping himself to a few marinated olives, he tried again. "Very good." His cheeks felt tight already from all the smiling.

However, they seemed gratified. Ali and his relatives patiently watched Dylan while he scanned his notes and chose a question. He reached forward and turned on the recorder.

Looking back and forth between his translator and the old woman, he said, "I was going to begin asking about the difficulties of being a woman at this time and place, but I think I'll start by asking your grandmother if she feels optimistic about a democratic Iraq."

Ali looked at her and spoke rapidly. Her eyebrows pinched together as she listened. She asked her grandson a question afterwards while Dylan looked on, curious.

Looking intrigued and proud, Ali turned to Dylan. "She asks why do you think democracy is coming?"

Her question, and his translator's reaction to it, confused and concerned him. Was her knowledge too limited to make this a worthwhile interview? He couldn't say.

Shifting in his seat, Dylan said, "Controversial political arguments aside, it's the reason our government gives for keeping our military here. We're supposed to be helping you get a new government in place, giving you time to form a democratic order for yourselves."

Ali relayed his response to the old woman and she spoke directly to Dylan, even though he couldn't understand. Her grandson translated. "She says democracy is a force of the people, for the people, and by the people. It can't be implanted from the outside. Holding elections before safety and order are restored is useless. How long do you think people will be satisfied with a government that can't protect them, or provide uninterrupted services?"

Dylan blinked. "Establishing a government to address those concerns takes time, but you're moving in the right direction."

"Elections only give us the appearance of democracy," Ali continued, translating his grand-mother's words back to Dylan. "I worry the West will be satisfied with that. It doesn't change the reality of our damaged institutions, our economy, or the bands of armed men terrorizing our population."

Dylan tried a new thought. "Without Saddam Hussein, you have a chance to reorganize."

When the old lady heard that name, she actually chuckled, as though she knew what Dylan said before Ali could repeat it. The kid had to shift gears when she began speaking over him. He held up his hand, trying to slow her as he relayed her response while she spoke it.

"Removing Saddam Hussein doesn't ensure democracy, nor does it address all of our problems, because it doesn't change the underlying structure of our culture. The conditions necessary for democracy to flourish are not present at this time. For this reason, she says we are not yet ready for democracy."

Dylan was blown away. This was proving to be a more interesting interview than he'd expected. "Could she explain what she means?"

Ali asked her to continue and she resumed. "Sunni and Shia fight each other, and the international presence. We are not one people, with one purpose. Our country is fractured by violence."

Dylan watched the old woman while she spoke to Ali directly. The young man nodded and faced Dylan again, his voice stilted as he translated what she was saying bit by bit.

"She says democracy grows from something else, a system that no longer satisfies or serves the people. It doesn't form out of chaos but, rather, from order."

She took a breath before going on. "Many would choose to have a stronger Islamic influence in government, but the emphasis on submission in Islam is at odds with your ideals of liberty. Without granting so many of the rights you'd consider essential in a democracy, would it be a true democracy? You forget, we are comfortable on our knees, facing east. Now you want us to stand up and face west instead."

Holy shit. Dylan reached for his tea. He needed it.

The old woman spoke to her grandson for a moment before looking at Dylan again. "If democracy is given to us prematurely, it will flow through our fingers like sand, and we will eventually find ourselves controlled by another dictator or bowed under Islamic rule. Anything resembling a young democracy will be fleeting."

Dylan kept his face impassive but he wanted to whoop out loud. "Please ask her how she came to these conclusions." He waited while Ali did just that.

With a smile Ali said, "She says she wasn't born yesterday."

Both men chuckled as she smiled serenely back at them. Ali explained, "My grandfather shared his work—his enthusiasm and rants alike—with all of us. Naturally, my grandmother absorbed the most."

"What does she recommend to improve the chances of democracy?" Dylan wanted to know.

Ali relayed the question. Jim and Ali's other aunt rejoined them as the old woman shared her thoughts, her hopes, and her love for her country with Dylan.

Jim set down his teacup and caught Dylan's eye from across the room. He nodded slowly. It seemed Dylan wasn't the only one surprised and impressed by this little woman.

"Ask your grandmother," he spoke to Ali again, "how soon she hopes to reach Canada?"

Something in Ali's expression disturbed him, but Ali repeated the question.

After she smiled gently, he explained. "She has no intention of leaving her home. It's all she knows, all she has. She expects to die here, and she isn't sorry about that." Ali reached out to hold her hand.

Dylan objected. "But your family is already re-locating. Wouldn't it be best to go with them? This is just a building."

Ali went on, while his grandmother's smile of acceptance never wavered. "She bore her children here. My grandfather brought her here after they were married. They made a home. She wants to be buried where he is. If she leaves, that will be unlikely. She also refuses to leave because she has a family legacy in her care. She keeps it safe until it can go to my father, then to me and my children."

Dylan wasn't following something, so Jim spoke up. "The shelves. I'll explain later."

Ali translated Jim's comment to his grandmother, and she nodded at him. "We must pass on more than blood to the future."

Jim nodded, apparently understanding perfectly.

Dylan was sorry to hear of her decision, but it was hers to make.

The old woman was obviously tired now, and they'd spent more time than was probably wise in their home, so Ali concluded the interview.

Dylan shut off his recorder. "Please tell her, thank you. Please thank them all. We appreciate their hospitality."

Ali did so, and then everyone stood. Dylan tucked his things back into his bag and humbly nodded to each lady in turn.

Looking at the visitors, Ali said, "I'll take you back to the Hamra Hotel now. That will be safest."

"Thank you." Dylan slung his pack over his shoulder.

The aunt who'd led them inside silently gestured them out

the back again. Dylan and Jim took off, moving stealthily along the house. They stopped at the corner of the building and scanned the area before darting out of cover to dive into the backseat once more. Jim crawled in first and turned to face the middle. He drew the dark blanket over them both as Dylan quietly pulled the door closed.

Jim tapped him and whispered, "Ali's aunt showed me a ton of books hidden behind a false wall. It was pretty narrow, but you wouldn't have believed it. I saw Arabic, English, French— titles covering a wide range of topics. Obviously, it's too dangerous to display them openly, and there's no way they can move them. It must have taken the old man a lifetime to build his library. I want to ask Ali about all this. That's the legacy the old lady is protecting for her family."

"We'll see what blanks he can fill in for us later. I'd love to talk with his grandmother again. My mind is already racing with thoughts I didn't get a chance to raise today. I'd like to come back tomorrow, if he can arrange it."

They overheard Ali say his goodbyes then leave through the front door. To any casual observer, his actions would seem perfectly natural. Gravel crunched under his shoes as he walked to the car. A second later, he slid into his seat and turned the key. The car moved off down the road.

They were only a few houses away when a small bomb detonated beneath the driver's seat. The impact blew the glass out of the windows and filled the interior with a metallic mist of blood.

The two passengers in the back were knocked out, their heads colliding in the concussion of the blast.

Fifteen

The angle of the sun had changed so it no longer beat directly on the still blanket in the backseat of the damaged car. Dylan jerked back to consciousness at the sharp sting of a bullet punching into his left thigh. His hand flew to his leg and he swallowed a groan when he found the fresh entry wound. Warm blood spread outward from the point of entry and soaked his pants. The salty sweat on his skin mixed with the fresh blood and burned the ragged edges of the wound. Investigating further, he discovered there was no exit wound. He hadn't taken a direct hit. Still, it wasn't exactly a comforting thought. The next bullet could just as easily take off the back of his head.

How long had he been out? The heat was suffocating. He wished he could move out from under the blanket, but giving himself away was suicide. Every inch of his body was drenched in sweat, the thirst it left behind almost unbearable. Even worse, the smell inside the car was getting to him, making his stomach churn. It was an alarming combination of odors he had no wish to identify. Vomiting would only make things worse, especially his throbbing headache.

There was a ringing in his ears, while everything else seemed muffled and yet, somehow, it didn't stop him from hearing the bullets pierce the shell of the car and embed themselves in the interior.

"Jim. Jim, are you all right? I've been hit," Dylan whispered. There was no reply.

Too afraid to lift the blanket for light, he touched Jim's cheek. His skin was cool, but Dylan found a weak pulse at his neck. His relief was heady, but their predicament couldn't be worse. How the hell were they going to get out of here?

Dylan shifted a little in order to check on Jim's condition. He ran his hand over him, searching for wounds. Everything seemed fine until he followed down Jim's left leg and his hand dropped off into space. Where the hell was the rest of it? Dylan choked back a gasp. Never had he been so reluctant to do anything in his life, and yet he knew he didn't have a choice. He had to confirm what he thought he'd felt, or rather *hadn't* felt. He took a steadying breath and ran his hand over the leg again. This time his fingers curled when the limb came to an end. He felt jagged bone and shredded muscle and tissue. Everything was wet and sticky. He fought down nausea as his hand came away coated with blood.

"Jesus, Jim, be glad you're unconscious."

Dylan rubbed his face with his clean hand, trying desperately to tamp down his rising panic. He needed to act fast, or Jim was dead. He didn't even want to imagine Ali's condition.

Anger and desperation seemed to close in on him as he carefully worked a shirt out of his bag and began the painstaking job of tearing it into strips without making any outwardly noticeable movements. It infuriated him to be forced to move so slow, or risk becoming an obvious target. He needed to stop the blood at both the stump and the groin or he was going to lose his friend.

Dylan packed the open wound with his clean underwear then tied it off as tightly as he could. Their confinement was working against him, impeding his movements, but he worked steadily on. When his knuckles grazed across a thick, sticky puddle of blood on the floor, it opened a whole new worry. Jim might have lost too much blood already. He needed a hospital—*now.*

Reaching carefully around Jim's upper thigh, Dylan apologized under his breath for cinching the tourniquet at the groin as tight as he did. Finally done, he leaned down and kissed the back of Jim's sweaty, clammy head.

"I hope I was in time, buddy," he whispered. "Hang in there."

Now he needed to deal with his own wound.

Making as little movement and noise as possible, he carefully rooted in his bag until he found a clean cotton sock. His body jerked instinctively when another bullet tore into the headrest above him. Dylan folded the sock into thirds. He brought it to his waistband, but couldn't work it down his pants without opening his fly. Expelling a shaky breath, he flicked open the button and drew down the zipper, taking the sock on a long uncomfortable journey down his sweaty, bleeding leg to the wound. He placed it carefully over the area and pressed his leg against the backseat, using it to hold the sock in place while he pulled his hand free and zipped back up. Dylan carefully shifted onto his hip, his left thigh in the air, and applied pressure.

Now he could really feel the burn of salt working against him in the wound. It didn't help that he'd clapped a dirty sock over the top of it. Just sliding the sock down his leg had compromised whatever cleanliness it had at the start. Under the circumstances, there wasn't much he could do about it. He tied what was left of his stripped out shirt around his thigh to hold it in place.

If he could feel fortunate about anything, and that would be a very loose interpretation of luck, it was that his eardrums hadn't burst when the bomb went off. Another bullet rocketed through the shattered driver's-side window and Dylan suddenly pictured the gas tank exploding. He hoped it wouldn't ignite right next to him. Then a more comforting thought followed. He realized shooting the tank was the last thing the sniper would want to do. Siphoning was a popular practice when essentials were scarce and expensive.

As more bullets peppered the car, he tried to sink deeper into the depression in the floor. Why were they shooting? Why didn't the bastards just rush the car and take any survivors out? Then a horrible thought struck him.

There had to be a good reason the sniper was keeping a safe distance back when no one was returning fire. Was he sitting on a minefield? Was there another bomb that hadn't gone off yet? Regardless, the continual gunfire was meant to guarantee no one survived this single, unremarkable episode on the streets of Baghdad, where violent acts were commonplace. The killers wanted to be thorough. Dylan dropped his head onto his bag and waited for death.

————

When she couldn't sleep, Ariela curled up in Dylan's favorite chair, wearing his big, soft shirt, with his scrapbook of articles open on her lap. She adjusted the lamp, angling it where she wanted it, then looked around. She had to chuckle. The guy didn't have much to be proud of in the furniture department, but he'd definitely made the right move when he bought this amazingly comfortable recliner.

Looking through his work brought Ariela closer to the man. It was easy to appreciate his obvious external attributes, like his luscious body, those intense eyes, even his playfulness. But in reading what he wrote, she gained more insight into *who* he was. He opened himself up on a level she'd never experienced with anyone else—not even Jean. God, she missed him.

He was a talented writer, clear and competent, but that wasn't all Ariela learned. Dylan was decent to the core, concerned, and outraged by hypocrisy. He was fearless when he took on issues, but even more so when going after people deemed too big to topple. He truly was a champion for those without voices and access. And she'd only been kidding when she'd called him her champion while hanging halfway out of the ambulance, strapped to a gurney. Who knew she'd actually nailed his character right then?

With every article, Ariela realized she'd just scratched the surface of his passion and intensity outside the bedroom—and the shower. Mmm, she liked his wild, almost feral side when he let it off the leash.

Oh, this wasn't good. She was getting aroused by his articles?

Well, not exactly, it just brought him to mind, everything about him. She wanted to see Dylan parading around the house again, shirtless, shoeless, tousled and sexy, and wearing those soft, faded jeans that hugged him so right. She wanted to pick his brain some more over another meal, laugh and taunt him while they played games. She wanted to walk the neighborhoods again while holding Dylan's hand, confiding things she'd never dreamed of telling Jean.

She knew she was safe, in every sense of the word, when she opened herself up to him. He'd protect her—body, soul, and heart. But she was selfish. All the qualities she admired most, Dylan's nobility, compassion, and strong sense of justice were the exact ones she feared would get him killed. He was heroic for pursuing truth, even when it wasn't always welcome.

He made people aware of what was happening around the world, without turning the focus on himself. How could a man be so driven, yet so modest? He wanted the pieces he wrote to get attention. He wanted the respect of his peers. But he didn't want fame. He seemed perfectly content with his salary, so it wasn't about money either. If he splurged on himself at all, it was to keep up with the technology that made his job easier, better, faster. She'd never known anyone like him. He was unique. No wonder she'd fallen in love with him.

When he came home, she'd tell him she trusted him and would support him in every way she could from now on, personally and professionally. She didn't want to be an obstacle in his career, his life. She just wanted to be the best part of it. She'd be his high spot to counter all the lows that came naturally for a man in his profession. She hoped. She wanted to be that person for him.

Ariela looked over at Dylan's other adoring fan. Her eyes turned misty and she smiled at the golden retriever snoring on the sofa. Even Dylan's stupid mutt was growing on her— irrefutable proof she was in love.

Without warning, her body suddenly jerked and she was hit by a sharp and unnerving sensation. Looking up with wide eyes, she had no idea why her hand rode down her leg and squeezed. Max lifted his head and looked at her, roused by her gasp of alarm.

"I'm okay," she assured him.

It was a lie. Ariela's heart was racing, her body tense with fear, the dramatic shift completely at odds with her tranquil mood a moment ago. She couldn't explain it, but it terrified her.

An ominous noise in the dark woke Dylan from a shallow sleep. Before he could focus on it, he was hit by a smell, unpleasantly reminiscent of food-encrusted dishes left in a sink too long. It filled the car, blending with the metallic overtones of blood. Whatever was left of Ali, added to the thick puddle under Jim, had begun to rot fast in the heat.

Struggling to control his gag reflex was only half the battle because now he realized what was so wrong, what was different. There was an eerie lack of gunfire. The change had been remarkable enough to wake him. Miserable and resigned to his fate earlier, he'd dozed off to the staccato sound of gunshots, a perverse variation of white noise, in the background.

Accepting the inevitability of his death had been easier somehow when he'd expected to be struck by another random bullet or two. At least it would have been impersonal. But now, tensing for who knows what, he wasn't ready to tolerate a very personal slaughter. He wondered how to handle the distinct possibility he was about to be dragged out by his painfully cramped legs and forced to his knees, with his hands clasped on top of his head.

Yeah, right—like that was going to keep it attached to his shoulders!

He reached over and touched Jim's cheek. It was cold, unreal, no longer living tissue. Still, just to be sure, Dylan searched for a pulse—nothing. As much as it broke his heart, he'd expected it. Not that it made accepting his friend's death any easier. His throat constricted with the pain. At least Jim never regained consciousness. He hadn't suffered.

Dylan put his forehead against the back of Jim's head and came to a decision. If he was captured, he was going to do his damnedest to inflict a little pain in return. If he was going down, he wasn't going down alone. He was fucked anyway. Why not fight it out?

Soft footfalls sounded outside the car. He froze, straining to hear everything. It took all the self-control he possessed not to scream when the door pressing against his feet suddenly opened. Now he was stuck. How had they known he was here? Had he moved and given himself away? What did they want? Were these just looters, or those bastard pricks who'd shot him and killed Jim and Ali? Should he kick out and hope like hell he snapped this guy's neck before he was executed by the guy's friends?

"Shh."

A woman? No. Yes. It *was* a woman and she was cautioning him to keep quiet. It could only be one of Ali's aunts.

Dylan tugged the blanket from his face and peered over his shoulder into the dark, trying to see her behind the black veil. She climbed around him, onto the backseat, and reached for Jim.

"No," Dylan whispered, stopping her hand.

She drew back as if burned. Then, collecting herself, she stretched out to look into the front seat. She let out a muted sob and dropped back, her body shaking violently. He could hear her deep, deliberate breaths as she fought through her anguish. In no time, her trembling subsided and something about her posture reassured him. She crawled backward off the seat and out of the car, waving for him to follow. He didn't understand the whispered words, but he certainly understood the need to move quickly and quietly.

Before climbing out, Dylan reached into Jim's back pocket and took his wallet. He slipped it into his own then eased out backward, pulling his and Jim's bags with him.

Sweat was running off of Dylan when his cramped feet touched the ground. It was all he could do to stifle his groan when his wounded leg was forced to bear his weight. Even without touching his thigh, he knew it was bleeding out, soaking the sock anew.

All of a sudden he found himself covered in a black abbaya, his arms trapped at his sides. The fabric hid the bags, as well. The woman settled the black veil over his head, shifting it so he could see, then with a finger to her lips, she led him to the shadows of the nearest house.

Ali's other aunt was waiting there. Together, they crept silently along the side of the building, away from the street. It was a slow and careful trip to their home. Every footfall was jarring as he tried to keep up—shaking, sweating, weak, and dizzy. He couldn't believe how painful it was to continue on with knees bent. The strain was more than he expected.

The old woman was waiting just inside the back door when they darted into safety. She looked more fragile than she had mere hours earlier. Her eyes glittered with tears, her anxiety impossible to mistake. The aunt who'd collected him from the car spoke, her voice cracking. Their wave of grief encompassed Dylan, as well.

He felt even weaker now, beyond fatigued. The muscles in his legs twitched uncontrollably, his bouncing kneecaps reminding him of chattering teeth. The room began to close in on him and in one mighty whoosh, everything went black. Dylan crumpled soundlessly to the floor, his arms still pinned to his sides, the bags clutched in his hands.

———

Ariela never returned to bed. She went back and forth to the computer, hoping a reassuring message would suddenly appear from Dylan. One never came. Keyed up on the pot of coffee she'd brewed around four a.m., she decided to head in to work early.

It was useless. She couldn't focus there either. A cold, gripping dread had spread through her, and hours later, try as she might to share in Jean's good news, her mood cast a pall over everything.

"The steaks were fabulous," Jean said in a happy rush. "I always overcook them, but this time Ron's had the perfect amount of pink. Of course, by then, he was getting pretty buzzed. He's not used to wine. I'd poured him three glasses before everything was ready. We never even touched the salad. There's plenty for lunch, if you're interested. It's good. I had some for breakfast." Jean spun around in her heels, her face alight with joy. "Ariela! I'm getting married! I asked him. *I* asked *him* and Ron said yes!"

Ariela shared in the laughter, but it was half-hearted. "I'm so happy for you. Really, really, happy," she said, trying to placate Jean. "I've just got this horrible feeling something happened to Dylan. I know that sounds crazy, but I feel it."

Jean sighed and slouched down in her chair. "Don't do this to yourself. That's fear talking. So, he's a little late sending you a message—big surprise. He warned you that would probably happen. Now look at you, you're falling apart right in front of me for no reason whatsoever. I can't stand to watch it."

"Then don't watch."

"Why don't you call it a day here? It's not like you're getting anything done, anyway," Jean snapped moodily.

Ariela agreed.

———

Once she'd let Max into the yard and brought the garbage out of the bathroom, Ariela went on a hunt. She picked up Dylan's scrapbook and began flipping pages, looking for anything that might give her a clue, or a contact. *A contact…*

Setting the book aside, she went over to his desk and claimed his chair. There was something going on. It harassed her like an itchy scab. She considered trying his phone again, but what was the point? She'd already left him two messages— not that she expected him to have cell phone service wherever he was. She'd also tried his satphone number, but that was futile too. Of course, there was an even more disturbing reason why she chose not to call again. What if she inadvertently made whatever situation he was in worse? It scared her to think she might put him in danger herself.

Forget it. This was better. At least that's what she thought until she found herself stymied by his coded address book. Why hadn't she expected this? Of course he'd protect his sources and contacts. And she wasn't going to get anywhere on his e-mail without his password. *Damn it.*

Shaking with desperation, she began rummaging through his desk until she found an old appointment book tucked into the top drawer. She flipped through it, her eyes crazed with hope. One number, running along the margin, looked promising. She picked up her phone and dialed. She was connected to the automatic-answering system for his paper. After listening to the options, she pressed a button for the editorial department, hoping for the best. A woman answered.

"Hi, yes, I'm trying to reach Dylan Bond. It's an emergency."

"I'm sorry. We're not allowed to give out personal information."

"I realize that. I'm not a stalker. In fact, I'm…" she faltered for a second, "his girlfriend. I'm staying at his house and taking care of his dog. I know he's in Iraq, but I need to reach him. Please, it's very important."

"Have you tried his phone?"

"Yes, many times. All I get is voicemail." Ariela squeezed her head in frustration.

"He takes his computer. I suggest you contact him through his e-mail."

Now she was really losing patience. She tried to control her temper as she explained, "We've been sending e-mails back and forth. He hasn't responded to my last one."

"Sometimes they can't, when they're in the field."

Duh!

Ariela took a deep breath, but she couldn't help the pleading in her voice. "Listen. I know this sounds ridiculous, but I have a bad feeling something's gone wrong with him."

"I'm sorry. I wish I could help, but I have no hidden doors beyond leaving a message for him with our Baghdad bureau. I can do that for you, but if he were in contact with them, he would most likely be in contact with you."

Ariela hated this woman. "Would you call me if you hear from him, or about him?"

"Are you on his emergency contact card?"

Her heart sank. "No," she whispered miserably.

"Then I'm sorry, but I can't help you. Policy restrictions."

Before she could badger her further, the woman cut the call.

"You bitch!" Ariela spun in fury, nearly flinging the phone at the wall. Only a flash of reason stopped her.

She went through the appointment book again, but after ten minutes, it was thrust back into the drawer. It took every ounce of control she had not to break down.

Picking up her phone, she hit redial. When the options came up, rather than hit the number for the editorial department again, she went directly to the operator to make a more specific request.

"I need to reach the editor in charge of international stories."

"One moment." She was transferred.

"Hal Cooper." The man had a rough and direct manner. This might not work.

"Hello, I'm Ariela Perrine, Dylan Bond's girlfriend. I'm trying to reach him. It's an emergency."

"I don't know what I can do to help. You can leave a message with us, and if he calls in, we'll pass it along, but that's about it."

Ariela fought hard to sound calm. "Listen, I realize this sounds crazy, but I know Dylan's in some kind of trouble. He's been really good about keeping me informed through e-mails, but it's been days since I've seen anything from him. He was supposed to send me a message with his flight information. That message never came. This isn't like him."

There was a pause on the other end of the line then she heard the squeak of a chair as it moved under the editor. "No one's reported back to me that he might be missing. I would have heard. I'm sure it's probably something as simple as his batteries being low and he isn't able to recharge. Everything he's carrying runs on batteries. If his satphone is down, so is his laptop. Don't let your imagination run away with you. This is just part of the business over there."

She trembled and her voice shook. "Please. I know something's wrong. I don't know how I know, but I do. I feel it."

He didn't even try to hide his sigh of annoyance from her. "What do you expect me to do?"

"Could you check with your people over there? See if they know anything? Please?"

There was a pause followed by another irritable sigh. "Give me your number."

For the next two hours, all Ariela could do was pace. She was so wound up she nearly dropped the phone she'd been stroking when it rang.

"Hello?" she asked in a breathless rush.

"Ms. Perrine?"

Every muscle in her body clenched tight. "Yes."

"Hal Cooper calling back. Well, Dylan hasn't been in contact with anyone at the Baghdad bureau. They said they'd keep an eye out for him. He hasn't been around the base, either, but that's nothing new. I'm sorry, there isn't much more I can do. Bond's dropped off our radar at the moment. I wish there was more I could tell you."

Ariela couldn't stop her sob.

Hal Cooper broke in, his tone reassuring. "Calm down. This isn't unusual, especially for Bond. He keeps tight control over his sources, especially over there, and we've had to learn to trust him. He's got good instincts. He's a professional. He'll be in touch." The phone went quiet in her hand.

Numb, she closed her phone. Maybe she *was* reading too much into this. So, why didn't she believe it?

Rather than make dinner, she loaded Max into the car and they went for ice cream, her favorite comfort food.

Sixteen

Dylan jerked awake to the sound of a distant explosion and instinctively curled into a protective ball before noticing where he was. Moving was a mistake. Searing pain ripped through his leg and left him gasping for air. Twice, he thought he was going to float out of consciousness again, but didn't. Gradually, he was able to look around the unfamiliar room. He must have been carried here.

His leg was killing him—quite possibly, literally *and* figuratively. Without disturbing the dressing, he was able to tell immediately, by touch alone, there was swelling around the wound. The entire limb felt thirty pounds heavier and forty degrees hotter than the rest of him. Not that the temperature difference mattered all that much because he was simultaneously burning up and shaking with chills. Not good, definitely infected.

One of Ali's aunts came into the room with a tray. She must have been listening for him. Setting the tray aside for the moment, she felt his forehead. Her eyes were troubled, but she gave him an encouraging smile. Apparently there was a basin near the bed. She bent and he could hear her wringing out a cloth before she pressed it to his face.

Putting down the cloth, she urged Dylan to sit up. He didn't have the energy without her supporting his shoulders. Then she held a bowl of broth to his lips. He was thirsty, no question, but he didn't know how much he'd be able to manage. A few swallows later, he shook his head and tried to pull away, but she persisted in getting him to drink more. Only when she was satisfied did she put it away and help ease him down to the pillow. She pulled the blanket up to his chin, feeling his forehead one more time. His eyelids were heavy, but he caught her worried frown as his lashes fluttered then closed. He listened while she picked up the tray and left the room.

He was so cold his body trembled and shook uncontrollably. *She isn't the only one worried about my fever*, he thought just before he fell back into darkness.

———

Ariela stifled a yawn as she walked into the office at seven-thirty on Friday morning. Dropping into her chair, she set her cell phone on her desk and turned on the computer. It was unlikely she'd find a message already. She'd checked minutes ago, just before leaving Dylan's house. There'd been nothing on his computer. Still, it made her feel better to have the screen up. She'd become obsessive about monitoring her mail while she worked on other things. Her heart broke a little more when she logged in. Tears prickled her eyes.

"I'm going mad, slowly going mad," she whisper-ed, clutching her head in both hands. She speared her fingers into her hair and pulled until her scalp tingled. She needed to feel something, *anything*, if only to distract her from this nightmare.

She was staring into space, practically catatonic, when Jean came down to the office thirty minutes later and flipped out.

"Holy shit! What's going on?" Jean rushed over.

Ariela forced herself to look up. "Still no word. Jean, I've tried everything. My hands are tied. I know, deep in my gut I know, something's happened to him. Call it intuition, I don't care. But I know he's not okay." Tears trickled down Ariela's cheeks, and she made no effort to stop them or even wipe them away.

Jean grabbed a tissue and blotted at the trails herself, her compassionate face full of pain.

Ariela stared bleakly back at her silent friend. "I was supposed to pick him up this weekend. Dylan said he'd let me know when and where by now. Or tell me if those plans changed. Nothing," she added with a soft sniffle.

"Oh, honey." Jean sat on the edge of the desk and smoothed Ariela's hair. Had she even remembered to comb it this morning? She had no idea.

"I have his car," she mumbled, at a loss.

Jean squeezed her shoulder. "Have you slept?"

"No. I just lie there and smell his pillow."

"Go upstairs and lie down. I'll take care of things down here today. And I'll keep your computer up. If he does try to reach you, I'll be upstairs in a flash. Please, let me hold vigil for a while, okay? You need rest."

"Does that mean you want my phone too?"

"Yes. It's the only way." Her face softened. "Trust me. I know how important this is. I won't screw it up."

A tremulous smile twitched at the corner of Ariela's mouth. "All right."

Her arm around her shoulders, Jean led Ariela to the back staircase. "Shut the phone off upstairs and lie down."

"I was going to drop by Mrs. Corley's job today," Ariela said as she climbed the steps.

"Mrs. Corley can wait until Monday. I'll call her and explain you're out of the office."

Hearing that, Ariela turned and gave Jean her first genuine smile in days. "Thanks. I appreciate this."

"What are friends for?"

———

Jean was sitting alone, lost in thought, when Ron dropped by. She looked up at him and he smiled. "I missed you at lunch today."

Coming over, he perched on her desk. She moved into his arms and laid her cheek on his shoulder, comforted by the familiar scent of her man, overlaid by the equally familiar industrial-strength hand soap he used at the garage.

She sighed. "I'm worried about Ariela."

He kissed her temple. "I can see that."

"I feel so powerless. There's nothing I can do to make her feel better. This isn't like supporting her through hangnails and inconvenient pimples, pollen and food anxieties. Do you realize since Ariela got together with Dylan, she hasn't mentioned omega three or mercury levels in fish *once*?"

"Is that big?"

"That's major."

———

Dylan lost all track of time as he slept around the clock. He was only marginally aware of how hard his attendants worked to bring down his fever and keep his wound clean. Somewhere in the dull and murky recesses of his mind, he knew the bullet had to come out, but Ali's aunts weren't equipped to handle it here. No doubt the thought of digging deep into the muscles of his leg, and doing even more damage, kept them from attempting anything beyond bandaging him.

He drifted in and out of consciousness whenever they roused him to force fluids down his throat. On the one occasion he tried to speak, he wasn't coherent—not that they understood him anyway. But he knew. His voice sounded foreign to his own ears.

His fever must have subsided slightly because he woke on his own to find the two younger women engaged in a hushed and heated conference just outside his door. They were speaking of him, clearly. They had to know they couldn't keep him here much longer without proper medical attention. If they didn't move him soon, he might not make it. His eyes drifted closed as he wondered what they planned. Options were limited and all would be risky.

He found himself jostled, vigorously, his name spoken with a heavy accent. "Mr. Bond. Mr. Bond!"

She slapped his cheek and Dylan worked his eyes slowly open. Even that took some effort. Looking at her, he realized his head no longer hurt. How long since his ears stopped ringing? Those were the only positive changes he noticed. Unfortunately, the heat radiating from his thigh was more intense than the overall warmth he felt from his lingering fever.

Ali's aunt pulled on his shoulders, forcing him to sit up. She was stronger than she looked, and he was weaker than normal. It was no contest. She pointed at him, then to the door. Where had the other woman gone? Distracted by the thought, he didn't respond, so she made the gesture again.

He sat there, comprehending what she wanted, but not sure he could manage it. "I'm tired. Too tired." His throat was dry. His voice broke from disuse. He waved her away. "Tired."

Before he could drop back onto the pillow, she called out and her sister hurried in with her arms full. She dropped what she was carrying and together they spun him so he sat on the edge of the bed then dressed him in what he assumed was the same black abbaya he'd worn when they smuggled him here.

There was a minor battle over the veil when they placed it over him. He tried to pull it off.

"It's too hot," he argued, but they insisted, determined to see this plan through, whatever it was. While one woman secured the veil, the other pressed a glass of water on him. He drained it without coming up for air. How long since he'd taken a pee? Dylan had no idea.

They left him alone to manage his shoes. That was a mistake. He dropped forward like a limp noodle, his head swimming. It took a lot of effort to keep from blacking out as he struggled to tie his laces without falling on his face.

More alert when the sisters returned, Dylan was resigned to whatever was coming. He took a steadying breath then got to his feet, staggering out of the room between them.

Ali's grandmother was waiting at the back door. Dylan saw his and Jim's bags on the floor at her feet. The two younger women each took a bag. They wrapped them against their bodies. Clearly, they didn't think he had the strength to carry them. They were right about that.

The women led him outside and surrounded him like a precision military formation, shielding him while still somehow managing to give the impression they weren't doing anything other than going on a routine trip to the market.

The old lady reached over and touched Dylan's shoulder to get his attention. When he turned, she pressed both hands down to the ground, crouching slightly, willing him to understand. She was telling him he was too tall. He bent his knees and tried to adjust his height, feeling the strain and the pain running through his thigh. At least the robe helped hide his unnatural posture.

They took side streets, cutting toward the heart of the city.

When Dylan needed to rest, they stopped, but always urged him on again, even when he didn't feel up to it. There was no way to avoid other pedestrians once they reached the business district, but that turned out to be a good thing. It actually helped them blend in. At one point, they saw a roadblock, presumably set up by the Iraqi police. Without a word, as a unit, they moved him away, in a different direction.

The buildings were taller here, though their surfaces were pitted by bullets—rubble was a given. There were more broken windows than intact ones now. Daily life carried on amid obstacles and debris, the scars inflicted by three different sets of fighters, each with their own agendas.

Ahead, a convoy of Hummers approached, moving down the center of the street. Gunners were positioned in each vehicle, ready to respond to potential threats. Dylan swayed weakly, his skin clammy, his knees struggling to keep him upright in such a tiring, bent posture. Sweat dripped from his hair, and his damp clothing under the abbaya clung to him. He could scarcely take the smell of his own body.

How had everything gotten so fucked up? What day was it anyway? How much time had he lost in a sweaty, fevered delirium? How was Ariela? She had to be absolutely frantic with worry. That's all he needed. He imagined her reaction to what he had to tell her and wondered if they could survive it. He hoped so, but doubts gnawed at him.

The foursome waited for the vehicles to close the distance. Before Dylan realized what she intended to do, the old woman stepped off the curb and walked right at the first truck with her hands in the air. The convoy stopped rolling.

"Stop!" the gunner shouted at her.

She did. Men came out from around the trucks. The guns

that weren't pointed at her fanned the street, the men holding them warily watching for any sign of an ambush. The old woman raised her open hands even higher to show she was unarmed and peaceful. That didn't mean anything. How could they know her intentions? Those robes could hide anything, including bombs. All a bomber needed was the chance to get close enough to take out as many people as they could when they detonated.

Anxious to diffuse the situation, Dylan stumbled down from the curb and limped over to Ali's grandmother. He held his breath as a number of the guns swung around and trained on him. The tension was so extreme he was afraid even straightening up to his full height would be risky. Who knew how that would look to them? He stopped beside the old woman and slowly pulled his headscarf back, just enough to expose his face to those closest to them.

Dylan saw one soldier's mouth drop open as he stared in shock. It was safe to say, the last thing this guy expected to see under a Muslim woman's garments was a scruffy man with deep blue eyes looking back at him.

"My name is Dylan Bond. I'm an American journalist. My photographer and interpreter were killed. I've been shot. I need medical attention."

He held out his CPIC press badge and one of the soldiers came forward and snatched it from him, handing it off to his superior.

Reading it, that soldier lifted a radio to his mouth and spoke quickly, his eyes locked on Dylan. Then he lowered the radio and returned Dylan's ID. "You can ride in the second truck."

The first Hummer pulled forward and the second came to a stop in front of him. The soldier pacing it waved him over. "Get in and stay down."

Dylan climbed into the back then tensed at the sound of the gun behind him suddenly swinging around. Ali's aunts had approached the vehicle with the two bags. The soldiers didn't trust them.

"Those are mine," Dylan intervened.

Ignoring him, the soldier made a motion at the bags. "Open them."

The women looked to Dylan, silently seeking his permission.

He nodded. "Do it."

Setting them on the ground, they each unzipped a bag then lifted them to show the contents. Once they were deemed safe, the bags were handed into the vehicle. Dylan placed them safely on the floor and turned to thank the women. They'd already disappeared into the gathering bystanders.

———

It was ten hours before Ariela put in an appearance. When she shuffled listlessly out of her room she overheard Ron and Jean talking in the kitchen. They were discussing her. Grinding the heel of her hand into her forehead, she let out a big sigh and walked in. They both looked up with guilty faces.

Her shoulders slumped when she looked at Jean. "You never woke me." The heartbreaking implications of that fact devastated her.

"I'm sorry. There was no reason. I swear I've been checking your email every ten minutes." Jean looked as unhappy as Ariela felt. "And the only call you got was your grandmother," she added softly.

Ariela's hand flew to her chest, as if to protect herself from the pain. But who was she kidding? There was nothing there to protect. Dylan had taken her heart with him. She felt like an empty shell without it—without him. Being alone used to be her comfortable default position. Now, it was excruciating.

Ron bounded out of his chair without warning and came to her, wrapping her in his long arms. Stunned at first, Ariela hugged him back. Then she cried—a good, hard, cleansing cry. The support of her friends helped her let it all out. Ron was a sweetheart, and a surprisingly good hugger—just not the *right* hugger. Her sobs gradually eased and she fell quiet. The steady beat of his heart under her left ear, combined with the ticking second hand on the wall clock behind them helped calm her.

"Thanks, Ron. I needed that." She gave him a squeeze then stepped back, flopping down on a kitchen chair. Meeting her roommate's eyes, Ariela confessed, "I feel lost and empty." The two women reached for each other, gripping hands across the tabletop.

Jean's eyes glittered with sympathetic tears. "There's a pot of coffee."

Ariela dabbed at the corner of her eye and sniffled. "I'd love a cup of coffee."

Turning to Ron, Jean gave him a sassy smile. "Since you're up, I'll take one too. Milk and sugar in both, please."

Ariela found she could laugh through her tears. "You guys are great."

"And you look better," Jean told her. "The dark circles under your eyes are gone."

"Replaced by watery, bloodshot eyes, and snot—big improvement."

Chuckling, Ron came back and dropped a handful of napkins on the table. Ariela grabbed one and quietly blew her nose while he set down the coffees. Ah, she could smell it now. It was nice to be able to breathe again. Relieved, Ariela pulled the mug close to her body and wrapped her hands around it, soaking up the comforting warmth.

"Thanks, Ron. Hey, you know, I haven't seen you since the big news. Congratulations."

He flashed a guilty grin at Jean. "Yeah, she finally broke down and asked me. I guess I was dragging my feet. I always assumed we'd get married. I just didn't realize she was getting antsy waiting for me to bring it up."

He took Jean's hand and kissed it. Ariela had never seen her friend melt before. It was sweet. Looking on with affection and envy, it struck her they'd never have to face the situation she was in. Then they turned to her with guilty expressions and pulled apart. Did they think she was too fragile to handle open displays of affection? She hoped not.

Jean picked up her mug and asked Ariela, "Are you hungry?"

She gave a listless shrug. "I haven't really thought about it."

"Ron's going to run for subs. You're going to have one too."

Ariela knew better than to argue when Jean decided to play mother hen.

"Maybe I should ride along. I need to feed Max and let him out."

———

Dylan woke up in an infirmary. He squinted at the sunlight streaming into the room and looked around. Someone was sitting in a chair in front of the window, their back to the glass. He struggled to make out who it was.

"Paul?"

Captain Paul Barnes set his magazine aside. Coming to his feet, he approached the bed. "Bond, it's good to see you up."

The horror of what he'd been through came rushing back. "Jim's gone. Ali's dead."

Paul nodded. "I know. We found the car two days ago. Pretty easy to see what happened, from the looks of things. There was a second bomb, under the passenger seat. It failed to go off. You're lucky to be here. Whatever there was of Ali was gone. We think his family must have collected what they could of him for burial. He'll be just another death that goes unreported."

"And Jim?"

Barnes looked away, obviously weighing his words carefully. "He was the reason we stopped. He'd been dragged from the car and mutilated on the street."

"Damn it, no!" The thought of what was done to his friend sickened him.

"You said he was dead when you left him?"

"Yes." Weariness strained Dylan's voice.

"Well, that's something anyway. At least he didn't suffer through it, unlike some poor bastards."

"How can people do shit like that? It's barbaric." Dylan rubbed a hand across his face, wishing he could erase the images behind his eyes.

Paul shrugged a shoulder. "Righteousness. Convince the devout their cause is justified and there's no telling what you'll unleash."

"These are the men who'll control the fates of the women and children in this country when we leave. They'll be at their mercy."

"Don't kid yourself. They already are."

Dylan looked away, feeling defeated, disgusted, and so disappointed he could hardly breathe.

Paul's tone shifted from grave to angry. "What the hell were you doing out there?"

Dylan bristled. "My job."

Barnes looked like he was struggling not to say something. He started to speak, stopped himself, took a deep breath, and tried again. "This isn't like the other conflicts you've covered, Bond. You can't move freely here. You're a target, a potential hostage. If captured, you could be valuable leverage." He pointed to the window. "There are bastards out there right now who'd execute you, on camera, just to make a fucking point. I don't want to find *your* body next."

In no mood to argue, Dylan let it go. "What day is it?"

"It's Sunday—closing in on five p.m."

Damn.

Seeing it was useless to badger his friend, Paul shifted gears. "They took the bullet out of you late yesterday and filled you with antibiotics to fight off the infection. In a day or two, when you've recovered some of your strength, we'll be able to shuttle you out of here by air, but only as far as our base in Germany. From there, you'll have to go commercial."

Dylan nodded and looked around. "Have you seen my bag?"

Paul went to the cabinet and opened it. "Which one?"

"Mine's the dark blue."

He brought it over and set it on the bed so Dylan could go through it. Pulling his computer free, Dylan checked for damage.

"I can't believe it," he said, stunned. "Other than a few scuffs on the case, it looks fine." He handed the end of the power cord to Paul. "Would you mind?"

Paul snorted and plugged it into the outlet next to the bed.

The screen burned on and Dylan looked up. "So, when do *you* finally get out of this place?"

"Not really my call. I have another two years on my enlistment."

"So much has happened since we met."

Paul thought about it and nodded. "I was pretty pissed to be saddled with you in the beginning. The last thing I needed to worry about was keeping tabs on a nosy writer on top of everything else. I thought, *Who the hell came up with this brilliant idea*? Embed journalists on our march into Baghdad, without knowing what we'll encounter? Give me a fucking break. I half expected you to get a few of us killed. If you had, I would have set you down in the desert and left you there, without a backward glance."

"Nice," said Dylan dryly, understanding the comment was pure bullshit.

Paul chuckled. "Why don't I scrounge up some grub for you?"

"See, you care. I knew it all along."

"I'll deny it." Paul smiled and left to inform a staffer their patient was awake and hungry.

Only now did Dylan notice his lean wrists. He took an exploratory survey of the rest of his body, feeling his way up his arms, down his legs, marking how pronounced his ribs were in just a matter of days. He ran his hands over his hard hip bones. It was a shock. He'd lost more than water weight. No wonder he was weak.

What was Ariela going to say about all of this? She had every right to be angry with him. This whole trip had been a disaster. Hanna was beyond his help and her story would remain unwritten. Jim was gone. He held himself responsible for that. And Ali Hadad, another bright kid forced to adapt in a difficult and dangerous environment, had been robbed of his promising future. The risks, the sacrifices he'd taken to get this story, all of it had been pointless.

Dylan brought up Ariela's picture and his eyes softened on her face. He traced the outline of her cheek and jaw with his fingertip and wished he was touching the real thing. *Soon.* He was going to make it up to her, somehow, if she'd still have him. Checking flights first, he opened his email.

TO: arielap@
SUBJECT: Did you forget about me?
MESSAGE: Man I've missed you. I hear you've been pestering my editor. I'm sorry you were so worried. I wish I could have spared you the anxiety. There's a lot I have to explain when I see you, but not now. I only want to talk about it once. You'll be relieved to know I'm in one piece.
I'll be flying out of Munich the day after tomorrow. I hope you're still willing to pick me up. My flight is scheduled to land at nine-fifty p.m. your time, on Wednesday. Let me know if I need to catch a taxi. I can't wait to see your pretty face and just hold you— hold you until my arms cramp. Dylan

Seventeen

TO: dylanbond@

SUBJECT: It's about time!

MESSAGE: I've never been more frantic. Now I know what a rollercoaster of emotions feels like. I want to get off before I puke. I'm not exaggerating when I tell you I've been a basket case. I thought I was losing my mind. I could try to explain how much I've missed you, but if you can wait to share things with me, I'd rather demonstrate how I feel instead. I recommend you sleep on the plane because I have plans for us. Of course I'm picking you up and I'm going to wrap myself around you and knock you to the floor on sight. Be prepared. Ariela

Dylan smiled and closed out of his e-mail. He looked affectionately at Ariela's face on his desktop, drawing his finger down the delicate sweep of her nose to her lips. After sending her one final, telepathic message of unexpressed love, he shut down and closed the screen.

Now the hard part.

He picked up Jim's wallet and opened it, extracting his friend's battered wedding band and a worn picture of Cara. Dylan slipped the ring over his pinky and twirled it around, wondering idly how many times Jim had done the same thing. He never talked about his divorce, but he'd kept his ring— close. Clearly it had still torn him up.

It was the job that had killed the marriage. Cara needed a partner, a father for their son, someone to stick around. Her second marriage provided what Jim couldn't. Their son was still two, according to the back of the photo tucked behind Cara's. What was his true age, anyway? He had to be close to ten now.

Dylan recalled Jim's skepticism about his own decision to quit foreign assignments. Jim hadn't thought he could do it, but his friend was wrong. Jim had loved getting out in the world, even when he'd griped about it. Obviously he'd had regrets but, having known Jim, if a family was something he'd truly wanted, he would have fought for them. Dylan tucked the photos and the ring back into the wallet and zipped them away in the duffel.

Paul peeked in the door. "You ready?"

"Yes."

Dylan handed Jim's bag to Paul then pulled his own off the bed and slipped his arm through the strap, tugging it up to his shoulder. As they walked down the corridor together, his gaze strayed back to Jim's duffle gently swinging between them.

"You'll get that to the states, then?" he asked.

Paul clapped him on the shoulder and nodded. "All taken care of."

———

Ariela got to the airport an hour early. She couldn't wait at home, couldn't stop pacing. At least here she could people watch, work her excess energy out, and keep an eye on the arrivals.

Waves of travelers moved through, dragging their luggage behind them. So much activity. Was this becoming her normal—always waiting for Dylan at the airport, or dropping him off? Would that eventually bother her? She preferred to have him here, with her, but if the alternative was not having him at all, then yes, she would have to adjust to his job.

Unable to help herself, she pulled her phone out for the fourth time to make sure it was turned on and set to ring. Talk about tense. She was losing it. Nevertheless, now she chose to tuck it into her pocket rather than risk having to search through her handbag, should he call.

Walking over to the television screens, Ariela found Dylan's flight number. His plane was on time. She exhaled a grateful sigh and edged toward his gate, as close as she was allowed, and waited some more.

She watched the flow of people with detachment. Like her, they seemed perfectly content to be overlooked in their haste to get wherever they were heading. Only one face mattered to her. She couldn't believe how anxious she felt at seeing him again—so excited, so eager, so timid, and yes, a little afraid.

For fifteen minutes, she paced before finally walking over to an empty bench to take a seat. When she lost patience with herself, she tried to focus on the general activity around her and was finally distracted by the boisterous and emotional reunion of a couple across the concourse. She smiled faintly with the other observers, touched by the sight.

———

Dylan spied Ariela first and a rush of heady emotions—tenderness, affection, and desperate love—swept through him.

The corner of his mouth twitched when Ariela turned, and they made eye contact. He saw the very same emotions surging through him suddenly transform her lovely face. Her radiance staggered him. Blinking rapidly, she shot to her feet, but her dazzling smile collapsed when she got a better look at him. He'd expected this, but it still hurt. He tried hard to hide his slight limp, but he knew the instant she noticed it. They closed the distance and her gaze lingered on his face, noting the changes.

"My god, what happened to you? You're so thin." Ariela's hand went to his cheek, her thumb riding along the sharp bone. Then she began to blink, rapidly, and her glittering eyes welled with tears.

"Hey, shh." Dylan pulled her in with one arm and embraced her. "Long story, but I'm okay. My leg is just a little stiff."

Her uneasy smile flickered back on and, brushing her eyes, she returned his hug. He buried his face in her hair, her neck, grateful to have her in his arms again. He'd missed this woman—the sight, the smell, and the feel of her.

He suspected she thought his leg had simply gone to sleep on the plane. This was not the time to correct the assumption. Turning her in his arm, Dylan kept Ariela fused to his side as they walked out, his good leg brushing hers as they matched strides.

"You could have eaten while you were away," she told him.

Dylan shot her a smile. "I thought you were going to knock me down?"

She laughed. "That was the plan, but you ruined everything by coming home lame."

"I'll try to avoid that next time," he teased.

"You'd better."

"And how's Max?"

"He's a dog. You know something? I think he finally likes me."

Dylan chuckled softly. "He liked you on sight—just like his old man." He pulled her close so he could kiss her head just before they passed through the glass doors and out into the exhaust-choked night.

The stars were obscured by a thick blanket of clouds, flashing and rumbling with portentous indigestion. There was weight, density to the air, and a suggestion of turbulence ahead. They both looked up uneasily as the first ponderous splashes of rain hit the pavement.

———

Ariela's surreptitious gaze kept returning to Dylan's shadowed profile while she drove. He was awfully quiet. The steady sweep of the wiper blades made her more uneasy with every mile. Taillights blurred and headlights blinded her. She needed to pay attention to the road, but his silence was a physical thing between them. She wanted to chip away at it, batter it down with a sledgehammer, if that's what it took.

"Are you going to talk about it?" she finally asked.

The strong yet gentle hand that had been lazily stroking the top of her thigh stilled. Dylan shook his head slightly and gave her a ghost of a smile.

"Not yet. Is there any liquor at the house?"

Oh god. "Sorry. I finished it."

"Let's stop."

Ariela's eyes flew back to him, but he stared straight ahead. She swallowed, feeling all her old worries and fears mingle with new ones as alarm rose inside of her again. She tamped it back down, for a moment, but it was a tenacious thing. It returned, bringing stiffness to her neck and shoulders as well.

"That sounds ominous," she said quietly.

Dylan changed the subject. "You're a sight for sore eyes."

The abrupt shift in topic didn't soothe.

——

Dylan unlocked the side door and turned his body so Max didn't hurt him when he burst out of the house. Still, the dog was so excited to see him it took them both to get the golden under control. That accomplished, Dylan carried the paper bag to the counter and drew out the bottle of whiskey.

Without a word, he reached inside an upper cabinet and took down two shot glasses. He brought them to the table and uncapped the bottle.

"Join me. Please?" He gestured at her usual chair then poured the deep amber liquor into both shot glasses.

She sat down and he slid a glass in front of her before sinking onto the opposite chair. "Are we drinking to something?" She heard the stress and anxiety in her voice, but there was no way to control it. The invisible cloud they'd brought inside was even more oppressive than the one actually flooding the curbs and flattening the peonies outside.

"Yes. This was Jim's favorite drink." He laughed, bitterly. "I used to give him grief about it. There are a hell of a lot better, and smoother, whiskeys on the market than this foul crap. But hey, for whatever reason, Jim preferred to feel his booze all the way down. I hope you don't mind. I didn't want to do this alone." Dylan lifted his shot and reached across the table toward her, waiting for Ariela to do the same. He smiled faintly when she tapped her tiny glass against his. "To Jim."

His sad toast made the hair on the back of her neck stand up.

"To Jim," she repeated. The whiskey scorched its way down her throat. Coughing and sputtering, she stared at Dylan, stunned at how easily he'd downed his. "That stings," she croaked. "I see you've done this before."

"Many times. Always with Jim."

"Couldn't you just keep with that tradition and leave me out of it?" she asked, hoping to forestall what she felt was coming. Dylan met her gaze, and the sadness she saw in him broke her heart. "What happened?" She was afraid to hear the answer, but needed to know just the same.

He shook his head. "We have two more toasts to make first." After refilling their glasses, Dylan lifted his again and waited for her to join him. "To Ali."

Ariela reluctantly raised her glass. "To Ali." As little as she relished this next swallow, she took it. The second was only slightly easier to choke down.

"One more," he said softly and poured again.

"Who now?" she asked, blinking back tears.

"Hanna."

"No!"

Dylan began to weep and she reached for his hand, squeezing it.

Ariela raised her glass first, this time, and waited for him to join her. "To Hanna."

"To Hanna," he repeated and they threw back their drinks.

Ariela couldn't stop swallowing, over and over, first the whiskey, then the sobs that threatened to escape. She felt awful. She couldn't imagine how much worse Dylan must feel.

He sat before her, rolling his shot glass by the bottom rim on the table, making little circles. Brooding, he watched it spin and tip. "Six days ago. All three. I knew about Hanna first. The morning of our interview, Ali was late coming to pick us up because she'd disappeared. He found her in the morgue," he finally said, without looking up.

Ariela actually felt her heart pick up the pace, like a kettle drum in her chest.

"Ali's contact, the one we'd been counting on, he disappeared. These things happen. It isn't a pretty reality, but they do. In order to salvage something of my assignment, we were forced to make alternate plans."

Dylan went on to explain, in detail, everything that had happened to him while she worried half a world away. When he described the bomb blast, she blanched. Going to her feet, she went and uncorked the bottle of wine on the counter. She poured them each a glass while he continued to describe how he'd administered first aid to Jim with the little that he'd had. He told her how he'd felt, waiting for the shooting to stop. She nearly sobbed when Dylan admitted his terror, when he suddenly woke up and realized that it had. He'd expected to die. His helplessness at not being in a position to save his friends brought fresh tears to her eyes.

He seemed to appreciate her gratitude for the women who'd risked their lives to sneak him out of danger. When she learned they'd risked themselves again to smuggle him to safety, her gratitude tripled.

After Dylan finished his recitation, Ariela reached over and took his hand. "Are you ready for bed?"

He nodded.

———

Ariela worked at Dylan's buttons herself then helped him out of his shirt.

"You're so thin," she murmured with concern.

"It won't last long. Now that I'm home, I'll bounce back." He toyed with her hair while she unfastened his belt. When she drew his zipper down, Dylan caught her wrist and stopped her.

"There's one thing I didn't mention yet." His eyes sought hers, and she waited.

He didn't explain, he just opened his pants and slid them down his legs. She saw the edge of the white bandage on his thigh immediately.

"You were hurt, too," she whispered, her hands shaking as she reached out to him.

He shrugged. "Just a bullet in my thigh. I was lucky it wasn't a torso or head shot, or worse, the second bomb could have blown. Had that gone off next to me, like the one under Ali, I wouldn't be here at all."

"Just a bullet," she whispered and stepped into his arms, pulling his head down to her shoulder. They held each other for a long time, Dylan's trousers pooled around his ankles, Ariela still completely dressed. She finally stepped away. "Lie down. I'll be right with you."

He did as she'd ordered. Stepping free of his pants, he slipped between the sheets and watched her undress. Dylan opened the blankets and she moved into his arms and snuggled close. Without speaking of it, they both seemed to feel this wasn't the time for a passionate reunion. Instead, they fell asleep, comforted by the arms that held them.

————

Dylan gasped out loud waking them both sometime after two a.m. Ariela stroked his chest and kissed his cheek, murmuring softly to reassure him she was there. He ran his hand down her arm and over her breast, scooping the weight into his hand. Ariela didn't know whether to discourage him, or let him carry her where he needed to go, where *she* needed to go. When Dylan slipped down to draw on her breast with his lips, his tongue, suckling rhythmically, she gave up debating with herself.

They let all the tenderness, all their love, flow freely between them. Their grateful hands explored each other. She was careful to keep her right leg from touching his wound as he moved up over her and buried himself inside her, one heady inch at a time. He stilled, holding her in his arms, their loins locked just as tight as their embrace.

His lashes were wet when he whispered, "I never expected to see you, or hold you, again."

Ariela cried at that herself and pulled Dylan's face down so she could cover him with kisses. "I was afraid I'd lost you too. My world was crumbling around me with you gone. I wanted to help, but I didn't even know how."

"I know." He kissed her tenderly. "I'm so sorry that I put you through that."

Dylan gave himself to her, body and soul. Ariela's heart absorbed it all and transmitted it right back to him, the love they felt coiling around their hearts like a bandage of security. Every thrust went worlds beyond the physical pleasure they felt. There was no Ariela, no Dylan. There was simply this—the absolute perfection of being together.

They loved as if they had all the time in the world. Neither understood exactly where this patience came from, nor was there any urgency to move things along. Ariela seemed genuinely startled when she suddenly seized in Dylan's arms. He held on as she took flight and finally surrendered himself.

———

When Ariela peeled open her eyelids the next morning, she found Dylan sitting on the edge of the mattress, holding a glass of orange juice for her.

"You're up already?"

"What can I say? I think just being here with you is what helped me finally get the rest I needed."

She sat up. "I'm glad. Is that for me?"

"It is." He handed her the juice.

She was right in the middle of drinking when he caressed her breast, startling her so badly she inhaled some pulp.

"Dylan! I was drinking. God, give a girl some warning."

"Sorry about that—impulse." His smile was fleeting. "Come on. I made breakfast."

"You did? That's a first."

"I decided I didn't want to send the woman I love off to work without a hot meal."

She groaned. "Work. That's right. I have to go to work."

"And so do I." He lifted the glass out of her hand.

Then it hit her. Ariela caught him by the arm and yanked him back. "You just said you love me."

Dylan gave her a strange look. "Yes," he said slowly.

"That's the first time you've said that to me."

He pondered a moment, chuckling to himself. "You're right." Then he dipped his chin and stared her straight in the eyes.

She gave him an innocent smile. "Waiting for something?"

"Coward."

"I love you too." Once it was out, she felt a little shy with him.

"There it is." He caressed her cheek, a tender look in his eyes. "Now if you don't get your pretty little bottom out of bed, I'm going to climb back in with you, and we'll never leave the house today."

"Promise?"

"Ariela."

"Okay, I'm getting up," she grumbled.

"I'll go pour you a cup of coffee, *after* I get one of these."
He bent down and kissed her good morning.

———

The table was set when Ariela joined Dylan in the kitchen.
He removed the covers he'd set over both plates and put them
in the sink. "Dig in."

"Aw, scrambled eggs and toast." Thinking back, she
realized he might very well be the first man to ever fix her
breakfast. It made the morning, and her lover, all the more
special to her.

"Since I don't know how you like your eggs, I thought this
was the safest bet."

"As long as I don't have to cook them myself, I'm not picky.
How do you like your eggs?" She took her first bite and sighed.
They were perfect, light and buttery with just a dash of salt and
pepper.

"Anyway I can get 'em." He winked at her. "I make a mean
deviled egg."

"Why doesn't that surprise me? You're a man of many
talents."

After breakfast, Ariela still felt uneasy about leaving him
alone his first day back, but when she offered to call Jean and
make an excuse, he was firm.

"No. I really do have things to take care of myself. I'd like
to bring you to work, though. It'll give me an excuse to pick
you up later."

"Okay," Ariela said slowly. The hairs on the back of her

neck were standing on end again. Why did she doubt him all of a sudden? What else was he keeping from her? Did she have to put a suicide watch on him? People did not simply bounce back after an ordeal like his, not to mention losing three of his friends in the bargain. The last thing she wanted to do was leave him alone now.

Unaware of her thoughts, Dylan picked the keys off the counter. "All set?"

She went, but not willingly.

Tara Mills

Eighteen

When Dylan got back to the house after dropping Ariela at work, he poured himself one more cup of coffee then shut off the machine. Nothing in life was easy, especially the most important things. He glared at the condolence card he'd just tossed on the counter. There was no way that piece of shit was gonna cut it. It was pathetically inadequate.

He turned to the window and watched the preschoolers playing in the fenced yard across the street. They were loud and rambunctious today. Not a job he'd ever choose. The thought made him smile, briefly, before he picked up his phone and made a call to his resource connection at the paper.

"Hey Dana," he said, relieved when he got through. "It's Dylan Bond...Yeah, I made it back. Say, can you find an address for an Abdulla Ali Hadad? He's somewhere in Canada, maybe Toronto. I can't be sure...Mm-hmm. You have my number, right? ...Okay, I'll let you get to it... No, he left Iraq in two-thousand four. I'm not sure if he took a direct route there...Mm-hmm. He's an academic. He could be connected with one of the universities...Thanks a lot. I appreciate it."

Dylan was typing out his notes twenty minutes later when the phone rang.

"Yeah, this is Dylan. Right. That was fast. No kidding, a fellowship? Great, I'm writing it down. Uh-huh. Got it. Thanks, Dana, you're amazing. I appreciate it. Bye."

He rubbed his eyes long and hard, pushing deep into the corners with his fingers. He wasn't ready to make that condolence call, but it had to be done.

Looking at the number he'd taken down, he dialed Ali's

father. He was sent to voice mail. Taking a deep breath, he waited for the beep. "Dr. Hadad. My name is Dylan Bond. I was working with your son when he was killed. I'm very sorry. If you'd like to talk more with me, here's my number." He rattled it off then hung up, feeling empty and responsible.

Anger welled up inside of him. He needed to lash out. It was time to make things uncomfortable for one of the men pulling strings from a comfortable distance while making sizable profits from the sacrifice of others. No one should be getting rich off this godforsaken mess. Dylan wasn't ready to release the evidence on profiteering yet, but he had something else. Something guaranteed to make the bastard sweat.

Energized at the thought of the confrontation to come, Dylan made one more call, tapping his fingers impatiently on his desk. Max jumped up when Dylan did, eager to go along.

"Sorry pal. I've got an errand to run."

He shut down his work and pushed back from the desk. Snatching his keys off the counter, Dylan ran to intercept Max before he blocked the door. The dog beat him anyway, and he had to wrestle the golden retriever back.

"Sorry, boy. Just me this time. I'll make it up to you, I promise." Dylan slipped out, with a very disappointed animal staring at him through the window as he left.

———

Once you start antagonizing a U.S. senator, there's going to be a response. Dylan expected it. It didn't worry him. He had other avenues up his sleeve now that he was banned from the senator's offices. One phone call to his old source and he knew where the politician would be eating lunch today. He had access to the senator's itinerary too, if he was interested.

Not today.

Dylan loitered for ten minutes outside the Ambassador Hotel, waiting while the senator dined inside. When the man's car pulled up to the curb out front, he straightened and headed over to the double doors. The youngest man in the politician's entourage, dressed like one of the big boys but clearly not one of them yet, pushed through the door first, holding it wide for the senator and his party to pass through. This was it. Dylan moved to intercept him.

"Hey, Roger!" he called out.

The senator stopped short, his smile crumbling away in icy shards when he saw who it was. His beady stare was hostile as hell, and quite impressive. "That's Senator Norton to you, Bond, if you have any respect for the office."

Dylan gave him a charming smile. "Oh, I have plenty of respect for the office…" He let his words trail off, leaving the implied cut unspoken. One of the senator's lackeys shoved Dylan back. He gave the man a cool, speculative look. "Do you really want to face assault charges?"

The man sneered. "Do you want to face harass-ment?"

"Last I checked we still had freedom of the press in this country. Someone has to keep our representatives in line."

The senator snapped around and faced him. "Keep away from me, Bond, or I'll see that you're covering bake sales next."

Dylan felt himself grow before their eyes, his small recorder extended toward the blustering man. "Care to clarify your Hardiman connections senator?" Norton blanched and Dylan pressed his advantage while he had it. "Maybe you could explain why you railroaded a no-bid contract through committee, without disclosing that a certain Mildred A.

Copefield, who upped her six-hundred and fifty shares of Hardiman stock to twelve hundred just before the deal went through, is your mother-in-law, and your lovely wife, Beatrice is overseeing her affairs as power-of-attorney? This has turned into a pretty sweet deal for Mildred or, should I say, you? Poor Mildred's been in a nursing home for over three years because of Alzheimer's. I understand she can't even recognize herself in a mirror. Would you care to comment?"

"Go to hell, Bond!" The senator's face had gone from paper white to tomato red in a heartbeat.

His aides hustled him into the limo and climbed in after him. Abandoned on the sidewalk as the car pulled away, Dylan cracked a smile when one of the men in the back thrust his hand up against the rear window—the gesture violent, the finger unmistakable. Chuckling to himself, he turned and headed in the opposite direction. It was a good day when he got to scare a corrupt politician into watching his back, at least for the short term.

———

It was just before noon when Ariela walked back into the office. She headed right for Jean, holding out a set of car keys. "Thanks for the loan."

Jean looked up with raised eyebrows. "You're back already?"

Flopping into her chair, Ariela stared at her in disbelief. "He wasn't there. When I snuck over to check on him, I half expected Dylan would be spiking his coffee with whiskey by now— or worse."

"I'd be drunk as a skunk if I went through the hell he did."

"I guess he was serious when he said he had things to do

today."

Jean rapped her pen on her desk. "Any idea where he is?"

Ariela's laugh fell flat. "DC."

"He drove to Washington, DC?"

She threw up her hands. "Apparently, his method of coping is to throw himself into his work."

"So what now?"

"I'm here. I might as well get some work done myself."

Kicking out of her shoes, Ariela turned to her computer.

Jean drifted over a little later as Ariela's printer was feeding out a diorama of a kitchen with breakfast nook. She looked at the page kicking out of the slot.

"Can you print up the virtual view next?" she asked, tilting her head to see the layout.

"Already on its way."

Jean picked up the printout and studied it. "Is this Beverly Campbell's job?"

"Yep."

Jean frowned as she tried to figure it out. "Where am I standing here? I'm all turned around."

Ariela grinned. "You're not. The whole kitchen is."

Jean looked at her. "Say again?"

"Let me show you."

Ariela pulled the current floor plan, along with the accompanying photos, from her file and laid them out on the desk for Jean to compare. As understanding began to dawn on Jean's face, a growing smile of wonder and delight replaced it. Ariela kicked back and crossed her ankles, lazily bouncing her pretty little pump off the ends of her toes while she basked in her own brilliance.

"You've completely changed things," Jean said in amazement.

"I did."

She pointed to the new layout. "You moved the doorway and wrapped the cabinets. And look, these weren't there before."

"You're right."

Jean looked up at her and smiled. "She's going to love this."

Ariela agreed. "And because I shifted the cabinets against the interior walls, both the kitchen and the nook benefit from the natural light coming in through these new windows."

"They really make the room. I like this little extension off the counter here." Jean followed it with her finger.

"People spend a good part of their day in their kitchens. It's one of the most important rooms in a house so it needs to be properly designed and comfortable. Before, this kitchen was a dead end. Now it's going to be Campbell Central."

"She's going to love the extra cabinets too."

"I don't know how she got along without them." Ariela admired the design herself, pleased with it.

Jean handed the printout back. "So when are you gonna bring Dylan around again?"

"Hang out with you and Ron?"

"Well, duh."

Ariela laughed. "I don't know. Maybe we should make some plans."

"How about tonight? Now that he's back, I'll probably never get to see you outside of work anymore. You two will be holed up in your little love nest again."

"You'll see us." Then she realized Jean was probably right. She did tend to spend all her free time with Dylan when he was around.

"I want to see how he's doing for myself," Jean went on. "Not to mention, with the wedding plans underway, we need to talk about a few things ourselves, like our apartment upstairs, living arrangements, etcetera."

"Oh god, you're right." What was going to happen in two months when Jean and Ron were suddenly expecting to live together? Someone had to move. How had she managed to overlook that fact?

"And what do you think about making Friday a half day?" Jean broke into her thoughts. "You can help me find a dress."

Ariela glanced up at her. "I thought you didn't want big and traditional?"

"I don't, but I'll still need a dress. I was thinking of renting one, unless I can't find what I want. I'd love to find something sleek, like a nineteen-thirties–style, nightclub gown. Picture Constance Bennett or Veronica Lake standing in front of a big band. I want to look as sexy as possible while I still can."

Ariela's eyes popped. "What are you saying?"

Jean's shoulder took a quick little hop. "I think I might be pregnant."

"Are you kidding me? How?"

Jean rolled her eyes at the obvious.

"I mean, you're on the pill, same as me."

"I wasn't always good at remembering to take them when I spent the night at Ron's, and he wasn't the greatest at reminding me to grab them, either."

"Does he know yet?"

"I told him."

"And?"

"He said, 'Well okay. Call me when you know for sure.'"

Ariela frowned in confusion. "What does that mean?"

Jean toyed with a couple of paperclips, absently hooking them together. "Ron's taking it in stride. If I am, I am. If not, I eventually will be so what's the big deal?"

"Huh." Ariela slowly swiveled side to side in her chair, lost in thought. "How soon will you know?"

"I dropped off a specimen at the doctor's office this morning. I was hoping to hear from them by now."

Ariela grinned. "You want it to be positive, don't you?"

Jean smiled back. "I kind of do. I just don't want to deal with morning sickness on my honeymoon."

Jean's phone interrupted the conversation, and she broke off to answer it, leaving Ariela to wait impatiently.

As Jean talked, she shook her head at Ariela. Bending down, she pulled a file from her drawer and opened it to fabric swatches while conferring with her caller.

Ariela gave her a commiserating smile after she hung up. "Maybe next call."

———

Dylan was driving back to Lewiston when Dr. Hadad returned his call. He pulled off the highway and parked so they could talk. The forty-minute conversation that followed grew organically in a direction he didn't expect. A mutual sense of purpose arose between them. When he finally hung up, Dylan was shaking with adrenaline all over again.

Oh god, what had he just committed to? He pressed the heels of his hands into his temples, groaning as he made deep circles. He had no choice. This was a debt that demanded payment. He owed Ali—the entire Hadad family.

Dylan felt his precariously balanced life shifting beneath him. His relationship with Ariela, the story he'd so doggedly pursued, even his very survival wasn't enough to counter the heavy debt on the other side.

Whatever anticipation he'd felt for the confrontation with Senator Norton had been spent. The one that was destined to come from this decision filled him with dread.

———

He sensed tension in the air the minute he walked into the design studio. It gave him pause, but Jean's welcome relieved a little of his anxiety. She stood and came right over with her arms open. They embraced.

"How are you, Dylan?" She stepped back to look him over, her brows pinched with concern.

"Managing," he admitted with a weak little smile, hoping it was enough to ease her worries.

"And your leg?"

"Pain meds are a wonderful thing."

She laughed softly at that then moved aside so Ariela could take a crack at him.

It was obvious she was upset with him. "I can't believe you drove to DC and back again today."

Dylan gave her an apologetic squeeze and kissed her on the forehead. "I told you I'd be busy. I've got stories to write and irons in the fire."

"I was worried. Don't take off like that without telling me from now on, okay?"

Yeah, he probably should have mentioned it. "Sorry, I forget there are rules when you're in a relationship. It's been a while."

Ariela slipped her hand into his and towed him away when Jean picked up her phone and began to dial. He sat down on the corner of Ariela's desk. She settled in her chair.

"Aren't you about done here?" He hoped so.

"No," she answered slowly, her eyes locked on Jean.

"I'm on hold," Jean told her while drumming rapidly on her desk with her pen.

Interesting. "What's going on?" Dylan asked in an undertone.

Jean sat straight up and dropped the pen, her eyes wide. "Yes, speaking. Uh-huh. You're sure? Okay. Afternoon is better for me. Great, I'll be there. Thank you." She looked up with a big smile, her face glowing.

Ariela squealed and bounded out of her chair so fast it knocked over her waste basket. She never noticed. Dylan picked it up and tossed the trash back into it while the friends hugged and chattered with excitement. He looked on, completely bewildered.

Jean reached for a tissue and dabbed her eyes. "I have to call Ron and tell him we're going out to celebrate tonight. You're joining us, right?"

When he saw the hopeful smile on Ariela's face, there was only one answer to that question. "Of course." Then he waved Ariela over and whispered, "What are we celebrating?"

"Jean's pregnant."

Nineteen

When Ariela climbed into the car, she seemed a million miles away. Dylan touched her arm to bring her back.

"Something wrong? Do you want to talk about it?"

"I was just thinking about all of the changes that have come at me in the last couple of months. Six weeks ago, I didn't even know you, and now look, I'm in love." Her little smile was there and gone in a flash. "My two oldest friends are planning their wedding *and* expecting a baby. On top of that, it just hit me I'm going to have to move. They're going to need the second bedroom for a nursery."

Dylan stared straight ahead, his mind racing. This would be the perfect time to suggest she move in with him, for real. She was there anyway, why not make it official? But he hesitated. How could he offer her shelter in a storm when he was standing right in the eye of the hurricane? His life was total chaos. His career was in a serious state of flux now that he was focusing on national rather than international stories. It was the right move for him, but that didn't mean it was easy or he wouldn't experience pangs of doubt and regret now and then. He'd moved back to the states and made the transition from absentee landlord to homesteader only eight weeks ago.

Then there was Max. Living with a dog was a big adjustment for him. It wasn't the biggest. The major upheaval in his life was sitting right next to him. Dylan glanced surreptitiously at Ariela and wondered what the hell he was supposed to do about this one.

———

It wasn't surprising that dinner conversation broke along gender lines. The guys talked sports and politics, while Ariela and Jean focused more on the wedding and pregnancy.

"You have to tell me everything. Don't be stingy with the details. I want to know about morning sickness and cravings, mood swings and contractions." Ariela turned when she felt Dylan's focus directed her way. He looked spooked that she was even curious. "Take the terror down a notch there, big guy." She laughed. "Just because I'm curious doesn't mean I'm making plans. Relax. I just have no idea what to expect one day. Jean's my guinea pig."

Jean snorted and reached for her ginger ale. "Guinea pig? Nice."

"You know what I mean," said Ariela, placating her.

"I suppose I am breaking new ground, but I don't want to be the reason your back hurts or you think your ankles look swollen. I swear to god, if you go into sympathetic labor with me, I'll kick you out of the delivery room."

Ariela's face lit up. "You want me at the delivery?"

Jean nodded, her smile adding to her happy glow. "Well yeah! Ron will probably appreciate having someone around who isn't ready to chew his head off with the next contraction." Jean turned, poised to say something to Ron next when she caught the look of confusion on Dylan's face. It made her laugh. "What, you didn't know Ariela's a hypochondriac?"

"No," he said slowly, but he was grinning from ear to ear, obviously open to the possibility. He looked at Ariela and asked, "What else have you been keeping from me?"

She crossed her arms and shot back, "You should talk."

Everyone stared at her, and no one was smiling now. Regret over her peevish retort struck instantly. She chewed her thumbnail and slid lower in her chair like a sulky teen. "I'm sorry. That just came out."

Jean looked at her, hard, before turning back to Dylan with a forced laugh. "Ariela doesn't just get headaches; she imagines potential aneurysms or tumors. A pulled muscle makes her worry about a hairline fracture. Or it used to."

Let them laugh, thought Ariela, kicking her foot under the table. But he'd struck a nerve with his question. Dylan was the master of withholding information. It was how he carefully sidestepped unpleasantness without getting caught in a lie. For a journalist, he was pretty stingy with facts and details. Earlier today was a great case in point. He'd shuttled her out of the way then taken off for DC without a word. Apparently, she wasn't quite over being angry with him. She might have been more forgiving if she hadn't already come to recognize the pattern. Well, she'd be nice through the rest of dinner. No need to cause a scene. Tonight was all about Jean and Ron and their happy news.

Meanwhile, Dylan seemed ready enough to let bygones be bygones because he reached over and gave her a one-armed squeeze, his smile back in place.

"No way." He shook his head. "The first time I saw Ariela, I thought she was one tough little nut. There she was, knocked out cold one minute, then fighting with the paramedics the next. Not only would she not admit she was hurt, but she insisted on going back to work. I actually wondered if I was the only reason she finally cooperated and agreed to go in for a check-up."

"You were," Ariela admitted sheepishly.

Jean slapped the top of the table. "I don't believe it! Who are you, and what have you done with my best friend?"

Dylan laughed, linking his fingers with Ariela's. "Don't kid yourself, Jean. She's a fighter."

Just for that, Ariela rewarded him with a tender, lingering kiss.

Jean raised a glass to them both and winked. "At least your finickiness finally paid off."

Dylan drew back from the kiss with a smile. "Care to explain?"

Ron and Jean both chuckled.

Ariela rolled her eyes. "Why don't I take this one—and feel free to correct me if I get anything wrong, okay?"

"Only too happy." Jean agreed rather sweetly.

Ariela snorted. "I knew I could count on you." Turning to Dylan, she said, "From what I understand, Jean and Ron think my standards have always been a little too high where men are concerned." She glanced over and they both nodded. "I imagine I've been the object of a lot of discussion and speculation on the subject. Right, again?"

Jean laughed and Ron grinned.

"Which explains the eight months," Dylan added, understanding a little more now.

He remembered the length of my sexual dry spell? Incredible.

"Eight months? What's eight months?" Ron asked.

"Never mind," the other three answered simultaneously, setting off another laugh around the table.

"Why am *I* different?" Dylan asked Ariela, his voice soft.

"I've been wondering that myself." Jean broke in. "No offense," she added when Dylan looked at her.

"None taken," he excused her easily enough.

Ariela wasn't exactly prepared to discuss this on the spot,

but when she looked into his dazzling lapis eyes, she wanted to try. Squeezing his hand, she said, "When we met, I literally didn't know what hit me." She laughed, and he smiled. "I was in a pretty vulnerable position right then. But when I woke up and saw your eyes and heard your voice, somehow I knew I was in good hands—the right hands. It was strange, because I've never trusted anyone instantly before. I knew you were looking out for me. I was safe. That's why I agreed to go to the hospital, even though I felt ridiculous."

She was still amazed at how this man came into her life. "So many other people would have left me with the bike messenger, made him take the responsibility. You didn't. You stayed with me."

Dylan squeezed her hand. "Walking away from people who need help is harder than you think."

Ariela bristled at the private reminder those innocuous words held. She turned from his intent gaze, furious with him all over again. And they'd been getting along so nicely too.

"But, one look at you, and I knew where I had to be," he finished.

"I get it." She crossed her arms, feeling peevish now. "You would never turn your back on someone."

She was shocked when his face fell and he no longer saw her, though he was looking right at her.

"A lot of times you don't have a choice. I can't load up every single refugee and haul them to safety. I can't walk up and disarm the guys with machine guns, scaring people away from the only water source for a hundred miles. I can't feed every desperate person I meet or take their starving children with me. If I couldn't disconnect, I'd be haunted right over the side of a bridge."

He took a swallow of water and tried to wave the dark and depressing mood away with an apology, but Ron and Jean wanted to hear more. Ariela, however, didn't. His words, his passion, cut her to the bone.

Dylan relented when pressed. "In my job, I've seen everything humanity has to serve up—the good and the bad. Some of it'll give you nightmares. You try to remain objective, or at least appear objective, but even that can be a challenge. For instance, say you finally land a choice interview with a violent warlord and he glibly justifies his actions and all the murders with bullshit. If you aren't careful how you couch your questions, or your expression gives your true feelings away, you won't live long. At the very least, it'll make it tougher to keep working. So you bury your reactions to keep them from eating away your insides. To be a journalist, you have to learn to separate yourself professionally in order to do the job. On my own time, I refuse to do it. I need to counter that detachment whenever I get the chance."

"That's why you went back for Hanna." Ariela stared at him, finally understanding how much she'd asked this remarkable man to give up. Would he eventually hate her for it? He'd said he could walk away from it—that he had—but was that true? Who was he actually lying to here? The more she thought about it, the more she believed he was lying to himself. How many people had he lost before it sent him into a haunted retreat and into her arms? With the three she just learned about this week, she knew of four people he cared about in the last five months. How many hadn't he mentioned to her? How many nameless people had he mourned? She'd had two. She was way behind his numbers, and yet, she'd tried to play the sympathy card to justify her ultimatum. What was wrong with her?

Journalism was in his blood. The time would come when he felt that relentless pull to return to the work so admirably suited to him. She couldn't stand between him and a calling like that. Obviously he'd needed more balance than he'd had. He found her when he was most vulnerable, most in need of love and comfort. Even a man could long for a little security, especially after so much insecurity. But how much time did that give them before he felt the tug again? Was she strong enough to kiss him goodbye when he left?

To Ariela's horror, she finally understood her mother a little better too. She wasn't as weak as Ariela supposed. She'd endured the daily risks of her husband's job with a brave smile, steady in her love and support. It wasn't until his death that she'd cracked. Even without her parents' history and commitment, her love for Dylan made her appreciation for her mom's pain stronger than ever.

It looked like her choice would come down to eventually being the woman he had to leave in order to be whole, or the person he wanted to return to because she made him feel whole. Either way, he'd eventually pack his bag.

"Ariela?" Dylan broke into her thoughts.

"Huh?" She jumped and looked around, startled to see all eyes on her—again.

Dylan took her hand. "I might have helped you in the beginning, but I never expected you'd help me too. You restored my optimism, something I didn't even know I'd lost." He looked over at Jean. "Thank you for including me in your little celebration tonight." Lifting his glass, Dylan raised his eyebrows at Ariela, waiting for her to join him.

Oh god, another toast? Unable to forget the shot glasses

they'd raised the night before, she picked up her champagne flute.

"Here's to your future and your coming baby. Congratulations." Everyone reached into the middle of the table and clinked rims.

"Congratulations," Ariela repeated with a shaky smile.

———

"Maybe you should move in with me," Dylan suggested on the way home.

Ariela turned her head so fast, her neck cracked. "What changed your mind?"

"I never changed my mind."

"Here we go again," she muttered, watching the city streak past her dark window.

"What's that supposed to mean?"

"You're telling me you didn't change your mind simply to avoid hurting my feelings for hesitating earlier."

"*What*?"

"You hold back."

"I do not." He fell silent, pensive. "Okay, maybe I do sometimes. You were reviewing the changes taking place in your life. I was doing the same thing."

"Do you honestly want me there?"

He glanced at her, the left half of his face lit by the dashboard, the right in shadow. "Yes. We're already living together at my place. Might as well call it what it is." He chuckled. "I've never even spent one night in *your* bed. We always camp out at my place. You've taken over half the closet. For crying out loud, your clothes are mixed with mine in the basket. We do our laundry together. I've gotten used to thinking of it as our place. You belong there."

If that was off the cuff, he was good. He couldn't have written it better.

"Really?" Her eyes went soft and misty and she leaned over to kiss him on the cheek. Dylan turned into the kiss, capturing her head and claiming her mouth while he kept one eye on the road.

Ariela pulled away. "Easy stud. Focus on driving, please." She settled back in her seat and added, "We have a lot of details to work out."

He gave an easy shrug. "I figured you'd say something like that."

"Well, it's a small place." She considered all the pros and cons as she watched the scenery fly past outside her window. "You might get sick of having an extra person around all the time."

"We can expand the upstairs. I need an actual office, anyway."

She was beginning to feel like Linda Blair with the rapid head spins. "What are you talking about?"

"I own the house. It was already divided into two apartments when I bought it, but since I only needed the smaller space, I rented the upstairs and left it partitioned off. Their lease is up in August. I can give them notice we won't be renewing it."

"You'd boot out your tenants for me?"

"I'd sell the whole damn house if I had to."

Stunned and relieved by his declaration, she was just as confident she'd never ask it. "We'll talk about this some more."

———

Ariela woke when she stretched out her arm and Dylan

wasn't beside her. Slipping into her robe, she went looking and found him at the computer in the living room.

"Let's move your desk tomorrow," she whispered, coming up and hugging him from behind.

"I didn't mean to wake you," he apologized as he typed.

"You didn't." She read over his shoulder. "Going after Senator Norton again, I see. Did I tell you I read through your scrapbook of old articles while you were gone?"

He turned with a smile of surprise. "No. You did?"

"Very engrossing." She nodded at the computer. "What's the old boy been up to now?"

"Where do I begin?"

Ariela walked over to the sofa and sat on the arm, facing him as he read what he'd written so far. "Sixty billion?" she asked in astonishment when Dylan finished.

"And counting. There are more people involved, which is why I keep turning up sources. People start talking. But the truth is, we may never know just how much money was misdirected because no actual record exists for a lot of these 'transactions'."

"Unbelievable."

"Appalling. Criminal. These people should be behind bars."

He leaned back in his chair, swinging around to face her. "What really gets under my skin isn't that Norton's corrupt, so many of them are, but he makes no excuses for it. He's brazen. He dares people to call him out, and no one does. He's never faced a serious challenge to his office. Hell, he's won four straight elections, just because voters recognize his name on the ballot. The worst part is, he doesn't give a damn whether he hurts his own constituents at home or those guys in hostile territory across the world, just as long as he gets his cut. The prick has never had so much money. War's been pretty lucrative for him."

"If spelling it out hasn't accomplished anything yet, and what you've uncovered so far hasn't had any noticeable effect, why beat yourself up over it?"

"It's my job. I know what that asshole does. Someday, the voters might just take an interest too."

She gave him a quick smile. "I actually toyed with the idea of calling his office to ask for help in finding you."

Dylan laughed and reached for her. "You're a gutsy woman, honey. I'll give you that." He towed her over to him and wrapped his arm around her waist, nuzzling her breast in the process. "I think Senator Norton can wait a few hours. I just needed to rant a bit." He eased her robe open and tongued her bare nipple. Then his mouth closed over it.

Ariela's eyes fell closed and she cradled his head to her, combing through his hair. Maybe writing about domestic issues like this one would be enough to keep him engaged and safe at home with her. She hoped so, but niggling doubts remained.

———

Dylan stepped out of his sweats, his eyes locked on Ariela as she slipped off her robe and dove under the covers.

"Join me," she said, holding up the blanket and sheet for him.

The mattress sank as he accepted her offer. They rolled into the center of the bed and held each other for a minute before easing back. Tonight was about touch, taste, texture, and tenderness. Her skin, under the pads of his fingers, felt warm and silky. He followed along her hairline with all eight fingers, fanning them out across her brow. He smiled when Ariela moaned. Then he swept back around and began again, following the arch of her nose, down around her eyes with a delicate touch. He rubbed her temples as his thumbs stroked along her cheekbones. That brought a sigh.

She laughed at the tickle when he lightly brushed across her lips with the back of his finger. He had to kiss that mouth. *No,* he pulled back and moved up to the space between her brows and pressed his first kiss there instead.

Smiling, she murmured, "I like that."

"Good," he replied, just as softly.

He slipped his fingers into Ariela's hair and held her in place while he kissed her eyelids, one at a time. They fluttered under his lips. Only then did he kiss her mouth. She kissed him back, the kiss deepening. She held him tight, drawing him down to her. Her legs wound around his and she pressed her body against him. He gripped her back, her breasts crushed between them.

Dylan was exactly where he was meant to be, where he wanted to be. When Ariela arched up beneath him, inviting him into her body, he'd never felt more welcome anywhere. He was home.

There was no reason to rush. No alarm clock set to go off in the morning. The stiffness in his leg faded into the recesses of his mind as Ariela consumed him, body and soul. She was his. He was hers, for as long as she'd have him.

She looked up at him, tracing his dark outline as they moved as one. Even without the light, he knew how those eyes were looking at him. He felt it with every slow thrust, every gentle caress. They didn't speak their love tonight, they expressed it. The dark brought clarity to their feelings, openness to their thoughts, and unity of purpose. The world receded and it was only the two of them, straining to fuse their bodies into one harmonious whole.

Muted gasps and ragged breaths escaped them. Ariela's fingers dug into his arms. Dylan's clutched her buttocks as he raised her higher, entered her deeper. A powerful rush of heat swept through her and she cried out as it carried her away. Feeling it, responding to it, Dylan stiffened, momentarily braced against the force, but he couldn't withstand the wave of ecstasy when it hit either. They clung to each other, shaken and shuddering, as their bodies were buffeted by invisible blows. Only when they fell silent did they hear an anguished answer to their passionate cries.

Max was pacing outside the door, anxious and howling.

They collapsed, amused and exhausted.

"We're okay, Max. Go lie down on your couch," called Dylan to reassure him.

The dog settled down, and so did they.

"I love you, Ariela," he said softly.

She gave him a tender kiss. "I love you."

Enough to forgive me for what I'm about to do? He wondered, squeezing his eyes shut at the promise he was going to break.

Twenty

Dylan wandered into the kitchen and poured himself another cup of coffee. Lifting it to his nose, he took a deep drag of the aroma, glad he'd brewed it strong. The flavor was rich, bracing, and *oh so necessary* given what he was about to do. He tried to put the prospect of Ariela's predictable and justifiable anger out of his mind. Losing her over this was a terrifying possibility to contemplate.

"Damn it, Jim. I don't want your fucking life—*or* your death. I hope you enjoy your last laugh, wherever the hell you are."

Dylan had loved the man, but despised his flippant predictions. His friend had made his choice where his love life was concerned. Dylan didn't feel he had one. He reached for his phone with a heavy heart and dialed.

"Hello, Dr. Hadad. It's Dylan Bond again. I'm sorry to call you while you're working, but my friend Paul just got through to me. It's like I thought. He can't help us personally, but he did give me the names of two private contractors who'd be willing to take a little business on the side. He said they're trustworthy and professional...Right, that's what I thought too. He warned me, though, they won't come cheap...I'll see what I can do on my end. I might be able to arrange something...Uh-huh. Sure. I'll call you again when I know something...That would be better, yes. Let me write that down...Okay, got it. I'll be in touch."

Dylan closed his phone and tossed it onto the counter, watching it skate across the top before it struck the toaster. *Fuck.* He downed the last of his coffee in one painful gulp then put down the mug harder than intended. He was losing it. Gripping his hair in frustration, he kicked the lower cabinet with his bare foot. The regrets were mounting this morning. He limped back to his desk, swearing the entire way.

There was one avenue he couldn't afford to ignore, as tempting as it was. If what they were planning was going to work, he needed some important strings pulled, by someone with the clout to do it. Time was of the essence. Sometimes you had no choice but to make a deal with the devil. No one said he had to be happy about it.

Hand curled around his mouse, Dylan opened the file he'd named I Spy. That was where he kept his more identity-sensitive contacts. Leaning over the screen, he searched through the names, finally finding the one he wanted. Time to make another call.

"Yes, can I speak to Marcie Spaulding, please?" He waited while he was transferred. "Marcie, Dylan Bond calling. Listen, I need you to set up a meeting for me with the senator...It's important...I know, but work something out. I *need* to talk to him...Don't say that. You're my only shot here...Well, transfer me over then...I realize that, but I think he's going to want to take this call...No, I'm not kidding. I have a proposition for him. Trust me, he'll want to hear it...Of course, I'll hold."

———

When Dylan finally hung up, he felt weighted down by conflicting emotions. His proposal to Senator Norton had been distasteful, but necessary. Now that the deal had been made, he felt sick. He'd compromised his principles in order to get the plan moving and temporarily muzzled himself for the sake of others. Sometimes that's just how things had to work. He'd also obliterated the line between observer and participant and ignored his rule to not get personally involved where his job was concerned.

Scrolling through his numbers, he made the next call, already sick and tired of phones.

"Dr. Hadad? Dylan Bond again…Yes, I just talked with, well I can't say who, but it's a go. Are we shooting for Monday then? …Uh-huh. And you can send them word? The faster we get in and out, the better for everyone …Yeah. I'll have my friend set it up for us. How about we meet in New York and fly out together? …That's fine too. I'll meet up with you in Montreal. Will that work? …Good. You have my number. Let me know specifics and I'll do the same…Right. I'll talk to you soon."

Dylan set his phone aside and sent off a quick e-mail to Paul before turning his attention back to his neglected article. He had to reread it twice just to get back into the right frame of mind before he was able to finish it. Once it was posted, he dealt with the next item on his agenda. This time it was personal. He updated his emergency contact information, stipulating Ariela should be notified in the event of accident or death. That went straight to Human Resources under separate cover.

Shutting down the computer, he realized what he really needed was a will, but he didn't have the time. Ariela would be back soon from shopping for wedding dresses with Jean. He'd tell her then.

Max wandered over and laid his head on Dylan's leg. Reaching down, his heart heavy, he ruffled the dog's soft, floppy ears and wondered if he was about to give up any hope of ever seeing Ariela in a dress of her own. She'd make a beautiful bride. He sighed, feeling even sicker than he had when he'd hung up after speaking with Norton.

"I could really use a beer about now. I'll bet you'd appreciate a walk too."

Max went wild and Dylan smiled sadly at him, envying the animal his uncomplicated life.

———

By six-thirty that evening, the spaghetti sauce was bubbling away. Dylan had just stirred it again when the phone rang. He grabbed for it, throwing the kitchen towel over his shoulder.

"Hello?"

It was Ariela on the other end. "Hi babe, I'm not sure how much longer we'll be. Jean has a very specific idea of what she wants and we've basically given up on bridal gowns altogether. Now we're looking at eveningwear. To be honest, I don't think she'll be entirely satisfied with anything. Wait a second." Dylan could hear Jean's distant voice as she spoke to Ariela. "Oh god, I'm back. Now Jean's talking about a silver dress." Ariela fell silent for a moment. "Actually, that might be pretty cool in the style she wants, especially if Ron is dressed in black. They'd look really great standing together."

"Hi, honey." Dylan's smile traveled over the line to her.

That's when Ariela must have realized she hadn't given him a chance to say anything beyond hello. She laughed. "Just hearing your voice is like getting a shot of adrenaline. You've revived my flagging energy."

"Glad to hear it."

"Honestly, I'm trying to move her along. Have I fouled up your dinner?"

"Spaghetti will wait. I'll just munch a little until you get home."

"I'm sorry about this."

"Why? What you're doing is important. She'll probably do the same for you in the future."

Ariela snorted. "Don't tease me."

He chuckled. "Hurry home. We miss you."

"I miss you too," she said softly.

He hung up, feeling a little relieved at the delay. It would give him time to gather his thoughts for the ugly scene to come. What was her breaking point? He was about to find out.

———

Dylan was sprawled on the floor, Max pressed against his side, an old Game Boy held over his face, when Ariela got home. The electronic music was playing when she shut the door.

"*Noo*...crash and burn," he groaned, letting his arm fall in defeat. The Game Boy dropped from his hand, startling the dog.

"Your sauce smells good." Laughing softly, Ariela walked to the end table and set down her purse.

Dylan rolled to his side and grabbed her ankle. "Where are you going?" he asked, loathe to let her go now that he had her.

Ariela dropped down on top of him and gave him a kiss. They had to push Max back with their elbows when he tried to nose his way between them as they sank deeper into the kiss. It was probably their moans that did it.

"Mmm, I'd be willing to skip dinner if you want to get naked instead," Dylan murmured against her throat.

"Later. I'm starving." She pushed back from his chest and straddled his hips, moving seductively against his bulge before standing.

"That wasn't nice." He gave her a woeful, disappointed pout.

"Aww, don't look so sad. Consider it a preview of coming attractions." She smiled and extended her hand to tug him up from the floor.

She had no way of knowing his emotions were genuine.

Dylan took the bread from the oven, and while they served themselves at the stove, Ariela chattered on about her day. She repeatedly told him how exhausting it was to shop for so long. "I don't think I can face another store for at least a month."

He smiled, happy she had plenty to talk about because he sure as hell didn't want to discuss his day yet.

Handing her the parmesan, he grabbed his fork off the counter. "I bought a bottle of red. Can I pour you a glass?" he asked.

"Yes, please. But I need a big glass of water too. I'm dehydrated."

She got her own glass and drank it while standing at the sink. He dealt with the wine.

Finally, ready to eat, he prodded her over to the table with the stem of her glass. "Come on." He set her wine by her plate as she sat down and took his own chair.

Her brows slightly pinched, she studied him. "You're uncharacteristically broody today. Anything wrong?"

"I'd rather not talk about it right now. I just got to a point where I can finally relax and forget everything."

Her frown deepened. After a silent beat, she nodded. "Okay. I won't push."

Dylan felt a fresh wave of guilt when he imagined the love in her eyes turning to pain. No, he wasn't ready to see that, cause that. He had to, but he could stall a little longer. He needed this. He needed her smiles while they were still his. They'd be gone soon enough.

"Hey, do we have any plans this weekend? Any more shopping on your schedule?" he asked, twirling pasta onto his fork.

"Nope, nothing. Why?"

"No reason. I'd just rather have you all to myself, that's all."

"Mmm, that sounds pretty good to me too."

There was so much love in her eyes when she looked at him he had difficulty swallowing without a wine chaser.

"Tell me, did *you* try on any dresses while you were out?" he teased, trying hard to lighten his mood.

Ariela laughed. "Wouldn't you like to know?"

Her secret beat the hell out of his.

——

They walked Max around the neighborhood that evening and retired early. Saturday was far more difficult. As the day progressed, Ariela could no longer ignore the dark cloud hanging over Dylan. She'd played along, hoping it would clear, but it never did. He was remote, distant, even when they held each other, loved each other. He was keeping something from her—again.

Trying to pretend everything was fine was draining her now too.

When Dylan's phone rang, he took it into the bedroom, leaving her waiting in front of the Scrabble board. The second time the telephone rang, he disappeared outside. Uneasy, Ariela shifted, trying to hear what he was discussing with the mystery caller. It was no use. When the third call came, Ariela hooked her finger through his belt loop and held on, giving him a look he couldn't ignore. She wanted an explanation.

He sighed and turned his attention to the phone against his ear. "Hello, yes I'm here. Let me bring it up on my computer."

He took Ariela's hand, and with a serious nod, slid her finger clear so he could go over to the desk. He didn't bother with his chair, just faced the screen and typed. Ariela looked over his shoulder and saw he was on a travel site.

"Here we go. I'm booked on flight seven-sixty-two, ETA ten-fifty a.m. your time. I can put us both on flight nine-oh-eight from there…You did? …Okay, I'll just worry about my own ticket…Sure. We'll talk more on Monday…Yes. I'll look for you. Good-bye."

While the printer spit out Dylan's travel information, he turned back to Ariela. Desperation and sadness shot at her from his beautiful blue eyes.

"Why don't you tell me what you've been up to?" she said carefully.

He clutched the back of his head. "I'd rather not."

Ariela wasn't amused. "Where are you going?"

Dylan glanced at the computer and moved to block it before she could read the screen. Then he sighed and gave up. "You're not going to like it."

"I figured." She knew already. Somehow, she just knew, even before he turned back with the paper in his hand and gave it to her. She looked down and her blood boiled "You *told* me that was it!"

"I thought it was," he said softly.

"You ass. You stupid, reckless, crazy ass!" Her bitter words rose to a scream at the end as she beat his chest with both fists and the paper floated to the floor. "You nearly died over there!" Her voice actually broke when she reminded him of that.

"Ariela, stop." He caught her wrists before she could hit him again then held them so she couldn't pull away.

"Why?" Her question a soft, tortured whisper.

"Come here. Please?" He tried to bring her in, comfort her, but she broke free and stalked off, her arms crossed defensively over her chest.

When she spun back around she was livid, terrified, and heartbroken, all at the same time. He looked lost, lonely, and helpless.

"Just tell me why you'd do this again." The look in his eyes came damn close to breaking her heart all over again.

"Because this is who I am, Ariela," he said simply. "Ali's father is going back to bring his family, and their books, to safety. With Ali dead, and no one else to look out for them, they're in even more danger now. He asked for my help."

"You couldn't help him from here?"

"Not with this. Besides, I owe them. I made his family's situation even worse by meeting with them directly." His eyes pleaded with Ariela to listen. "We were targeted, Ariela. They got to Ali's contact, then Ali, then Jim. Do you think they won't retaliate against those women next? It's a wonder they're still alive. *I* wouldn't be, if it weren't for them."

She gave a tremulous laugh. "So you're just going to barrel in there and whisk them out Rambo-style?"

"Not exactly." He paused, then conceded with an uncomfortable shrug, "Well, sort of. We want to be quick, in and out. We're hoping it'll take us thirty minutes or less. Plus, we're going in with armed professionals, just in case. We'll be completely outfitted: vests, helmets, everything."

"Will you be armed?"

"This time—yes."

"Oh my god," she cried, pulling at her hair. She spun around, facing the ceiling for a moment. When she turned back, she glared at him. "Don't expect me to be here when you get back."

His gaze softened on her. "I'm counting on it."

Tears glittered in her eyes. "I told you I didn't think I could handle caring about someone in a dangerous job. I don't think my life can stand another heroic type." There was a hitch in her voice. "Not knowing what happened to you once already was too hard, too damn hard on me."

He closed the distance between them and embraced her. Ariela cried against his shirt while he rubbed her back, her hair. She couldn't push him away this time.

"I can't pull out now. I won't. I understand why you're afraid of me going back, but I can't let that change my decision."

"You're lucky to be alive. You've got the bullet wound to prove it." She shuddered against him.

"I'm fit to go, and I have to help them. They helped me."

"You don't. At least, not like this."

He shook his head at her. "I do. If it were my grandmother over there, I'd hope someone would do the same for her. I'd do it for yours too."

Ariela wouldn't meet his gaze. She slipped out of his arms and walked over to his big comfy chair, dropping heavily into it. "I don't want you to die."

He raked his fingers through his hair. "I don't want that either."

Dylan followed and crouched in front of her, grabbing the arms and caging her where she sat. He needed her to understand.

"How did we meet, Ariela?" he asked softly.

His question surprised her. "On the sidewalk."

He smiled. "You had an accident, and I helped. Who knew that my good-guy act was going to land us here, waist deep in love so fast? This wouldn't have happened if I'd been a different person, would it?"

"Probably not."

"Ariela, I can't change who I am. I came to your aid, they came to mine, and now I'm in a position to help them in return. If you asked me not to go, and I stayed, you could never see me the same way again. I'd be diminished somehow—weaker. I don't want to lose your good opinion, but even more important, I don't want to lose my own self-respect. I have to go, but I'd like you to support me, and be here when I get back."

Tara Mills

Twenty-One

They didn't discuss his Monday departure for the rest of the weekend, not even when Dylan pulled a small case out of his closet and headed to the local gun club for a little target practice. Ariela chose to take Max for a walk by herself rather than think about it.

When he got home, Dylan was especially affectionate. Odd as it seemed, they'd reversed roles from the day before. Now, she was remote and distant while he wanted nothing more than to penetrate the shell she wore like armor around her.

To his surprise, it was easier to woo her into the bedroom, than to get a smile out of her. As they tangled together among the sheets, their hands and lips soothed, but their bodies belied their inner turmoil. Each drive of pelvis to pelvis carried with it an edge of desperation. His plunges into her were so forceful, so determined, that when they finally cried out, it was as much from release as emotional exhaustion. They collapsed on their backs and panted for air, reaching out to twine their fingers together. Neither could summon the energy for a simple kiss.

They woke early Monday morning and Ariela drove him to the airport. Their parting embrace stretched on, neither willing to end it. Finally, Dylan drew back and took her face in his hands. His eyes possessed her, drinking in every detail of her beloved face. When she blinked back tears, he sighed and kissed her softly, wrapping her close one last time before releasing her to hoist his bag onto his shoulder. When he moved off to join the crowd, their arms stretched out between them until their fingers lost contact and their hands dropped away. It reminded him of that first time, when she was rolling away, strapped to the gurney, and their fingers pulled apart.

He hadn't wanted to let her go then either.

———

Ariela couldn't handle watching Dylan disappear down the corridor without her so she turned and fled, needing to leave the pain behind, and knowing there was no chance of that. Assuming the best way to cope with disappointment was to immerse herself in something else, she went straight to work. Jean was just coming out of the bathroom looking peaked and shaky when she arrived.

"We need mouthwash down here," Jean said before making her unsteady way back to her desk.

"Maybe you should lie down?"

"No, that only makes it worse—if that's possible."

Ariela looked at her sympathetically. It was strange to find herself nursing her nurse for a change. She forced a few crackers on her friend.

"I'm getting nervous about waiting six more weeks for the wedding. What if we bumped it up?" Jean took a bite.

"Why?"

"I don't want to start showing too much tummy in my dress."

"The way you're keeping food down? Not a chance."

"You sure?" she asked, clearly worried.

"I'm sure. You'll still be able to wear a two-piece on your honeymoon."

That brought a smile. Jean picked up her bottle of juice and took a good, long swallow. "Now it's your turn," she said, coming up for air. "How are you holding up?"

"You're a good distraction. I'd much rather talk about your

worries than mine. Yours seem a lot more manageable."

"Nice try. How's Dylan?"

"I wish I knew," Ariela said honestly and her brave mask cracked.

"Oh, honey." Jean's eyes started to tear up too.

"I'm so confused." Ariela threw out her hands. "I love him so much, but loving him is terrifying. I don't know if I can handle it. Whenever he leaves, and he's always going to leave, he takes a piece of me with him. How can I live like that? Sometimes at night, I'll lie there thinking about the future. What if we get married, have kids? How much time will I have with him, or will I be raising our child, our children, on my own half the time? Do I want to be a single parent? I don't know."

Jean nodded, understanding. "But if you had a child together, you'd never be lonely. You could look at them and see a little of Dylan in them too. It would make missing him a little easier to handle, don't you think? And there's always Max. You know he'd be a big help," she added with a laugh.

Ariela snorted with the giggles, dashing the tears from the corners of her eyes. "What if I'm not strong enough to handle the stress of losing him?"

"I don't know if I'd be strong enough to handle losing Ron either. The difference is I'm going to marry him anyway, and not obsess over things I can't control or predict. He's stuck with me."

Smiling, Ariela blotted her nose with a tissue.

Jean went on. "Your choice is whether you lose Dylan now, or forty years from now."

———

Dr. Abdullah Hadad was an older version of his son. It was

easy to see Ali in the man, even if he was slightly shorter and carried the solid build that often followed maturity. When they met in the airport just before boarding, Dylan could feel the man's grief radiating off of him like waves of desert heat.

It was during the flight that Dylan was able to offer his condolences in person. He described Ali's invaluable contributions to his work, and expressed his genuine affection and friendship for the young man. Dr. Hadad graciously accepted the kind words. Now that the awkwardness was removed, he went on to tell Dylan about his other two children; a thirteen-year-old boy, and a nine-year-old girl, both already in Toronto.

"You know, sons are our pride, but daughters are our treasure." He smiled when he said this, one of his few smiles.

Then the professor turned the conversation by expressing an interest in Dylan's children.

Dylan smiled. "I haven't gotten around to starting a family yet."

The professor patted his arm. "You're still young. Men have the luxury of time, if they don't have parents wailing for grandchildren. You shouldn't be concerned."

Trying to hold back a chuckle, he said, "Don't worry—I'm not. I assure you."

Yet, his thoughts betrayed him when they slid back to Ariela. He imagined her pregnant with his child. Talk about a pipe dream. He wasn't even sure if she wanted *him* anymore.

The older man dropped the subject, admitting instead how much he regretted putting his sisters in the position of laying down the law to their mother about leaving. It couldn't have been easy. He confessed he'd even given them permission to trot out the old *head of the household* argument on her if she proved too difficult.

Dylan laughed. "Guilt always worked in my family."

Abdullah rubbed his chin thoughtfully. "Ah yes, I can imagine." He glanced over. "I'll think on the best approach, something tailored to her particularly and which she can't withstand. One way or another, she's coming with us. I'd rather not drag her out bodily. There'd be no dignity in it for either of us. Once the books are gone, there will be no reason for her to remain, especially if I promise to bring her home to be buried. That will take some work, but hopefully there'll be plenty of time to worry about those details later."

Dylan liked the idea. He liked the man even more.

———

Not long after the plane touched down, they were choppered over to the Green Zone and met just off the pad by their hired contractors, Bruce and Rich. Both men looked like they'd come straight out of Special Ops, with biceps as thick around as a man's thigh, and pistols resting comfortably on their hips. They were both well over six feet tall, seasoned and serious.

Captain Paul Barnes sat in on their briefing, without getting involved, while Dylan listened to their plan for the next day. Afterward, Bruce and Rich asked Dylan to join them on the shooting range so they could see how he handled small arms. Since the professor preferred not to carry a weapon, he wasn't included in the invitation.

Dylan had serious nerves when, after ten minutes of hitting the target, not necessarily in the center but always within the rings, Bruce walked over and took his pistol away and put a rifle in his hands.

"Ever fire one of these?" Bruce asked him.

"I used to hunt with my grandpa when I was a teen. But this isn't exactly a hunting rifle."

Rich looked over at him and snorted. "No shit. That's a standard issue M-16 semi-automatic. Let's see what you can do with it."

Bruce chuckled. "It's loaded and ready to fire. Just remember the kick and go easy on the trigger. That baby wants to pump like a dog in heat. Think you can handle it?"

"I've got it." Dylan seated the stock against his shoulder and eyed down the tip, lining up his shot. Bruce stepped back, and Dylan squeezed the trigger. He struck the target dead center, exactly where he wanted to be.

He turned with an amazed smile to see Bruce cock his head at him. "Okay. Do that again, a few more times, and I'll be satisfied."

Bruce returned with a sleek, no-frills gun, and Dylan stopped to stare at it. "What the hell is that?"

Bruce laughed. "M-1014. It's a joint-service shotgun, and this baby is mine. I just wanted to play with her a little."

Afterwards, they didn't offer any comments—positive or negative—about Dylan's ability, but they must have found him satisfactory because they didn't look worried when they broke for dinner. Dylan found a little time alone in a corner of the commissary to send Ariela a message.

> To: arielap@
> From: dylanbond@
> Subject: Safe and sound.
> Message: I wish I felt as good about *us* as I do about what we'll be doing tomorrow. We left so much unsaid before I left. More than anything, I want you, and need you, to forgive me for doing what I have to. When I get

back, I hope you're willing to work things out between us. I need to know what you want from me as a man, not just a journalist. Somehow, who I am always seems to get lost behind what I am with you. Can you accept that there's a person inside me too? I can't think of my future without seeing flashes of you at the center of it. What do you see? Do I figure at all in your plans? I hope so. I'll always love you, regardless of your decision. With stopovers and connecting flights, I won't be back until Saturday morning, flight 5480, ETA 7:40a.m. I guess I'll know your answer then. I miss you. Dylan

———

Bruce, the bigger of the two contractors, met up with Dylan outside his room. He acknowledged Paul with a nod as he strode down the corridor to intercept them. Dylan closed the distance and handed Paul his duffel.

"I wrote down Ariela's address and put it inside—just in case."

Paul was grave when he took the bag. "I won't need it. It'll be here when you get back."

Dylan gave him a quick nod and followed Bruce out. Paul walked away.

Rich and the professor were already standing beside the vehicle. The armored truck barked, *Don't fuck with us,* clearly and in no uncertain terms, to whoever saw it. It was testosterone on wheels. Just the sight of it made Dylan feel better about what they were about to do.

Bruce handed Dylan a bulletproof vest, and he put it on. Body armor had been a necessary part of his life over here—in certain situations. Abdullah, however, seemed to be having trouble dressing in his gear, so Rich assisted him.

Next came a shoulder holster, not necessary, but it was something Dylan had requested since he was more familiar with a pistol. After that, he was handed an automatic rifle. Every weapon was pre-loaded, and Bruce pointed out Dylan's back-up cartridges inside the truck.

"Hey, Scribe." Bruce tapped Dylan on the shoulder. "The pistol is only for up close and personal, got it? Hang on to the M-16. Warn them the fuck off with the big boy."

He walked around to the other side of the truck and opened the door, leaving Dylan to wonder if he'd be able to take someone out at point-blank range. He hoped he didn't have to face that test.

"Put a lid on it," Rich called out as they climbed inside. Four helmets went on.

Their Humvee kicked up dust as it rolled down the road, garnering little interest from the people going about their business. What felt pretty damn momentous to the men in the truck heading toward the gate, was little more than business as usual to those living inside the fortified compound. Dylan looked out his window, his hands cradling his weapon, and knew, in spite of how routine this appeared to everyone else, to him, it was an experience of a lifetime. He held his breath when they were waved through the large, intimidating gate. His eyes darted from side to side, sweeping the streets and crowds for threats.

———

Ariela went in to work early on Thursday. She couldn't sleep in Dylan's bed, in his house now, without tossing and turning. Ever since he'd sent his e-mail, she'd been an emotional wreck.

He'd raised a fair point. She did use his job as an excuse to hold him at arm's length. Or she tried to anyway. Her heart had accepted the man far faster than her head had accepted the journalist. But he was so much more than that. She'd wept when she read his message. His pain had sliced her chest wide open, deservedly. She'd wounded him, withheld her affections, and for what? To make a point?

Even though he'd said he still had hope, she could read between the lines. He was letting her go. He'd given her up as lost already. Did he expect her to leave just before he got home? Just set his house key on the counter on her way out? Maybe he did. If he'd been any other person, she very well might have to avoid a scene. Well forget it. That's not how she wanted this to play out.

She couldn't stop shaking now, and it had nothing to do with the pot of coffee she'd polished off before driving over here. This was one bullet she wasn't going to let him dodge.

Jean must have heard her, because she hurried downstairs in her bathrobe and slippers and dragged Ariela up to the apartment.

The television was on, and a black-and-white image from an old movie was frozen on the screen. Jean was as hyper as Ariela when she pointed to the nightclub scene. Ariela moved closer, finally comprehending her friend's excitement. "That's beautiful."

"I know. I want that."

Ariela glanced over. "You could totally pull this off. Are you going to do the hair too?"

"Maybe. Just a little less complicated. I love the side part and that sexy swoop, don't you?"

"It's fabulous. I wonder what color that dress actually was?"

"I don't know."

"I see why you've chosen silver. It looks like it might have been silver. It's gorgeous, like she's dressed in a waterfall the way it hugs her all the way down to the floor and pools behind her. Liquid. Quicksilver. Can I advance the frame to see more?"

"Actually, you'll want to go back instead. There's a good shot of the back of the dress."

Ariela picked up the remote and reversed the action. A huge grin spread across her face. "Now I get what you meant by a fan at the back. Wow. Stunning."

"I can't believe how long it took me to put two and two together. I knew I'd seen it somewhere." Jean rocked back and forth, foot to foot, with absolute adoration for the dress in her eyes.

"I have an idea. Can I take this DVD?" Ariela asked.

Jean's eyebrows popped up. "Yeah, just don't lose it."

"No worries. I'll meet you downstairs." Ariela pulled the disk out of the machine, shut off the television, and headed down to her computer. She now had a mission of her own, something to distract her from her worries about Dylan. The last thing she wanted to do was bring him up and screw up Jean's happiness. This was a positive outlet for her energy, her thoughts, and she hugged it to herself like a float ring.

Minutes later, the third view of the dress was just rolling out of the printer when Jean joined her in the office.

"What a great idea!" Jean picked up one of the images with a smile.

"Now we have something to go on. Grab the telephone book. We have calls to make. We're going to get you this dress."

They were able to find the perfect seamstress, recommended to them by the second woman they called, and they sent the images over the computer to her. When she called them back, she was very excited about the job, and working within their time constraints wasn't going to be a problem. She looked forward to the challenge. Jean was glowing when she got the news.

Ariela grinned. "Ron is going to fall in love with you all over again when he sees you in that dress."

"I. Can't. Wait."

Would *she* ever be that happy? Only time would tell.

———

Driving through the unpredictable city without an escort made all four men in the Humvee-from-hell feel extremely exposed. Even tanks could be blown up.

Every muscle in Dylan's body was vibrating with tension as his gaze swept the moving landscape for danger. His finger rode the side of the gun, ready to slip instantly to the trigger. Slow, steady breaths, his attention to every little detail sharp and focused, he was poised for trouble.

When he began seeing familiar buildings and intersections, he grew even more alert. He'd walked this way, sick and lame, escorted by the women he'd come back to rescue. Not far from here, he'd been shot and his friends killed. Familiar didn't always translate into comforting.

Abdullah looked over at him. "We're getting close."

Dylan nodded without turning away from the passing scenery.

When they turned down the women's street, Dylan felt a momentary wave of nausea hit him. He'd huddled under sniper fire for hours, mere yards from here, and now he wasn't even sure where to look for the threat he'd felt.

Bruce drove right onto the yard from the street, bouncing over the neglected landscaping and throwing the truck into reverse. He backed right up to the front door, only allowing enough room to open the back. Leaving the engine running, both armed escorts kicked open their doors and dropped to the ground, using the doors as shields while they swept the area for risks.

Rich barked, "Clear!"

Dylan and Abdullah leaped out and made their way to the house as fast as they could while the other two kept guard. The women must have been watching for them because the door opened at exactly the right moment, letting them inside.

Rich moved backward, shoving the professor's truck door closed in the process, and went to throw open the back of the vehicle. Only after it had completely shielded the front door did he follow them in. Bruce remained outside, alert and on guard behind the driver's door.

The ladies had been busy. Parcels and stacks of books were tied together and piled around the room. After a quick and emotional greeting between the family members, everyone started a fast hustle, loading the books and a few of their precious belongings into the truck. It was a relief to see that the old woman had resigned herself to flight, but tears glittered in her eyes as she prepared to leave her home and the majority of her possessions behind. She knew she wouldn't be back.

Everything was loaded in ten minutes, faster than expected. Rich hoisted Abdullah's youngest sister into the back then closed the hatch. Tucked against the books and parcels, she lay down, out of sight.

Rich waved the other sister forward, and she left the house, falling back for a moment when he threw out a hand and peered across the street. Once he deemed it safe, he waved her into the vehicle. From behind his door he pointed at Dylan and nodded. Being armed, he knew he was expected to help cover the professor and his mother as they hurried into the vehicle.

Dylan looked at Abdullah, and the older man took a deep breath. Nodding once, the older man grabbed his mother around the waist and moved her out behind Dylan. She somehow managed to pull her front door closed behind her as he dragged her away. Dr. Hadad boosted her into the truck and followed after her. Dylan fell back and ran around to the other side and jumped in. Only when they were secure did the two security men jump into the front.

They managed to get the women out without firing a shot. Still, the tension inside the vehicle was high as they drove off. Though they hadn't encountered any threats so far, that didn't mean they wouldn't. Urban warfare didn't allow for comfort when out of doors. They remained vigilant, all the way back to the Green Zone. Lives depended on them.

———

Dylan felt drained, exhausted as he stowed his pack under his seat on the plane. Sinking into the cushions, he drew the belt across his lap. The roar of the engines lulled him into a sleepy state, his mind drifting back to the last twenty-six hours. Now that the adrenaline rush had faded, he was amazed at how smoothly everything had gone.

Though he'd been prepared to return hostile gunfire, no one had shot at them nor, thankfully, had they run into any roadside bombs. It was a hell of a relief. He would have fired his weapon, instinct and training had prepared him to respond, but shooting an actual person rather than a target, wasn't something he wanted to do if he could avoid it.

Once safely inside the compound, the Hadad family were able to greet each other properly. Dylan meant to give them their moment, but to his surprise, they drew him over and each family member embraced him, warmly, beginning with the old woman. She ran her hands up over his flak jacket, straightening him up just like his mother used to tidy him before school. Only when Mrs. Hadad was done did she step aside and allow her son and daughters to thank him themselves.

Dylan asked Dr. Hadad, his friend Abdullah now, to translate his thanks to the ladies for risking their lives to save him. He could see it meant a great deal to them. One of Abdullah's sisters asked through her brother, what Dylan was going to do now and whether he was going to continue to work in the region.

Dylan shook his head and felt a bit bashful when he said, "I'm going to go home and get married, if she'll have me."

When that statement was translated every face looking back at him lit with joy.

The old woman said, "Who could refuse you?" and clearly meant it.

She patted Dylan's cheek with affection then stepped back as a man approached. He informed them their transportation was already waiting to carry them to the Canadian Embassy in Jordan, and from there, to an even bigger family reunion in Toronto.

Dylan had been happy to see them go. Then it had hit him there were a lot of people he'd never see after this. He'd gone looking for Paul to retrieve his bag and they'd said their goodbyes for the last time right before he hitched a ride back to the airport and the cargo plane heading out. It was unlikely they'd ever meet again, but it didn't weigh on him. Dylan was ready to move forward. His focus had changed.

He honestly couldn't say how his career would evolve next. He couldn't discount the possibility he'd want back in the thick of the action in the future, but for now, he knew where he wanted to be most, where he needed to be. He loved Ariela, enough to make some painful sacrifices.

He couldn't help thinking about Jim and his failed marriage. Jim never could find a balance in his life. He thought he had to choose. He'd chosen the job. But he couldn't forfeit his wedding band, or the pictures of his wife and son he'd carried in his wallet. They were worn and frayed at the edges from being handled so often. Did Jim ever put on his ring and wind it on his finger as if he could turn back the years and change his decision? He must have. All evidence pointed to a man unsettled with his choice and plagued by regret.

Was there a compromise to be found with Ariela? Dylan wanted it, he wanted it all. He wanted her, the home, and the children to offset the stress and strain, and incalculable rewards he got from his job. He honestly didn't know.

Preparing himself for the disappointment of his life, Dylan drifted off to sleep as the plane rose in the air.

———

Ariela was leaning against the railing bisecting the wall of windows in the airport concourse when she spotted Dylan's head bobbing in the crowd. She stretched up on her toes and looked hard for anything she could see of him as little flashes of his body were exposed, then closed out of sight, between the moving crush of people surrounding him.

He was walking into the afternoon sun, his brilliant, blue eyes glittering like sapphires, so he couldn't see her yet, but she could tell he was searching for her too, craning his neck and casting looks around people. Despite how hard she tried to hold it together, tears started to collect in the corners of her eyes. She swiped them away, irritated at anything that might interfere with a clear view of him. Then a gap opened up in front of him and Ariela took it. She charged Dylan like a linebacker, colliding hard with his body and knocking him back a step as he tried to identify what just hit him.

It might have been her scent, or maybe the familiar feel of her body pressed to his, but whatever it was that he recognized first, it tore a groan from his throat, and he grabbed the back of her shirt and lifted her off her feet, crushing his mouth over hers. They laughed and cried as they embraced. The pedestrians divided around them, without breaking stride.

He kissed her salty tears then went back to her mouth for another taste before breaking off to say, "You're here." He said it as if he still couldn't quite believe it.

Ariela reached up and touched his beautiful cheek, her heart breaking that he still doubted her. "I figured something out."

"Oh yeah? What's that?"

"I was so afraid of losing you that I was going to lose you."

The corner of his smile twitched. "Took you long enough."

"Hey." Then she gave a little laugh. "I'm sorry. I can't promise you won't see the occasional episode of worry and insanity from me, but if you're willing to tough it out, I'm willing to love the man and support the journalist."

"You mean it?" He nuzzled into her neck as he hugged her again.

She sighed, squeezing him tight. "I do."

He eased back, one eyebrow raised. "Remember those words."

The End.

Tara Mills

Friends and Lovers

He lost touch with her once.
There's no risk he won't face to keep her.

Lauren McKay and Wes Dunlop saw their moment slip away when he left for college. Now, fifteen years later, Detective Dunlop just walked into the domestic violence shelter Lauren runs and the sparks fly, reminding her why she never got over him.

Sylvia Coulter knows if she could go back and give her younger self some hard-earned advice, it's unlikely she'd get through to the misty-eyed romantic. She'd tell her a day is coming when she fears her husband. Sadly, innocence truly was bliss—bliss with an expiration date.

Just as Lauren and Wes are beginning to imagine a future together, the Coulter's marriage implodes. When Sylvia flees to the shelter, trouble follows. Confronted by the violence first-hand, a terrorized Lauren has to ask, is this where *her* newfound happiness is destined to end too?

Get caught up in this gripping and emotional romantic suspense today.

Take a sneak peek.

After lunch, once the dishwasher was humming away and the table and counter were wiped clean, the four friends sat down to a game of Trivial Pursuit. Ken claimed his wife because he said she had the memory of an elephant, so by default Wes and Lauren were paired as the opposition.

"That was during Johnson's administration, wasn't it?" Wes asked Lauren.

She stared at him. "How should I know?"

He turned back to the other two. "Then we're going with Johnson."

Ken groaned. "He's right. Next time its guys against the girls."

"Fine. We'll kick your asses." Sherry sneered.

Lauren wasn't so sure about that. There were a lot of things she could say with utter confidence about Wes: he was hot, no question; he was compassionate, he'd proved that on numerous occasions; but smart? The man blew her mind. He was kicking butt without much help from her. Lauren was embarrassed because she didn't know enough to actually contribute anything important. Oh, she'd gotten a few inane answers, not that it mattered. Wes was carrying her deadweight.

"Well, finish us off," said Ken with a sigh when Lauren rolled their pie into the middle of the board. He looked at Sherry. "What should we give them for a category?"

Sherry pursed her lips and considered the opposition thoughtfully. "Wes blows at Arts and Literature."

"I do not."

"More than the rest."

"Arts and Literature it is." Ken pulled a card and read it without a word before showing it to his wife.

Sherry's face changed from curiosity to disbelief and she raised her voice in protest. "No way. New card."

"Not fair. You have to read the card drawn," Wes argued.

She read it, but with a noticeable trace of testiness. "What British author brought The Hundred Acre Wood to millions of children around the world?"

Wes and Lauren looked at each other with astonishment then burst out laughing. "A.A. Milne!" they shouted simultaneously.

"I cannot believe you finished us off with that," Sherry grumbled, tossing the card onto the board.

Wes and Lauren shared a high five. "Poetic justice," he told his sister.

"We won fair and square," Lauren agreed with her partner.

Ken was looking at his wife with concern. "Sher, you look tired."

"I'm fine."

"Are those circles under her eyes?" he asked the other two.

"Afraid so." Wes nodded, sweeping the game pieces unto the Ziploc.

Lauren closed the box of cards and gave Sherry an apologetic smile. "You look like you could use a nap."

Just hearing the word nap made Sherry yawn. She gave in. "Hate to break up the party, but fine. Have it your way."

Ken hugged her shoulders. "That's my girl." She rolled her eyes.

Wes enjoyed a big stretch when he stood up. "I've been here long enough. I'll let you have your house back."

"And I should get going too." Lauren rose as well. "Thanks for having me over. This was fun."

"Let's do it again. Maybe next week, okay?" Sherry worked herself up from her chair.

Lauren lit up at the suggestion. "I'd love to."

They said goodbye to their hosts at the door then Wes and Lauren set off on their own.

She didn't know what to make of it when Wes hovered behind her as she unlocked her car door.

Then he asked, "What's next on your agenda?"

It was difficult to face him now that she wasn't looking to him for clues. "I'm going home," she said simply.

"But it's early yet. Why don't you come over to my place?"

Lauren closed her eyes—tight. "Wes."

"Before you shoot me down, hear me out."

She turned and finally looked up and into his eyes. It was a mistake because it was too damn easy to get lost in them, to feel sucked in and drugged by them.

He went on. "I know you aren't exactly comfortable around me right now because of yesterday. Can we talk about it, clear the air? I don't want this hovering between us like a bad stink. Please?"

She exhaled a weary sigh. "I already know what you're going to say. You'll tell me it was just an impulse. You don't know what came over you. You'll ask me to forgive you so we can go back to being friends, right? Listen, I know pity when I see it. You were only responding to my emotional vacuum. I don't hold it against you, and you *are* forgiven. All better now?"

Wes stared at her, stunned. "*That's* what you're thinking?"

She nodded, too depressed to go on.

"Fuck that!"

He spun her around so suddenly Lauren gasped. Then her back was against the car and her feet left the ground. Wes's mouth came down hard on hers. Lauren's fingers bit into the front of his shirt as he bent her backward and his body forced her spine to mold itself to the cool metal while the hot bite of his hips, his solid chest, pressed into her. She couldn't have stopped her helpless moan of surrender if she wanted to.

His kiss was bruising, an irritated lesson and her mouth was buzzing when he finally eased back and their lips peeled slowly apart.

"Maybe I was wrong," she mumbled stupidly, too dazed to see straight.

"You *think*?"

Friends and Lovers
Available in digital and paperback.

Read it today

Shadows and Doubts

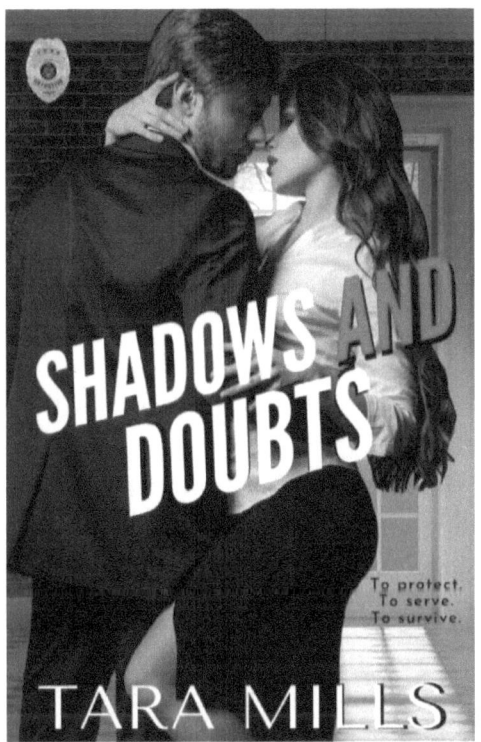

*When defending her clients puts an attorney
in the crosshairs, her safety falls to a cop with
personal demons of his own.*

Eden Hennessey, champion of social justice and attorney with
the non-profit Civil Rights Watch, just won her biggest case
yet—and made a dangerous enemy. Now the anonymous hate
mail has turned to threats. Someone is following her, taking
photos of her, and proving nothing she's done to guard her
privacy and protect herself is enough.

Recently returned to duty after an emotional crash over the

death of his former partner, Detective Glen Gold knows he can't afford a single infraction. But when he's assigned the Hennessey case, the challenge of identifying who's behind the threats grows increasingly complicated by their deepening attraction.

As the line between personal and professional begins to blur, Gold's badge isn't all he could lose if he doesn't shut down Eden's stalker in time.

Enjoy this sensual and exciting romantic suspense today.

Take a sneak peek.

He was done talking about his past. Having lived it was punishment enough.

"Do you still plan to play broomball on Thursday?" he asked, switching subjects on her.

The thought of Eden on the ice throwing elbows and insults blew another understandable misconception about her right out of the air like a clay pigeon. As much as he wanted to advise her against going, he couldn't help smiling at the image he had of her out there.

"I can't let my team down, but I'll be careful." She stood and began clearing the dishes.

He rose to help. "Then I'll be there."

"You think that's necessary?" She set their empty bowls and plates in the sink and ran water over them.

"Yes. But it's also an opportunity."

"Hm." She pondered that a moment then asked, "Are you having more tea?"

He set his empty cup on the counter and backed away. "I should go." Lingering would be too easy. Acting on the attracttion that was growing with every interaction they had even harder to avoid. "Thanks for the meal. It doesn't count, you know," he told her with a teasing smile.

Eden laughed. "I never said it did. Close my case then you'll get the real meal."

"I don't know how you're going to top this one."

"Just wait," she promised with a beguiling look in her eyes.

"Well, I'd say *that's* incentive."

"Exactly how I meant it."

She followed him down the steps and waited while he put his shoes on. They were cold and damp, inside and out. The downside of hating winter boots almost as much as he hated galoshes, or worse, rubbers.

He put on his coat. Eden tugged his scarf off the smaller hook and stepped forward to loop it behind his neck while he zipped up. She didn't move back. If anything, she seemed to tip closer so her chest was practically touching his.

Glen cocked an eyebrow at her and she gazed placidly back as if she weren't challenging a professional line and stirring up all kinds of mischief for him.

"I can't," he told her, his regret absolutely genuine. "I'm already on thin ice with the department."

"Can't what?" the vixen asked in a husky whisper, the challenge, shit, the invitation as heavy as his balls. Damn her sexy smile.

"This. Not yet. We can't." His words came out as an apologetic plea.

It was enough. They stared into each other's eyes, mutually acknowledging this was going to happen. *They* were going to happen.

"Funny," he said with a little snort. "Bedford asked if we'd slept together yet."

"Did he?" She didn't sound surprised, more *impressed*. "What did you say?"

Facing into the light like this, her eyes shimmered. It was mesmerizing.

"I don't remember," he said.

"Liar." She smiled. "In any case, you should go."

He really should. "I should," he said just above a whisper, his lips mere inches from hers.

"I'll be at the rink by seven on Thursday night. See you then?"

How did she make such a simple statement sound loaded with potential?

"Don't look for me."

Her brows shot up. "O-*kay*."

Her reaction amused him. "Just trust that I'll be patrolling the periphery and watching for trouble."

"And I'm to pretend I'm not aware you're close but out of reach. Again. We seem to have a theme going here."

"Evidently." He dipped toward her, tantalizingly close, and the fractals of her eyes reminded him of the frost patterns on the inside of his dark windshield. A windshield right outside, where he should be.

"Goodnight, Eden."

Her kissable mouth twitched with a smile and she took a step away. "Glen."

He reached blindly for the doorknob but instead of turning to it when he found it, he muttered a frustrated, "Ah, shit," and spun back, caught her around the waist, and dragged Eden flush against him. She arched backward over his arm as he kissed the hell out of that beautiful mouth of hers.

There was a sense of relief, triumph even, as her gasp of surprise turned into a rumble of pure pleasure. She drove her hands into his hair and gripped him by the head as she kissed him back, her response as potent as his.

When they finally eased apart to catch their breath, both were staring at the other and panting in mild surprise. It was Eden who started giggling first. Once she let loose, he was gone, laughing along and shaking his head.

"That was..." he began then let the thought go.

"Incredible?" she asked, glowing even as she fanned herself.

"I was going to say ill-advised, but let's go with your answer. I like it better."

"Ha!" She laughed. "Guess I'll see you Thursday."

He turned back from checking the dark street. "Don't—"

"Give you up," she finished for him and rolled her eyes. "I won't. But you don't make things easy, do you?"

"You must have talked to my captain." Snorting at his own joke, Gold ducked out into the cold.

Shadows and Doubts
Available in digital and paperback.
Read it today.

Tara Mills

Forest Fires

Beauty and the Brain—the adventure begins.

When rough-edged handywoman Charley Jensen stops to help a stranded motorist with a flat tire in the middle of nowhere, she writes the preppy biologist off as too soft to survive in her isolated and unforgiving wilderness.

But Drake Carver is more than just a brain in a pretty package, he's resourceful and, much to Charley's surprise, fun to be around. However, only when their lives are on the line does she learn he's tougher than he looks.

Suddenly, her secret, burning question, '*Are you strong enough to be my man?*' becomes '*Am I strong enough to love this man?*' Will they get the chance to find out?

Enjoy this opposites-attract, refreshingly different adventure into romance today.

Read an excerpt.

What is he waiting for? Charley ached to move into him, but Drake was holding back. Maybe he didn't see her that way. Was she the only one feeling an attraction? If she went up on her toes and kissed him, would he step back and set her away from him? She didn't think she could handle the humiliation. Then she remembered Heidi and moved back on her own.

The awkward moment ended abruptly when a raucous unkindness of ravens burst across the sky directly overhead. They both looked up at the deep *whoosh* of their wings beating the air. Their frantic squawks were unsettling.

Visually tracking the fleeing birds, she said, "I wonder what that was all about."

His posture rigid, Drake's nostrils flared. He frowned. "What is that? Do you smell it?"

Lifting her nose, she inhaled deeply and her eyes bulged in alarm. "It's smoke. I smell smoke. Come on!"

She took off, leading him higher. They circled the peak and stopped short at seeing the wall of smoke and red flame bearing down on their perch from the northwest. It grew and undulated as they watched.

Charley grabbed her head with both hands and whimpered in horror. "My truck!"

Drake pulled out his phone. "No signal. Think we can we make it down there in time?"

"No way." She gnawed uneasily at her ragged thumbnail. "Bad idea. Even if we could reach it, we'd be trapped down there with the fire. The road goes right into it. See that?"

She pointed west. It was hardly visible through the smoke.

He followed her finger as she explained, "We came in over there, which means we're cut off. There aren't any other roads."

Two pines towering above the canopy went up like torches in front of them as the nightmare unfolded in the distance.

"It's coming right at us," he said. "We have to get off this mountain or we're going to be in serious trouble."

Charley looked at him, her stomach in knots. "The only way we can get down safely is the way we came up, going straight into it."

"Then we have to head toward the lake from the other side."

She shook her head emphatically. "Absolutely not. No. That's not an option. I've seen it from that side. A fair part of it is sheer cliff."

"Well, what do you suggest?" he snapped with irritation. "We can't stay here and we can't go back. I don't see a lot of options, do you?"

"Have you done any climbing?"

"I was a boy, remember?"

"I'm talking *climbing*. Without the proper gear, we're not going to make it." She grabbed him by the front of his shirt and shook him. "Listen to me. The only reason you want to head down that way is because you haven't seen it. I have. Trust me, its suicide."

He covered the hands clutching his shirt and gave them a calming squeeze. "Charley, staying here is suicide. We have to reach the lake."

She turned to look back to the inferno building to the northwest and was hit by an even stronger belt of smoke. The front was moving steadily closer, the plumes whipping like a wicked storm. Another flock of birds screamed overhead. They convinced her.

Unable to control the tremble in her voice, she said, "I don't like this."

"I thought you didn't mind heights."

"I'm fine with heights. I'm not crazy about falling, and *I* know how insane this is."

Her answer prompted a fatalistic smile.

"Come on." Drake went back to where they'd eaten lunch and grabbed his bag off the ground. "Where to from here?"

She stared at him. "I said I've *seen* this cliff from the south. I didn't say I *memorized* it."

His eyes rolled shut as if he were fighting for patience. *Good luck!* When he looked at her again he was calm. "Give me something—please."

After an uncomfortable pause, she managed an uneasy decision. "I think we should head around to the right."

Drake nodded. "Let me go first."

This was one time Charley wasn't going to argue.

Forest Fires
Available in digital and paperback.

Read it today.

Bibliography

Books:

The Occupation: War and Resistance in Iraq by Patrick
Cockburn, London, Verso, 2006

*Reporting Iraq: An oral history of the war by the journalists
who covered it*, Edited by Mike Hoyt, John Palattella, and the
staff of the Columbia Journalism Review, New Jersey,
Melville House Publishing, 2007

*Beyond the Green Zone: Dispatches from an unembedded
journalist in occupied Iraq* by Dahr Jamail, Chicago,
Haymarket Books, 2007

Love Thy Neighbor: A Story of War by Peter Maass, New
York, Vintage Books, 1997

*The Hydrogen Economy: The Creation of the Worldwide
Energy Web and the Redistribution of Power on Earth* by
Jeremy Rifkin, New York, Putnam, 2002

Articles/Magazines/other sources:

Kill the Messengers, National Public Radio, This American
Life, March 2007, http://www.thisamericanlife.org/radio-
archives/episode/327/by-proxy?act=2 ,
What's In A Number?—2006 Edition
http://www.thisamericanlife.org/radio-
archives/episode/320/whats-in-a-number-%E2%80%94-2006-
edition

The ugly truth about everyday life in Baghdad—A Confidential Memo from the US Ambassador Zalmay Khalilzad, Baghdad to Condoleeza Rice, Secretary of State, dated June 20, 2006, http://www.independent.co.uk/news/world/middle-east/the-ugly-truth-about-everyday-life-in-baghdad-by-the-us-ambassador-404742.html

Theocracy Lite by Katha Pollitt, September 19, 2005

Nothing can quite describe life in Iraq by Tina Susman, Los Angeles Times, November 2008, http://www.latimes.com/news/nationworld/world/la-fg-iraqdispatch10-2008nov10,0,1647805.story

Zeinab Sadiq Jaafar and the Battle for Women in Iraq available at the Huffington Post, February 2009, http://www.huffingtonpost.com/madeleine-m-kunin/zeinab-sadiq-jaafar-and-t_b_163915.html

In the Twilight Zone by Orville Schell reporting for Salon. 2006, http://orvilleschell.com/in-the-twilight-zone/

An article on reporting in Baghdad by Wall Street Journal reporter Farnaz Fassihi, 2004, available online at http://www.pnionline.com/dnblog/extra/archives/000955.html

At War, Notes from the front lines by Erica Goode from the New York Times' Baghdad Bureau, September 2008, http://atwar.blogs.nytimes.com/author/erica-goode/

Covering Iraq: The Modern Way of War Correspondence by Michael Fumento for the National Review, November 2006, http://www.fumento.com/military/brigade.html

Inside the Green Zone by Brian Bennett/Baghdad for Time Magazine. 2007,
http://content.time.com/time/magazine/article/0,9171,161518 8,00.html

Outside and Inside Iraq's Borders: A Forgotten Exodus by Kenneth Bacon and Kristele Younes for the Washington Post. http://www.washingtonpost.com/wp-dyn/content/graphic/2008/01/22/GR2008012202690.html

War Reporting in Iraq: Only Locals Need Apply: *The Day of the Traditional Foreign Correspondent is Drawing to a Close* by Patrick Cockburn, Counterpunch, Weekend Edition, March 2007, http://www.counterpunch.org/2007/03/03/war-reporting-in-iraq-only-locals-need-apply/

Map of the Green Zone as depicted by CNN at http://www.globalsecurity.org/military/world/iraq/images/cnn-green-zone-map.jpg

Weapons information provided by http://usmilitary.about.com/od/armyweapons/l/aainfantry2.ht m

Maps of the region, and downtown Baghdad specifically, provided by National Geographic.com

*I also used the internet extensively to read up on local foods, time zones, tools of Dylan's trade, and to watch You Tube videos shot during the occupation of both patrols in Baghdad and within the Green Zone to get a sense of place.

Acknowledgements

No writer is an island, which is why I'd like to send an extra word of gratitude to my husband for reading all of my work—over and over again. Your input, suggestions, *and* criticisms have helped shape me as a writer. Mark Morris and Nola Cross—thank you both for agreeing to proof this. Your help and encouragement mean the world to me. Thank you to my family and friends who share my work and related announcements in whatever way works best for them.

Thank you.

Books by Tara Mills

Novels

Accidents Make the Heart Grow Fonder
Caution: Filling is Hot
Forest Fires
Friends and Lovers
Going Solo
Grading on Curves
In Love and War
Shadows and Doubts

Novellas, Short Stories & Teasers

Britt and the Butler
If You Want Me
The Senator's Wife
Falling
Stolen Moments
Holiday Kisses
It's in His Kiss

The Pelican Cay Series

Intimate Strangers – Book One
Tarnished Hero – Book Two
Dark Storms – Book Three
Sweetest Taboo — Book Four

About the Author

I write stories I like to read, with authentic characters and realistic themes. From laugh-out-loud romantic comedy to nail-biting suspense, I've got you covered.
Escape with me into books.

In the real world, I'm a happy wife, proud mom, doting nana, and dog owner—again.

Please visit my website
www.taramillsauthor.com
Stories with a heartbeat.

Follow me on Facebook, Pinterest,
Twitter, or Bookbub.

Did you enjoy this story? Please share the love.

Read. Review. Recommend. Repeat.

Thank you.

♡

www.ingramcontent.com/pod-product-compliance
Lightning Source LLC
Chambersburg PA
CBHW030935260626
47169CB00002B/488